A Hot Man Is the Best Revenge

Other Ellora's Cave Anthologies
Available from Pocket Books

NAUGHTY NIGHTS
by Charlene Teglia, Tawny Taylor, & Dawn Ryder

MIDNIGHT TREAT
by Sally Painter, Margaret L. Carter, & Shelley Munro

ROYAL BONDAGE
by Samantha Winston, Delilah Devlin, & Marianne LaCroix

MAGICAL SEDUCTION
by Cathryn Fox, Mandy M. Roth, & Anya Bast

GOOD GIRL SEEKS BAD RIDER
by Vonna Harper, Lena Matthews, & Ruth D. Kerce

ROAD TRIP TO PASSION
by Sahara Kelly, Lani Aames, & Vonna Harper

OVERTIME, UNDER HIM
by N. J. Walters, Susie Charles, & Jan Springer

GETTING WHAT SHE WANTS
by Diana Hinter, S. L. Carpenter, & Chris Tanglen

INSATIABLE

by Sherri L. King, Elizabeth Jewell, & S. L. Carpenter

HIS FANTASIES, HER DREAMS

by Sherri L. King, S. L. Carpenter, & Trista Ann Michaels

MASTER OF SECRET DESIRES

by S. L. Carpenter, Elizabeth Jewell, & Tawny Taylor

BEDTIME, PLAYTIME

by Jaid Black, Ruth D. Kerce, & Sherri L. King

HURTS SO GOOD

by Gail Faulkner, Lisa Renee Jones, & Sahara Kelly

LOVER FROM ANOTHER WORLD

by Rachel Carrington, Elizabeth Jewell, & Shiloh Walker

FEVER-HOT DREAMS

by Jaci Burton, Sherri L. King, & Samantha Winston

TAMING HIM

by Kimberly Dean, Summer Devon, & Michelle M. Pillow

ALL SHE WANTS

by Jaid Black, Dominique Adair, & Shiloh Walker

A Hot Man Is the Best Revenge

Shiloh Walker

Beverly Havlir

Delilah Devlin

POCKET BOOKS

New York London Toronto Sydney

Pocket Books
A Division of Simon & Schuster, Inc.
1230 Avenue of the Americas
New York, NY 10020

This book is a work of fiction. Names, characters, places, and incidents either are products of the author's imagination or are used fictitiously. Any resemblance to actual events or locales or persons, living or dead, is entirely coincidental.

First Pocket Books trade paperback edition August 2008

Manufactured in the United States of America

10 9 8 7 6 5 4 3 2 1

ISBN-13: 978-1-4165-7730-0
ISBN-10: 1-4165-7730-0

Contents

Good Girls Don't
Shiloh Walker
1

Irresistible
Beverly Havlir
105

Ride a Cowboy
Delilah Devlin
225

GOOD GIRLS DON'T

SHILOH WALKER

ONE

"DUMP HIM."

Lori looked over the fence at Mike and snorted. "We're getting married in three months, Mike."

"All the more reason to do it now instead of later. Divorce is expensive." He simply stared at her levelly, his wide-set green eyes revealing exactly what he thought of Dirk. Mike Ryan hadn't ever liked Dirk—it was one of the few things the two friends had ever seriously disagreed on.

Lori just arched a brow at him and replied, "I don't plan on getting a divorce."

"He doesn't make you happy. You all but said that."

"He does too," Lori muttered, turning around and leaning against the fence. Crossing her arms over her chest, she stared at the half-finished flower bed. She wasn't pouting. Seriously. Dirk *did* make her happy.

She just . . .

Hell.

She wanted more from him.

"If he made you happy, you wouldn't look so damn depressed right now."

A thick hank of blonde hair fell into her eyes and she shoved it back with a grimy hand, leaving a streak of garden soil on her forehead. "Couples have fights, Mike. That's perfectly normal."

"That wasn't a fight, Lori. Fights involve you yelling. Him yelling. Not him talking and you just sitting there, listening and looking like you want to cry. Hell, I've seen that happen four times in the past two months. You seem to be getting more depressed all the time and you want me to believe you're happy?"

A warm hand came up, cupping the back of her neck. His thumb rubbed in slow, comforting circles and Lori had to fight the urge to turn around, bury her face against Mike's chest and wail like a baby. "It's complicated," Lori muttered, blinking away the tears stinging her eyes.

No, it wasn't. Not really. But she wasn't about to tell her buddy Mike that the reason she was miserable was because her fiancé treated her like a child who couldn't think on her own.

Over the past year, Dirk had become more and more controlling. Lori had been having little doubts about things for a while, but lately—they weren't little doubts. They were more like Lake Superior–size doubts. Lori hadn't even realized how much he was controlling her until a few days ago.

It was hotter than hell, ninety-five degrees and the heat index had crept into the triple digits. She was jerking some weeds out of her flower beds, trying to get it done before afternoon came and it got *really* hot. Curls kept springing loose from her ponytail, and her hair was sticking to her neck and face, falling into her eyes. Usually, come summer, she had her hair trimmed into layers that made it a little more manageable and a lot cooler.

She hadn't this year. She had planned to. She'd even had an appointment but had cancelled it because of Dirk. Just like she had let him talk her out of buying a sporty little Mustang and talk her into buying a Corolla. *It gets better gas mileage and it will be a lot easier to maintain.*

Other little things here and there. What sort of clothes she should wear. She'd been offered a job at a special-needs school. It had involved a pay cut, but she'd really wanted that job. It wasn't enough of a pay cut that it would have caused her problems. Her folks had passed away a few years ago and left her enough money that she could have afforded the cut.

She could have afforded that new Mustang.

He had always been a bit of a control freak, but over the past year Dirk had become more controlling. He tried to tell her what she should wear, how to style her hair, the proper way to clean the house—she was feeling more and more like his drudge instead of his fiancée.

But even that wasn't all of it. It was like he was trying to take over her life completely. Make her decisions for her. Even the most intimate ones.

More specifically, Dirk didn't think she knew what she wanted in her sex life and basically tried to control that too. *No, we aren't going to the club. No, we aren't going to try this. No, we aren't going to try that.*

They had sex one way, missionary, in the bedroom with the lights out. The sex was wonderful, or it used to be until she started trying to convince Dirk to mess around a little more. To loosen up. Now the sex was just okay. Dirk said it was her imagination.

Any time she asserted herself, just a little, it ended up in a fight. Lori was tired of it. And more, although she didn't want to admit it, she had a sinking suspicion that Mike was right.

Mike might not know the whole story but he saw through her façade of happiness. Mom hadn't. Her friends hadn't. And if Dirk had, he didn't care.

Dirk didn't make her happy and he didn't seem too interested in trying to change that.

MIKE WATCHED LORI WALK AWAY, her tanned shoulders slumped, her head low.

She'd been getting more depressed by the day, it seemed. Today she'd been crying. He could tell by the faint redness in her eyes and it pissed him off something awful.

Dirk was an ass. Up until the past year, he'd been an ass who made Lori happy but something seemed to have changed that. Mike hadn't seen any signs that Dirk was messing around and Lori said that wasn't it, but there was something.

Lori wouldn't tell him what, and frankly, Mike didn't care.

The only thing he wanted was to see her actually *look* happy again.

The only thing?

Okay, that wasn't all he wanted. He would love a chance to push her pretty, muscled thighs apart and sink his cock inside her, but he wasn't doing that. Sex and friends weren't compatible as far he was concerned.

Especially not the way he liked sex. Lori was the ideal girl next door. Cute, sexy as hell and funny. She loved the outdoors, loved sports, and as far as Mike was concerned, that was too close to the perfect woman. For him, at least.

She taught kindergarten. She went to church. She was sweet and wholesome and he wasn't going to risk messing up a friendship by putting the moves on her, even if she hadn't been involved.

Wholesome didn't mix very well with the kind of games he liked. But he still didn't like seeing her look so damn miserable.

"Just dump him," Mike muttered to himself, watching as she disappeared inside.

A WEEK LATER, Mike's words came back with a vengeance to haunt Lori. She should have listened to him.

If she had listened to him, she wouldn't have had to see *this*.

Wouldn't have to feel like this.

How can this be happening?

That question kept circling through her mind, but oddly enough, in some part of her, Lori really wasn't that surprised.

Lori stood in the doorway, staring into her shadowed bedroom as tears rolled down her face.

That was *her* fiancé. The snarling wolf tattoo on his shoulder that she thought was so sexy, the thick sun-streaked blond hair that he kept cut just a little shorter than she liked.

And their neighbor. The pretty redhead with gray eyes and breast implants. Sara Mattingly.

Dirk and Sara. Together.

Sara was on her knees, her ass up in the air, her wrists cuffed at her back and Dirk was pumping back and forth inside her ass, his hands gripping her hips.

The sound of Sara's gasping scream finally pushed Lori to action. Reaching out, she flicked the light on and watched as Dirk turned his head to look at her over Sara's bound body.

Sara was too far gone and had only noticed that Dirk had stopped moving. "Please . . . please . . ."

With a brittle smile, Lori said, "Go ahead, Dirk. By all means."

Spinning on her heel, she stalked away.

Things felt surreal now. The gut-wrenching pain had faded, replaced by a distant sort of shock. Weird random thoughts kept darting through her mind and only a few of them were related to what was going on in her bedroom.

Her mind jumped to the conference she had left early and she actually started looking for her car keys, thinking maybe she should just go back there. It was a four-hour drive, but it was only nine o'clock. It would be late when she checked in, but she could still get some sleep and go to the last day of the conference . . . yeah. Yeah. That would work.

She finally realized she was still holding her keys, the Tinkerbell charm clutched in her hand so hard that the metal bit into her flesh. She stared at the keys for a minute and then shook her head, trying to clear away the thick fog that had wrapped itself around her brain.

"Need to get going," she muttered, shoving her bangs out of her face.

She didn't quite make it to the front door before Dirk caught up to her. "Lori . . . Lori, wait."

The sound of his voice snapped Lori right out of the nice, comfortable fog. Pain returned, biting and tearing at her heart with razor-sharp claws. With the pain came anger and she spun around to face him as rage bubbled up inside.

Dirk reached for her and light glinted off the titanium bracelet she'd given him for Christmas. She'd spent an arm and a leg on it. He had been wearing it while he fucked their neighbor. This made her anger spike.

Holding up one hand, she whispered harshly, "Don't touch me."

"Lori, please don't go. Let me explain—"

"Explain?" she demanded. "There's nothing to explain. I just found my *fiancé* screwing our neighbor."

"Lori—"

"Don't. Okay? Just don't."

Dirk continued to move closer and Lori shifted the keys in her hand, holding them so that her house key protruded between her knuckles as she made a fist. "One more step and you'll be lucky if I don't carve your eyeballs out," she warned, her voice a low, furious snarl.

Lashes flickered over his dark chocolate eyes and Dirk stopped in his tracks. "Lori—"

"Shut up!" Her voice broke on the last word and she snapped her jaw shut, waiting until she knew her voice would be level before saying anything else—until she knew she could keep the tears in check. "This isn't the first time, is it?"

Dirk didn't say anything. But they'd been together for three years. Lori knew how to read him, even if he hadn't figured out how to read her. The look on his face was answer enough.

It was bad enough that he was screwing around on her, but considering how she had found them—their neighbor was getting the things that Lori had asked for time and again. Dirk had told her each time she wouldn't like it.

Rage and hurt warred inside her, both vying to be let out. Lori didn't know if she wanted to scream or cry. But she wasn't doing either here. Not when she could smell Dirk's sweat and Sara's perfume on his body. And she'd be damned if she let him see her cry.

"I'm leaving," she said icily. "When I get back, I want you both *out*."

"This is my home, honey." Dirk had that pacifying, soothing tone he used when he thought she was overreacting.

"No. It's mine. It *would* have been ours in a few more days." On Monday, they had an appointment at the bank to add him to the mortgage and Lori was overcome by a sense of relief as she realized just how close she had come to screwing up her life.

She was damn thankful the appointment wasn't until Monday. "Now though? It's mine, completely mine, and it's staying that way. I want you *out*."

She turned around and stalked to the door. His hand closed around her right arm and Lori turned, reacting without even thinking. She swung out and punched Dirk square in the nose. Blood spurted and she relished the sight for one second before turning and opening the door.

Her keys were still clutched in her right hand and she knew a second's disappointment that he hadn't grabbed her other arm instead. She would have liked seeing the nasty cut her key could have gouged down his handsome face.

Her voice shook with fury as she said, "If you're still here when I get back, I'll call the cops."

Then she turned on her heel and stalked out.

IT HAD BEEN HIS EXPERIENCE that the voice of an angry woman carried.

This was no exception. Her voice interrupted Mike's contemplation of the late evening sky and just how damn bored he'd become with his life.

Rolling from the hammock, he sauntered around the side of his house to see Lori striding toward her car, and her jerk-off fiancé chasing her. Dirk Morrigan was naked as a jaybird.

Lori, sadly, was not. She looked furious. Even from where he stood, he could see the light of temper in her eyes.

Mike had overheard the sounds of two people going at it from her house and it looked like Lori had just gotten home. She was supposed to be at some teacher thing in Fort Wayne until Sunday. Using his brilliant powers of deduction, he figured that Lori had interrupted something Dirk would rather she never have known about.

"Dumb ass," he muttered. Not only was Dirk a jerk, he was obviously a stupid one.

Leaning against the white picket fence, he called out, "Y'all got a problem?"

Lori turned her head and stared at him. Even across the yard, he felt the power of her stare clear down to his gut. She had the softest, prettiest blue eyes. But right now, she was so damn pissed, they looked like ice. She stood stiff as a board, her hands clenched at her sides.

"No, Mike," she said, her voice brittle and sharp. She cast a narrow look over her shoulder toward her fiancé and added, "No problem as long as *he* is gone when I get back."

Mike glanced toward Dirk and drawled, "Might help if he got clothes on first." Then he noticed the swelling coming up around Dirk's right eye and he grinned. "Lori's got a mean left hook, hasn't she? I'd do what she says, unless you want to see if she can aim as well with her knee as she can with her fists."

Dirk opened his mouth, but Lori cut him off. "If he's smart, he'll get everything he can carry out of my house. Come morning, I'm having a bonfire."

Cocking a brow at her, Mike said, "Kind of a dry summer. Might want to think of another way to get rid of his stuff."

"Do you mind, Ryan? Lori and I need to talk."

Glancing toward Dirk, Mike said, "Actually, you need to get some clothes on. And unless your name is listed on the house payment, I think you'd better do what she says."

"This is a private matter, Officer," Dirk snapped.

"It's *Detective*. And private or not, if she wants you out of her house, you gotta get out." Mike decided this was the most fun he'd had in a long time. He hadn't ever liked Morrigan. Maybe the jerk wouldn't leave willingly. Mike would love to help.

His common sense reminded him it wouldn't look very good if one of the other neighbors reported a domestic disturbance and *he* was involved, but hell. It wasn't like he'd get this chance again, right? Looking at Lori, Mike asked, "You want him out?"

"Oh, I want him out, all right," Lori said. Then she jerked her car door open and climbed inside.

Dirk started after her, and Mike said levelly, "You make one move toward that car, buddy, and you and me are going to have a go. And I really don't want to wrestle you until you've got some clothes." Baring his teeth in a smile, he said, "But that doesn't mean I won't."

For a minute, it didn't look like Dirk was going to listen. But as Lori pulled away, Dirk swore and turned around, stomping back into the house.

Michael called out, "Be gone in an hour, Dirk."

Dirk turned and flipped him off.

Mike ignored him, focusing instead on Lori's disappearing taillights.

Well, he sure as hell wasn't bored anymore.

FOR MORE THAN AN HOUR, Lori drove around listlessly. With the window down and Aerosmith blaring, she tried to figure out how long this had been going on. Dirk hadn't been acting any differently, so either he was a hell of a liar—or this had not been going on long.

She ended up parked in the parking lot of Exposé.

The club had opened six months ago, and Lori had told Dirk repeatedly that she wanted to go. *It's not your kind of club, honey.*

Lori knew what kind of club it was.

One of her friends from work was a regular there.

Exposé was a sex club.

She'd heard that damn near any kind of fantasy, no matter how kinky, could be acted out inside those walls. And Lori had a lot of fantasies she wanted to try, but Dirk hadn't ever listened.

Not because he wasn't into it, though. From what she had seen just a little while ago, Dirk was more than into kink. Damn him to hell and back, he knew she'd wanted to try . . . *something*. Anything. Hell, with him, nearly everything. She had tried being subtle, then not so subtle, and he hadn't ever listened.

Lori had an image of Dirk pumping against Sara, his cock shuttling back and forth inside the woman's ass. Her stomach twisted, knotting so hard it actually hurt.

He gave it to Sara.

The hot humiliation of it twisted her stomach into such a hard knot that Lori almost doubled over from the pain.

"Not worth it," she told herself. Sooner or later, she'd believe it.

Tears burned her eyes and she dashed them away impatiently, still staring at the discreet lettering of the sign just above the door. The line seemed to be a mile long and as she watched, several couples were turned away. Exposé was a private club. Nonmembers were admitted, but it was at the bouncer's discretion who he let in and who he turned aside.

There was a second entrance, this one with no line.

A man wearing a simple white shirt with a pair of jeans sauntered up to it, his arm wrapped around the waist of a petite brunette. She was wearing a short black strapless sheath and a pair of heeled sandals that laced up over her knees. They nodded at the guy watching the second door and walked right in.

The members' entrance.

They'll never let you in.

Even as Lori reached for the handle, she heard those insidious words inside her head. They circled around, repeating themselves over and over as she climbed from the car and started for the line. She doubted her white T-shirt and jeans were what the women usually wore in there, but still, she didn't turn around.

She headed for the back of the line, her hands tucked inside her back pockets. She tuned out the murmur of voices and the hard, steady beat of music pouring from the club as she tried very hard to think of absolutely nothing.

Taking her place in line, she stood there and waited.

When a hand touched her arm, she jumped and spun around, her heart pounding in her chest.

"Grace."

Her friend was grinning, but as she stared at Lori's face, her grin faded. "Honey, what's wrong?"

Lori blinked and shook her head. "Nothing. Just . . . nothing."

Grace rolled her eyes and said, "Uh-huh. Come on, let's go get a drink and you can tell me all about it."

Resigned, Lori followed Grace into the club. She *really* didn't want to talk about it but Grace wouldn't take no for an answer. Besides, she could sit at the bar and get a drink. And just the thought of doing something that Dirk wouldn't like was enough to make her smile. Even if it lasted only a few seconds.

TWO

WHILE THEY WAITED for class to start, Lori and Grace took turns working the heavy bag. The impact of her fist against the leather sent a jolt singing up her arm and set her blood pumping hot and fast. She wore a bandana around her head to hold her hair back.

The day after she'd kicked Dirk out, she'd gone to the salon and had four inches chopped off her hair. The thinner, layered cut was a hell of a lot cooler and curled a lot better. With every snip of the scissors, she had smiled.

"You look a lot happier." Grace drew up one leg and pivoted, striking the heavy bag.

After Grace had finished her roundhouse, Lori took a turn. After she'd kicked the heavy bag, Lori looked at Grace with a smile. "I hadn't realized how much I missed class."

"There's something very therapeutic about butt kicking." The door opened and a short, rotund little guy walked inside. As he did, the senior student got up from the floor and clapped his hands together. "Or getting your butt kicked."

Lori smiled and fell in line with the other brown belts.

After they finished warm-up, Lori and Grace fell in across from each other for sparring. "Heard anything from Dirk?" Grace asked as they started to circle each other.

Lori feinted and then kicked toward Grace's padded head. "Nope. Don't want to either."

Grace's hand plowed into her rib cage and Lori fell back with an "Ooomph." She retaliated with a spinning heel kick and a punch. The kick didn't land but the punch did and Grace recoiled, rubbing her belly with one gloved hand.

"Geez. Ask a simple question . . ." But she was grinning around the blue mouth guard.

Lori grinned back. "I sort of expected him to call, but nothing."

They fell silent for a few minutes, trading blows until the whistle sounded. After shaking hands, they retreated to the sidelines and dropped to the mat to watch the other students. "Well, I'm still sort of disappointed you didn't get to burn his clothes."

Lori laughed. "Dirk isn't going to risk his Armanis. I could have told you that. Would have been a fun bonfire, though."

"Keep it down, ladies!"

Lori and Grace looked toward the instructor sheepishly. "Oops," Lori muttered.

Grace just grinned. Waiting until the instructor started working with a couple of junior black belts, she leaned over and said, "So I hear you've been given a trial membership to Exposé. You coming this weekend?"

The whistle sounded. Lori and Grace climbed to their feet and headed back onto the floor. "Not sure yet."

"Don't tell me you're getting chicken."

Lori jabbed at Grace's head. "Bite me."

Grace kicked instead, first a front kick, followed by a side kick. Grace circled away before Lori could counter. "I don't know. I'm just kind of . . . uh . . ."

"Ladies, are you here to chat or train?"

From the corner of her eye, Lori saw Master Leland approaching. "Sorry."

They focused on the class, but afterward, Grace asked, "So you're sort of . . . what?"

They sat in the sauna, stripped down to panties and sport bras. "Restless, maybe? Not sure what I'm looking for there."

"It's who." Lori glanced toward Grace and the brunette shrugged. "You aren't the kind of person who goes to Exposé just because you want to get some kinky sex. You're looking for somebody there. Somebody who can give you what Dirk couldn't. A lot of my friends, I'd tell them they need to accept some of the offers they've received. But you . . . well, you'll know when you need to accept it. Casual sex just isn't your thing."

HE WAS SEEING THINGS.

Mike convinced himself that was exactly what was going on. It had to be. Because there was no way in hell Lori was sitting at the bar while one of the local Romeos tried to coax her out onto the dance floor at Exposé.

Lori was cute. Lori was sweet. He'd admit, privately, that he'd had a thing for her for years, but because she was cute and sweet, he'd never acted on it. Cute and sweet didn't work very well when it came to the kind of things Mike liked from a woman.

Cute and sweet didn't belong at Exposé.

Ergo, neither did Lori. But she sat at the bar, looking entirely too comfortable.

Lori rebuffed the guy, seemingly more interested in her drink, and while Mike was glad she didn't seem too impressed with the moves being made on her, he'd be even happier if she got up and walked out.

He hadn't seen much of her over the past few weeks. Since she'd tossed Morrigan out on his ass, she hadn't been home too much. The few times he'd looked for her, she'd been gone.

Here? He couldn't help but wonder if this was where she'd been. Mike hadn't been to the club in months so there was no way he'd know unless he asked her.

"I'll do that," he muttered. And then he'd get her the hell out of here.

The crowd moved between them and he lost sight of her head of sunny blonde curls for a second. Weaving through the throng of people, he moved closer, muttering under his breath.

He'd come here hoping to blow off some steam and get laid if he could find some woman who didn't bore the hell out of him. He hadn't come so he could drag Lori Whitmore out of here before she bit off more than she could chew.

Damn it, the guys at the door were slipping. They were supposed to do a better job of keeping out those who just weren't cut out for this kind of scene.

Lori sure as hell wasn't and she didn't need to be here.

She sure as hell didn't need to be here alone.

A woman alone in here was considered up for grabs, and Mike doubted she wanted to know exactly how much trouble that could get her into. Lori was too sweet, too cute, too . . . *holy hell.*

Just as Mike broke free of the crowd, somebody tapped Lori on the shoulder, a girl who looked vaguely familiar to him. Lori spun around on her stool and Mike damn near swallowed his tongue as he took in what she was wearing.

No leather for her.

No, Lori was wearing wine red lace, nearly the same color she had slicked on her lips. The corset was designed to look as through she wore nothing under the lace, but as he moved a little closer, he realized it wasn't pale, soft flesh he was seeing under the overlay of lace but some sort of silky cloth that was nearly the same color as her skin.

The teasing hint of what lay under the corset was enough to make him want to tear the lace and silk away, stripping her bare. He wasn't the only one who had an appreciation for the picture she made. Just before he drew even with her, somebody who looked entirely too familiar slid up to her side and rested a hand on her shoulder.

It was Trask Boyett, one of the more serious club members. Unlike the Romeo from earlier, this one would know how to initiate somebody like Lori. And Mike wasn't about to see it happen.

Hell, no.

"Lori."

She looked away from Trask, her eyes meeting Mike's and widening. A soft flush stained her cheeks but she didn't look away. Her eyes were wide and round with surprise as she stared at him and Mike could only imagine the thoughts racing through her mind.

Looking over her shoulder at Trask, Mike cocked a brow.

Trask's blond brows rose over his pale gray eyes and he smiled slightly. "You shouldn't let her out alone in here, Mike. You know better."

Lori scowled, looking back at Trask, but he had already withdrawn, melting back into the crowd. She returned her gaze to Mike, her brows arching over her soft blue eyes as she demanded, "What in hell was he talking about?"

Mike ignored her, reaching out and closing a hand around her arm. "Come on. You and I are going to have a talk."

She resisted, trying to tug her arm away. "I'm having a drink here."

Mike reached behind her and grabbed the half empty tumbler. He tossed it back, grimacing at the overly sweet taste of rum and Coke. After he'd emptied it, he slammed the glass back on the gleaming mahogany bar. "No, you're not. Come on."

Still, Lori tried to tug away from him so he moved closer and bent low, murmuring into her ear, "You can either walk out of here with me or be carried. Believe me, not too many people will think much of it if I throw you over my shoulder."

Her eyes narrowed and the soft curve of her lower lip poked out in a slight pout, but she fell in step alongside him.

Mike had two choices. He could take her upstairs to the private rooms. For three hundred bucks, he could rent one until the club closed at four a.m. Or he could take her out to the trellised patio. The patio led out into a maze of hedges that had dozens of little nooks and crannies where they could get some semblance of privacy.

The private rooms were tempting, but Mike didn't want to be alone with her, not while feeling as edgy as he did right now.

So the patio it was.

Exposé was hopping tonight. Most of the good spots in the maze were already taken. They passed three different couples who were in various stages of undress. As they walked past the third, Mike glanced over his shoulder and saw that Lori's eyes were wide and her face was pink.

And she was staring at the three people to her left. The woman was on her hands and knees, her mouth full of one man's cock. Another man was kneeling behind her. Her skirt was pushed up over her butt and the man was riding her slow and easy.

Just before they passed out of sight, the woman jumped as one of her partners spanked her—once, twice, three times—leaving the smooth skin of her ass a soft pink.

Mike finally found what he was looking for, an empty alcove set back a little from the path. It wasn't completely hidden, but it was a little deeper than the other spots.

It was only the illusion of privacy. The maze was set up just for the express purpose of watching, being watched . . . listening to those nearby.

Somewhere behind them, a woman screamed in pleasure and Mike got his own little jolt of pleasure as Lori's eyes widened. She hadn't been to the club too often, he decided. And not out in the maze yet, he'd bet.

Good.

"Are you having fun?" he asked casually, letting go of her arm and dropping down onto the padded bench.

"Ahh . . . "

That was all she got out. A series of gasping screams, broken up by the words *"Yes . . . please . . . spank me . . . yes . . . please . . . Master . . .* " filled the night air and her eyes widened even more.

"You're at a sex club, sweetheart," Mike drawled, stretching his legs out in front of him. "Why do you look so surprised?"

Lori made a face at him. "I know where I am, Mike."

"Do you?" he murmured. Then in a louder voice, he said, "What I'd like to know is what you are doing here."

The blush that had been fading returned full force, staining her cheeks bright pink. But she didn't stammer or try to change the subject. She pushed a hand through her hair and Mike's attention was distracted for a minute as he watched the soft, pale strands float back down around her naked shoulders. He wanted to see her naked, stretched out on his bed, wearing nothing but that soft pink blush and those blonde curls. He could imagine those curls wrapped around his fist and that pretty pink mouth wrapped around his cock.

She spoke and Mike stifled a groan, shifting his legs, trying to ease the pressure against his throbbing cock. It took a minute for her words to make sense and when they finally did, his eyes narrowed. Shoving up off the bench, he closed the distance between them as he growled, "Say that again."

She rolled her blue eyes and made a soft little harrumph under her breath. *"I said,* why do people usually go to sex clubs?" She cocked her head and gave him a challenging look. "I'm sort of surprised to see you here. I didn't know this was your scene."

"You never asked, darling," he drawled. He ran his eyes over her soft, curving form, lingering on the low neckline of her corset. Then he raised his gaze, staring at her pretty, wine-red-slicked mouth for a long moment before he drawled, "I don't see the point in advertising where I like to spend my free time."

"And I don't see any reason to talk about where I want to spend mine," Lori said archly. Then she gasped as Mike reached out and hooked his fingers under the lacings on her corset, drawing her closer to him.

He spread his legs as he drew her nearer, bringing her to stand between his knees. Close enough that he could smell her skin and see her breasts rise and fall with each breath.

Mike said, "I wish I'd known you were such a curious little kitten, Lori. I'd be happy to help you out." He reached up, trailing a finger down the smooth curve of her shoulder, lower, along the edge of her lace and silk corset.

She inhaled a deep, harsh breath. It made her breasts rise and fall and Mike let his finger linger in the deep valley between her breasts and murmured, "You don't know what you're getting into, Lori. Go home."

Lori hissed and reached up, smacking his hand away from her. "Don't tell me what to do, Mike. I had enough of somebody trying to control me with Dirk. I'm done with it."

Smiling a little, Mike stood and circled around her, staying close enough that their bodies brushed together with each step. "Is that what this is about? Dirk? I can understand wanting to piss him off, but you shouldn't do something you'll regret just to do it."

Lori whirled on her heel and glared at him. Although she was a good eight inches shorter, she still managed to look down her nose at him. "No, it's not about pissing him off. I don't give a damn about Dirk. I'm here because I've wanted to come since the club opened. I tried to get him to come with me." A small, catlike smile curled her lips and she murmured, "Now I'm glad he didn't."

Mike decided he didn't like that smile. He didn't like the secrets that could be lying just behind that smile. "Lori—"

"Don't presume to tell me what to do," she snapped, spinning on her heel and heading back toward the maze. "You know me well enough to know how much that will piss me off."

Mike reached out and closed both hands around her waist. He stroked downward, cupping his hands over her hips, holding her still as he moved up behind her. He pressed his cock against the soft, rounded curves of her butt, rocking against her. "Maybe I don't know you as well as either of us thought."

He lowered his head to nuzzle her neck. Her head fell to the side and Mike almost groaned against the smooth, pale flesh she exposed. "You come to a place like this, darlin', you're going to get told what to do, sooner or later. Isn't that why you came here?"

"No," she snapped, trying to jerk away from him.

Mike just shifted his grip. Sliding one hand around her hip, he pressed low on her belly. He skimmed his other hand up her side and cupped one breast through the silk and lace. The corset was the real thing, though. Through the layers of fabric and boning, he could barely feel her. But the action wasn't lost on her. He could feel the reaction all through her body. "Yes, it is. You came here because you're curious, but you didn't come because you wanted to dominate somebody, sugar. You want to be on the other end. I can see it in your eyes, but I have to wonder if you really know what you're getting into."

Lori had fallen still. Her breasts rose and fell in a ragged rhythm as her breathing sped up. Slowly, Mike reached between her breasts and freed the heavy cord of wine red silk that held her corset closed. "Do you know, Lori?" he murmured, lowering his mouth to her neck as he loosened her corset.

Raking his teeth down her neck, he whispered, "Anybody could walk up and see me touching you. In a minute, I'm going to have you out of this. Anybody who walks by will see me touching you. You sure you want that?"

He turned her around slightly, moving so that he stood in front of her as he finished unlacing the corset. He slipped her out of it and tossed it toward the bench. "Does it bother you that somebody could see you?" he whispered. Reaching out, he tweaked one nipple, squeezing it between his thumb and forefinger.

The pebbled flesh was diamond hard and when he touched her, her entire body jerked. A soft, ragged moan escaped her lips. Mike stared into her face, cursing silently at the blind arousal he saw on her face.

So much for scaring her off.

Mike's control was strained to the breaking point, though. He had to do whatever it took to get her out of here, *before* he lost it.

Hearing footsteps on the path, he spun her around so that she faced out. It was Trask who appeared, walking by himself. When he saw Mike and Lori, he came up short, a small grin on his mouth. His eyes dropped lower, studying Lori's naked breasts as Mike reached around her and cupped the full globes in his hands.

"A total stranger is staring at you, Lori," he muttered, lowering his mouth to her ear. He bit down gently on her earlobe before he rasped, "Open your eyes." Her lashes lifted and he saw her gaze widen as she realized they were being watched. "He likes watch. You want to give to him a show?"

"I prefer to participate," Trask drawled.

Mike laughed, sliding his hands down Lori's narrow torso so he could cup her hips. "I'm not in the mood to share her," he replied.

"Share?" Lori squeaked.

"Hmmm. Share." Mike freed the button at the waist of her low-slung jeans and said, "Is that one of your fantasies, Lori? One of the reasons you came here? Two men at once? Or maybe you were hoping to add another woman to the mix . . . ?"

"No." She shook her head, still staring at Trask with a mixture of horror and arousal on her face.

The soft skin of her belly rippled under his touch as Mike lowered the zipper of her jeans. He slid the tips of his fingers under the waistband of her silk panties, just barely brushing the soft curls at her mound. "Good to hear, Lori. I'm not much interested in sharing you."

Across the distance that separated them, Trask said, "I don't think you're much interested in having her here period, Mike. Honey, he's just trying to scare you off."

"Fuck off, Trask," Mike said easily. He nudged his hips against the round curves of her butt, letting her feel him. "Does that feel like I'm trying to play games, Lori?"

As he spoke, he dipped his fingers lower, until he could feel the hot, wet folds of her sex. Slowly, he circled the hard nub of her clit, once, twice. Then he pushed inside the snug sheath. She was tight—damn tight—and so hot. Mike could already imagine it, stripping her jeans away, taking her to her hands and knees and working his stiff cock inside her. She'd close around him like a silk fist.

The image was almost enough to make him come inside his jeans, just thinking of it.

But this was Lori. No matter what was driving her right now, Mike knew enough about her type to know she'd regret this sooner or later. And that wasn't a burden Mike was going to bear again.

The women he took knew the score.

Lori still believed in fairy tales. Lori wanted to settle down, get married, live happily ever after. It worked for some people—Mike knew that. But she wasn't very likely to find her happily-ever-after here.

And as much as he wanted to, he wasn't going to satisfy himself with her soft, pale body. Neither was he going to let her get used and tossed aside.

Hardening his voice, Mike pushed his fingers deeper and asked, "Come on, Lori. Is this really what you want?"

The soft, broken whimper he heard from her drove him nuts. Mike tried to find something else to focus on, something other than the warm weight of her body against his, something other than the sweet, seductive scent of her skin, something other than how hot and tight her sex felt around his fingers.

Mike looked over her shoulder and met Trask's eyes. "He's watching you, Lori. I know you. Sex is a personal thing for you, something you don't treat casually. Standing here, in front of somebody you don't know, while I do this—" He emphasized his words with a twist of his wrist, screwing his fingers deeper. "This isn't what you want, Lori."

The hell it wasn't . . . the thought circled through Lori's mind, but she couldn't deny one thing. As much as she enjoyed having Mike's hands on her, she didn't want to be watched.

"Mike . . . "

"You want me to stop?" he murmured. "Or keep going? Because if you hang around here, you're going to get a lot more than this." He circled his thumb around her clit, teasing her closer and closer to orgasm and all the while Trask watched, a hot, hungry little light in his eyes.

She almost closed her eyes and tried to block him.

Almost.

But she was going to have to look at herself in the morning, and Lori wasn't so certain she could do that if she went any farther than this.

"Stop." Her voice sounded rusty—totally unlike her own. She swallowed and tried again, this time a little louder. "Stop, Mike."

His hands retreated from inside her clothes and she stood there, breathing raggedly, while he adjusted her jeans and her top. His lips brushed her ear and he murmured, "That's what I figured. Go on home, Lori. This isn't the place for you."

Three

HIS WORDS ECHOED in her head for the next two days.

Lori still couldn't believe what had happened Friday night.

She'd gone to Exposé several times since she'd kicked Dirk out on his sorry ass six weeks ago. While some of the guys hit on her regularly, most of them caught the hint pretty quickly and the few who didn't, she just ignored until they did.

But the first time one of those guys actually caught her attention, Mike showed up.

She couldn't have been more startled to see him there if he had shown up wearing a dog collar and nothing else.

Mike didn't need a dog collar to stand out. He did it just by breathing, but then, some people were just like that. They seemed to command attention just by walking into a room. He spoke—people listened. It was just part of who he was.

And *that* was the only reason she kept dwelling on what he'd said.

This isn't what you want . . .

He was wrong. Mike didn't know a damn thing about what she wanted. How could he?

He's only been one of your best friends for years . . . maybe that's how?

Lori scowled. She'd been talking to herself all damn day and it looked like part of her was losing the argument. Mike *did* know her. Did that mean that maybe she was just out looking for excitement and after it was over, she'd regret it?

It had been one of Dirk's arguments when she tried to talk him into taking her to Exposé. She hadn't listened. She'd insisted he was wrong.

But maybe . . .

No. "No." Shaking her head, Lori said it aloud, hoping to convince herself. "Dirk was wrong. Mike was wrong. I know what I want."

And it was something a little more exciting than what she had now.

Maybe she wasn't interested in a gang bang, and Mike had proven without a doubt that she wasn't into exhibitionism. But she did want more and Lori knew she could find it at Exposé and that was exactly what she was going to do.

And when you see Mike again? What are you going to say?

"I'm a grown woman and I can do whatever the hell I please."

"I'M A GROWN WOMAN and I can do whatever the hell I please."

Lori chanted it under her breath as she pulled into the parking lot of the club.

"I know what I want. I know what I want. I want . . ."

That. I want that. She saw him the minute she stepped through the door and her breath lodged in her throat.

Mike was leaning against the railing, a longneck held loosely in one hand, his eyes watching the dance floor. Her belly clenched with need and she had a strong urge to walk up to him and wrap herself around him. She didn't though. Even if that were the sort of thing she might normally do, the echo of his words were still too loud in her head.

This isn't what you want.

The way he'd said it—so certain, so sure—like he knew what she wanted, what she needed. Hell, how could he possibly know? Lori sometimes didn't know what she wanted. She just knew that she wanted more than she had. A lot more.

Mike could give it to me.

It came out of nowhere, that certain knowledge. Mike was a good-looking guy—Lori had always known that. He was sexy, confident and capable. More, he was funny, he could be as sweet as anything, and he was smart. Mike was never boring.

But Mike had never been more than a friend and Lori hadn't ever wanted more.

And damn him, if he hadn't put his hands on her, she might have been able to continue never wanting more. Lori turned away from him, sliding through the crowd and climbing the stairs to the second level. The dance floor there was smaller but suddenly Lori wasn't interested in dancing.

What interested her was downstairs, staring with moody eyes at the dancers. But Lori was going to settle for a drink, or five. Whatever it took to forget how good his hands felt on her. And to forget how certain he was that he knew what she needed.

Five minutes later, she was seated at the far end of the bar. She took another drink of her White Russian and tried to decide if she should just go home.

"You hiding?" The words were spoken directly into her ear, warm breath kissing her flesh.

Lori jumped and spun around, bumping into Trask. He backed up just enough to let her finish turning and then he grinned at her. Lowering his head, he asked, "Mike seen you here?"

She faked a bored expression, lifting one shoulder in a shrug. "How should I know?"

Wide shoulders stretched under a white T-shirt. "Well, he's downstairs and you're up here, hiding in the corner."

"I'm not hiding," she said loftily. "I'm having a drink. I don't feel very social tonight."

"And you came to a club? That's certainly a way to be left alone." He skimmed a finger down one of the skinny straps of her shirt. The layers of gauzy rose were see-through everywhere except for her breasts, and sequined, so that they caught the light with every breath she took. "Especially dressed like this. You aren't exactly saying *stay away,* not in that outfit."

Then Trask paused, looking into her face. He cocked his head to the side and murmured, "Well. Maybe from the neck down. Your eyes are saying *leave me alone*. Guess that's how you managed to get left alone here as long as you have."

Lori turned back to her drink and managed to scoot just a little bit away. His hand fell to the side but he didn't walk away. She could still feel his eyes burning into her skin. "I came for the drinks, not the company."

His snort had her skin flushing. "You came because Mike told you not to. You don't much care for being bossed around, do you?"

"Do you?"

He laughed, a low, husky sound. "Not one bit. But somehow I don't think you came here expecting to top somebody, now, did you?"

Blood rushed to her cheeks, hot and furious, staining them painfully red. She stared into her drink and mumbled, "Just go away, Trask."

He didn't though. Instead he called out to the bartender. As a beer was pushed in front of him, he said, "And if I do that, then you're going to have somebody else to deal with. At least I'm not going to try to talk you into going outside with me. Or into a room. Nor am I going to try and talk you into leaving. He might though."

He being Mike.

Lori turned her head and saw Mike working his way through the crowd. He hadn't seen her yet and she jerked her head around, bending over her drink and trying to make herself as small as possible. Next to her, Trask was laughing. "That's not going to work, sugar."

"Would you just shut up and mind your own business?" Lori snapped.

"But this is so much more fun." From the corner of her eye, she saw Trask wave at somebody. And she didn't need to look to see who it was. She could tell. Her skin burned as Mike's gaze came to rest on her, burning a hole into her shoulder blades.

Sending Trask a sidelong glance, she muttered, "Jerk."

Trask just shrugged. "He would have seen you anyway. Man's

got radar when it comes to something he wants." He reached out and skimmed his fingers down her shoulder. "You have fun convincing him you came here for just a drink."

"I don't have to convince him of anything," Lori said, but Trask was already melting into the crowd. By the time Mike reached her side, Trask was lost among the masses.

"What are you doing here?"

Spinning around on her stool, Lori gave Mike a bright, false smile and lifted her drink. "Having a drink. And you?"

"I'm getting ready to haul your ass out of here."

Lori arched her brows and studied him for a minute. Then she shrugged and took a sip, spinning back around to the bar. "No. You're not."

"Didn't we already go over this, sweetheart? This isn't your thing."

Indignant, she spun back around to glare at him. He stood there, staring at her with a condescending look on his face that reminded her all too much of Dirk's reaction when she tried to tell him about something she wanted. "No. *We* didn't go over anything. *You* just decided it wasn't my thing. Shouldn't that be my call?"

He reached up, cupping the back of her neck in a big, warm hand. He lowered his head and spoke directly into her ear. She shivered at the feel of his warm breath dancing over her skin, even as angry indignation filled her when he said, "I'll haul your ass out of here, Lori. Don't think I won't."

She couldn't pull away. It wasn't that he was holding her too tightly, though he did have a good firm grip on her neck. She just *couldn't* pull away. It felt as though there was something magnetic between them, pulling her closer and closer . . . and closer. Lori felt the warmth of his body against hers and realized she had slid off the stool and was pressed against him.

Damn it. Why in the hell was *he* doing this to her? And why now? Mike was one of her best friends; they'd been friends for a long time. Granted, she couldn't say that she hadn't ever noticed him before on that level. She had. But lately . . .

The scent of him flooded her senses and it was making her lightheaded. She licked her lips and fantasized, very briefly, about leaning forward and licking *him*. Right there, just above the pulse she could see in his neck. Instead, she lifted her gaze and met his. "I'm a big girl, Mike. Aren't you the one who was telling me I needed to find what made me happy? Guess what . . . that's what I'm doing."

"And you've suddenly decided that hanging out at a sex club makes you happy?"

Lori lifted a shoulder. "I don't know. But I really want to find out."

For a minute, he was quiet. He said nothing, just watched her with that intense probing gaze. Then he reached out and closed his hands around her hips. Her skin started buzzing from that light touch and Lori swallowed her whimper before it could escape. But when he pressed his hips against hers, rubbing his swollen cock against her belly, the whimper slipped past her lips, followed by a harsh, ragged gasp.

"I can help you with that, Lori. You're curious? You want to take a walk on the wild side? I can show you things some of the boys here can't even dream about." He skimmed his lips down her throat, then raked the skin lightly with his teeth.

Lori shuddered in his arms but before she could completely

melt against him, she pulled away. Wrapping her arms around her waist, she said, "And why in hell do you want to do that?"

A tiny grin curled up the corners of his mouth. Reaching out, he took her palm and placed it against the front of his pants, molding his fingers around hers until she cupped him through the denim, then rocked against her. "Well, here's one good reason. Another . . . well, you don't know what kind of trouble you're getting into. I can make sure it's just the sort of trouble you'd like."

He leaned down, taking her mouth with his. He pushed his tongue inside her mouth, tangling it with hers. Heat pressed into heat as Lori rocked against him, and for a second she almost ignored the voice of common sense in her head.

But she was damn tired of guys thinking she needed to be protected against what she wanted. Working her hands between them, she jerked her head to the side and arched away from him. His hands fell away from her hips, and as soon as he let her go, she backed away. She boosted herself up onto the stool and turned back to her drink. "Go find somebody else to beat your chest for, Tarzan. I'm not Jane, lost in the big, mean jungle. I can handle myself."

There was nothing but silence and when she looked back over her shoulder, Mike was gone.

But she could feel him watching her the entire night. And every time a guy approached her, she couldn't work up any interest.

HE'D PLANNED TO SPEND MOST of Sunday lying around watching football and drinking beer. Instead, he spent it brooding and staring out the window as he tried to resist the temptation to go over to Lori's.

Whether it was to apologize or kiss her again, he didn't know. He could still taste her. Silk and spices. That was what kissing her made him think of. She looked too sweet and golden to taste that exotic. She tasted dark. She tasted hot. And she'd been hot, arching against him in a way that had him ready to strip her naked and fuck her blind.

She hadn't left, but she hadn't ever gotten up and danced. And it wasn't for lack of being asked. Lori had sat there for nearly two hours drinking rum and cola, then switching to water.

When she had left, he had followed her outside and watched her climb into her car. He had watched her drive away and felt hollow inside.

He still felt hollow inside.

Didn't change the fact that he didn't want her at Exposé.

If she kept going there, she was going to end up getting exactly what she thought she was looking for. Mike didn't really care to see her with one of the guys from Exposé. Mike knew that Lori didn't belong there.

He just had to convince her of that.

When the phone rang close to five p.m., Mike glanced at the number out of habit and almost didn't pick up. It was his partner, Alexander O'Malley, but it was their weekend off. No reason to pick up and he didn't feel very social.

Finally, on the eighth ring, he did pick up and grunted an unintelligible greeting into the mouthpiece.

"You sound like you've had one hell of a weekend. Heard you were at Exposé. Have any fun last night?"

"Wasn't there looking for fun. Just wanted a drink," Mike replied curtly. And even if he had been looking for fun, he wouldn't have found it. Lately, Lori was the only woman he wanted and he'd be damned if he went down that road. "What do you want?"

"You sound like you're in a shitty mood."

"I am. What do you want?"

Alex laughed. "Hell, you're being such an ass, I don't know if I want to tell you."

"Fine. Don't." Mike started to hang up the phone and Alex muttered, "Hell, you really are in a shitty mood. I was going to bring a friend over but you'd probably scare her off in this mood."

A friend. Mike knew the translation of that, but for once, he really wasn't interested. What he was interested in was off-limits. "Don't bother. My mood is toxic today."

Alex snorted and said, "Yeah, I noticed." He hung up and Mike hit the disconnect button before tossing the phone over his shoulder. It landed somewhere in the vicinity of the couch.

A few yards away, he saw Lori's back door open. She came out wearing a pair of white shorts and a black halter top. As she carried a garbage bag over to the garage, he was treated to a view of her slender, tanned back. Her skin had always looked so incredibly soft.

Now he knew it was even softer than it looked and the memories of it taunted him. It was one of the reasons he hadn't gotten more than an hour or two of sleep last night.

She moved around the backyard for a few minutes after she'd pitched the garbage bag. She knelt down by the flower beds, plucked a few weeds, moved over to another flower bed and bent over to straighten one of the fairy statues. Mike's eyes were drawn to the taut curve of her butt as she bent over and his cock, already hard and aching, started to throb as he imagined stripping away those neat white shorts and pushing inside her. Her pussy first, teasing her closer and closer to climax. When she was begging and pleading, he'd lube up the tight glove of her ass and take her there.

Over and over, until she was too hoarse and limp to even moan his name.

"Shit," he muttered, turning away from the window and stomping across the floor.

Just go over there. It was such a tempting thought. If last night was any indication, then he had a feeling he could have her naked and under him, or kneeling in front of him . . . bent over the back of her couch . . . the images circled through his mind, one after the other, teasing him. Five minutes. He could get her naked and be inside her in five minutes.

He had wanted just that for years, ever since the cute blonde had moved in next door. He hadn't ever pursued though. Mike had taken one look into her summery blue eyes and known she wasn't the kind for one night stands and he wasn't interested in anything longer.

Then they'd become friends and it had been a little easier not to think about seeing her naked. And it had taken just one touch to totally ruin that. Mike wasn't sure if he'd ever be able to think of Lori in a purely "just friends" light again.

"You shouldn't have touched her," he muttered, swinging away from the window. He prowled the room, alternating between cursing himself and cursing Lori for showing up at Exposé and messing things up.

Hell. He didn't know if he could keep his hands off her. He wanted her too damn much and if she weren't one of his best friends, there wouldn't be a problem.

He didn't fuck his friends and he didn't fuck women who didn't know the game.

He stomped over to the window just in time to see her straightening from the flower beds, stretching her arms overhead and arching her back. Her breasts lifted with the movement and her top rode up, baring the smooth, tanned expanse of her belly.

"That's it," he muttered, stalking through the house. Lori was a big girl, right? She had gone to Exposé for a reason and who in the hell was he to tell her she shouldn't? And why in the hell shouldn't he be the one to give her what she wanted? He wasn't some stranger. He was the guy who had wanted her for years. And he'd be careful.

Mike knew how to be careful. Just because he usually didn't like to mess with being careful didn't mean he couldn't. He would be careful with Lori. He wouldn't take more than she was willing to give and he wouldn't push her any farther than she was ready to go.

When it was over, it was over. Both of them could walk away without regrets.

Right?

It was faulty reasoning. When his cock wasn't hurting like a bad tooth, he knew he'd find all sorts of reasons why he'd have regrets, but right now, he couldn't think of one.

All he could think was how damn bad he wanted her. The

jerk-off boyfriend was out of the picture and Lori had melted under his hands. That was all he needed right now.

Throwing open the front door, he got outside just in time to see her climb into her car and shut the door. By the time she was halfway down the street, Mike had stomped back inside, swearing under his breath.

FOUR

FRIDAY CAME AND WENT without Lori showing her pretty blonde head at Exposé. Mike knew, because he spent the entire damn evening watching the door. By the time last call rolled around, he had convinced himself that Lori had listened to him the past weekend and decided this wasn't the place for her.

Either that, or he'd scared her off.

Didn't matter, as long as she stayed away.

Despite the fact that he had been this far away from trying to seduce her out of her clothes, Mike knew how bad an idea that would be. People needed to stay in the element they were best suited to. Lori wasn't suited for this.

And this was where Mike was comfortable.

He left the club, telling himself that tomorrow night he'd come back and get laid. That was what he needed to do, but his lack of interest in doing just that was part of the problem. He needed to get his mind off Lori, stop thinking with his cock.

* * *

NEARLY TWENTY-FOUR HOURS LATER, Mike sat brooding over a half-empty tumbler of whiskey, watching as Trask led Lori out onto the dance floor.

Stop thinking of her! Yeah, sure. That was proving a hell of a lot more difficult than he'd expected.

Trask was one of the few regulars who didn't mind going out on the dance floor. Most of the men stood by on the sidelines, watching the ladies. They weren't there to dance.

Those who didn't mind the dancing used it like it was some part of a mating ritual. Mike figured that was all dancing really was. He'd done the same thing himself and hadn't ever thought twice about it.

At least until he saw Trask dancing with Lori.

Tossing back the rest of his whiskey, Mike pushed his way through the crowd on the dance floor. The song ended before he reached them and another one started up, this one faster, with a hard, driving beat. Trask lowered his head, murmured into Lori's ear, but she shook her head, backing away. Her face was flushed. From dancing? Or from whatever Trask had said to her?

She left the dance floor and Trask turned around, coming up short when he saw Mike. A wide grin lit his face and he arched a brow. Gold flashed as the hoop in his brow caught the light. "Hi, Mike."

Mike raised his voice, shouting over the music, and leaned in closer to Trask. "I see her leave this dance floor with you, you're going to need a doctor."

Trask shrugged. "Don't worry. She's not interested."

Mike watched as the other man disappeared in the crowd and

then he turned, searching for Lori's blonde head. He caught a glimpse of her moving through the outer fringe of the crowd. Keeping that blonde head in sight, Mike started toward her.

She disappeared into the women's restroom and Mike propped his back against the wall opposite the door.

The women's lounge was loud and crowded, just like it had been every other time Lori had been in there.

The bathroom was done in black, white and red with huge art deco prints on the walls and glossy black vases filled with fresh bloodred roses and sprays of baby's breath.

Lori sat on one of the long black lounges with her legs drawn up, staring at nothing.

Trask had asked her to go for a walk with him. A walk out to the maze.

Lori had declined easily.

She wasn't disappointed in what she'd found at Exposé, but she still hadn't exactly found what she was looking for either. She just wasn't interested in visiting the maze, walking by all those little alcoves with any of the men she'd met here. They just didn't interest her much.

What about Mike . . .

Mike . . . He was a different story altogether, and not one she wanted to think about right now. She pushed thoughts of him out of her head.

Thinking about him lately just made her itchy. She remembered the way he had kissed her when they were in the maze the first time she'd been here, the way he'd touched her the second time he'd seen her here. She remembered that confident, certain way he'd told her she didn't belong here. She remembered how his mouth tasted, how it felt on hers. She remembered the way he touched her, knowing they were being watched, doing it just to prove a point.

All in all, those thoughts worked to make her hotter than hell, *and* madder than hell.

Jerk.

Sexy, mouthwatering jerk, but jerk nonetheless.

For the past week, they had been ignoring each other and as far as Lori was concerned, they could keep ignoring each other. At least until he figured out she didn't need a babysitter.

Maybe it had been the Good Samaritan in him that had tried to warn her away. She didn't know. Tried to tell herself she didn't really care.

Except she did. She wanted to feel his hands on her body again. Wanted to kiss him again, wanted to snuggle up close against him and just lean on him, feeling his warmth and his strength. And she missed her friend. She missed leaning against the fence talking with him and she missed catching a movie with him every now and then. She just plain missed him.

"I need to just go home." Lori was too morose to enjoy the club and until she could stop thinking about Mike so much, she was wasting her time there.

With a sigh, she shoved to her feet and headed for the door, sidestepping the two women in front of her who were locked in a tight clinch. Modesty and privacy weren't big issues at Exposé. Lori had figured that out, but she couldn't see getting that hot and heavy in a public restroom. Even one as nicely kept as this one.

All in all, Lori decided that so far her quest for a little more excitement in her life had been a total waste of time. She hadn't found any excitement, and worse, she hadn't found anybody she really wanted to, ah . . . get excited with. Other than Mike.

Out of the blue, Grace's words came back to haunt her. *You'll know* . . .

When they'd been talking in the sauna a few weeks ago, Grace had told her that she'd know when she met the right kind of guy.

Her gut clenched and Lori blew out a breath. The right guy.

Hell. If she was going by the way her body reacted to Mike, then she'd met the right guy years ago.

He was just determined to protect her from everybody. Including himself.

As she opened the door, she was already digging into the small purse at her side for her keys. It wasn't until she plowed into Mike's chest that she even realized he had been standing there.

Waiting for her, apparently.

"Wow. Do I get another lecture?" she said sardonically as she extracted herself from his hands.

"I just wanted to talk to you."

"Not tonight."

As Lori started to walk away, his hand came up and gripped her arm. "Lori . . . "

She stopped in her tracks and turned to look at him. Carefully enunciating each word, she repeated, "Not tonight. I am tired. I am irritable. I want to be alone."

His eyes narrowed, his mouth tightened, but then he nodded and stepped back, his hand falling away.

Lori turned her back to him and walked out.

WHEN SHE OPENED HER FRONT DOOR, the last thing she expected to see was Mike and she almost slammed the door in his face just so she wouldn't have to talk to him. She was getting damn tired of his unwanted opinions. However, too many years of being nice kept her from being that rude.

Lori arched a brow as she faced him. "Oh, goodie. Are you here to fuss at me again?"

Mike didn't say a word as he closed the distance between them, moving so close the tips of his booted feet nudged her bare toes. So close she could feel the warmth of his breath on her face. "I'm coming inside. We're going to have a talk."

Lori snorted. "There's nothing to talk about. I'm a big girl and I can do what I want. And there's nothing you can do about that, Mike. Go away."

She reached out to close the door but he caught it with one hand. With the other, he reached out and jerked her against him, pressing her close. So close she could feel the long, hard lines of his body against hers. "I said, we're going to have a talk. You want to do it here?" he murmured. He slid a hand down her back and cupped her hip. Holding her still, he rocked his cock against her, sending a series of hot, shivery little thrills racing through her.

"I don't mind an audience. But what about you?" He nuzzled her neck and raked his teeth across the sensitive skin.

"Damn it, Mike." She shoved against his shoulders but he just held her closer. "Fine! Come in."

But if she'd been expecting him to let her go, she'd been hoping for too much. She figured that out real quick as he simply slid his arm around her waist and straightened, lifting her feet off the ground. He stepped inside and kicked the door shut behind him, all without removing his mouth from her neck.

A shaky sigh escaped her as he nuzzled her neck right where it joined her shoulder. "I know what this is about, Lori. You're going to Exposé because you're curious. You're not the first to do that and you won't be the last. Hell, *I* went because I was curious. I've been doing this quite awhile and I can tell you one thing for sure, curious people go there all the time, but they don't usually stay long."

He licked her neck, then bit down lightly, just grazing the surface of her skin with his teeth. Lori couldn't stop from melting against him, and honestly, she didn't want to. His touch was . . . sheer heaven.

She had to admit that, even if she was irritated as hell with him. "Then what's the big deal? Why does it matter to you so much? Every time you've seen me there, you look ready to spit nails."

Mike chuckled. Lori could feel the vibration of it against her breasts, and her nipples started to throb in reaction. Damn it, even his laugh turned her on. How had he gone from best friend to wet dream material?

"It's a big deal because I don't want to see you getting hurt. I don't want to see you get in over your head." He pulled away, reaching up to cup her cheek in his palm. He rubbed his thumb over her lower lip and Lori felt her heart melt. There was something gentle, almost sweet about the unconscious caress.

But the misty feeling started to evaporate as he continued to speak. "There are guys in the club who'll pull you into their lifestyle, Lori, and some of them have very twisted ideas of pleasure. Even I'll admit that. You get pulled too far in, you may have a hard time finding your way back. I don't want to see that happen to you."

"I'm not going to do anything I don't want to do, Mike."

His gaze lifted until they were staring each other in the eye. Sliding his hand down from her face, he cupped his palm around her neck so he could draw her closer. "That's the whole thing, Lori. You *will* want to do it. Maybe not right away and you might regret it later on, but that doesn't undo what you've already done."

Her irritation was almost as effective as a bucket of cold water. She arched her back, craning her neck away from him and squirming. "Put me down, damn it." This time he actually did, and she wiggled out from between him and the wall. "I'm capable of thinking for myself, Mike. I'm a big girl and I'm getting damn tired of men who think they know what I want better than I do. I'm tired of men thinking that they know what's best for me. I put up with it from Dirk and that was a big-ass mistake. I am *not* going to put up with it from you."

Mike's eyes narrowed and he stared at her with an icy expression on his face. "Don't you dare compare me to that bastard. I'm just worried . . . "

Lori smiled and said, "You're worried I'll get in over my head, like you just said. Which means you don't really think I can think for myself." She planted her hands against his chest and shoved with all her strength.

He didn't move much and the one step back he did take made her think he was taking it more to humor her than anything else. "I know you can think for yourself, Lori. But what you're looking for there . . . look, it's like a drug. You get into it, you start to crave it. Some people can walk away when they realize it's getting too intense. Others can't. And it can destroy them inside."

"For crying out loud, Mike. All I've done is go dancing there a few times. It's not like I'm running up to any and every guy there begging them to make me their sub or something. I'm not looking for an orgy and I'm not looking for recreational sex on the side. Stop worrying about me so much!"

"If you're not looking for recreational sex, as you put it, what *are* you doing there? What are you looking for?" he demanded.

Lori just glared at him, turned on her heel, and stalked away from him. He caught her arm and spun her around. As he crowded her up against the wall, pressing his pelvis against hers, Lori pressed her lips together to keep from moaning aloud. Man, the feel of him—it was something else.

She'd thought sex with Dirk had been good. But Dirk hadn't ever made her feel this hot, not even when he was inside her, bringing her to climax. The look of anger on Mike's face kept fanning the flames of her own anger and Lori had an insane, violent urge to reach up and jerk his head down and kiss him with all the fury she had inside her.

"I don't know. Just *something*." She snarled at him and squirmed against his hold. "Go away, will you?"

"No." He had lowered his head and muttered it against her neck. Then he bit her.

Lori felt the shock of it clear down to her toes. She arched against him, her body taut, then she slowly started to melt against him. She whimpered under her breath and started to rock her hips against his, trying to find a little relief from the pressure building inside.

"You got any idea what you're asking for, little girl?" he murmured. As he spoke, he trailed his fingers down the outer curve of one breast. When she arched into his touch, he cupped her flesh more fully and started to circle his thumb around her nipple.

His other hand rested on her waist, and as he massaged her breast, he wrapped it tightly around her waist. "You're out of your league there, Lori," he murmured, lowering his lips to her neck in a slow, gentle caress that was completely at odds with the rage she felt coming from him. "You have no idea of the things a man would want to do with you."

Lori tossed her hair out of her face and dared him. "Why don't you tell me?"

"I will tell you. I'll tell you what I'd do if you were there with me. I'd tie you up. You want to lie there helpless, while I strip you naked and tie you to a table?"

Heat ripped through her at the thought of it. If he thought he'd shock her, he was dead wrong. "Yes."

Against her, Mike stiffened. "That's not you, Lori. That's not how you are. You want to lie there helpless, while somebody uses you like a toy and then just throws you away?" he rasped against her ear.

"You wouldn't use me, Mike." She might not know about the

kind of sex he was into, but she did know *him*. "And I'd like to see the man who thinks he could just toss me aside. I've been there once. It won't happen again."

"Stop bringing him into this. He has nothing to do with it." His voice lowered and his hands closed over her waist. "Since you seem so certain, maybe I should give you a taste of exactly *what* you're asking for."

Lori forced a laugh. "You aren't going to scare me away, Mike. Don't even try. You don't have it in you to hurt a woman." Just the thought of him giving her a "taste" was enough to have her thighs going limp with need.

"Really." Mike drawled the word long and slow and then his eyes went dark. She received no other warning, just his mouth closing over hers in a hard, violent kiss.

He jerked her shirt and buttons went flying. Her breasts were naked underneath. Mike's hands closed over her breasts, but despite the fury she could taste in his kiss, they weren't cruel. Oh, he was rough. He tugged and twisted her nipples, kneading the plump mounds of her breasts, squeezing them with a force that was just shy of pain.

And Lori loved it.

FIVE

WHEN SHE MOANED into his mouth, Mike was torn between stripping her naked so he could fuck her blind and stripping her naked so he could paddle her ass. Then he'd fuck her blind.

Tearing his mouth away from her, he snarled, "Look, damn it. See how easy it is to leave a mark on you?" There were faint red marks on her breasts from where he'd handled her so roughly. "You want to know how much worse it can get?"

Incredibly, Lori just smiled at him. She slid her hands up his chest as she rose on her toes and pressed her lips to his. "With you? Absolutely."

As she stared up at him with drowsy eyes, Mike could literally feel the threads of his control snapping one by one. "I can only be pushed so far, Lori. Push too far and there's no turning back."

"Promises, promises."

With a snarl, Mike slid his hands under her shirt and jerked it off. Staring at her naked breasts, he boosted her up and braced her back against the wall. He pushed his thigh between hers, using that to support her weight as he lowered his mouth to her breasts.

Through the thin cotton of her pants, he could feel her. Hot and wet. Scalding him through his jeans. His cock jerked in reaction.

Plumping one breast in his hand, he bent down and nipped her lightly. Her nipple was tight and hard, and her skin tasted sweet. Craving more, he opened his mouth wide and sucked on her nipple, taking as much of her flesh into his mouth as he could.

Lori cried out and arched against him. Mike wrapped his hands around her hips and started to drag her back and forth across his thigh. The feel of her moisture soaking through her clothes and his, the scent of her was an aphrodisiac and Mike lowered her to the ground, intent on getting a taste of her.

He stripped away her pants and panties, using his hands to spread her thighs wide. He held her eyes as he lowered his mouth to her sex. The curls on her mound were trimmed and just a few shades darker than her hair. He nuzzled them for a second and then he licked her. She cried out his name, her hands fisting in his hair. Cupping her ass in his hands, Mike held her and started to spear his tongue in and out. She rocked against him. The taste of her flooded his mouth and he groaned, greedy and ravenous for more.

He pushed away from her and caught her hands as she reached for him. He shoved back up to his feet and stared down at her, struggling to breathe. He was sweating. His heart was pounding a mile a minute. He could still taste her on his lips and he wanted more. He had a bad feeling *more* didn't describe what he wanted. He wanted a hell of a lot more and he was going to want it often.

"Lie back."

Lori blinked, her lashes lowering over her eyes. Then she licked her lips and looked him square in the face. "Where?"

"Right where you are, little girl. If I wanted you someplace else, I would have told you."

As she lay down, Mike jerked his shirt off and undid the buckle on his belt. He started to take off his jeans, but decided against that. The minute he was naked, he was going to be on her, hard and fast, and he wasn't ready for this to be over before it started.

Lori lay on the hardwood floor, her hair spread around her head and shoulders. Her nipples were hard, her breasts were full. She had long, well-muscled thighs and full hips. Her belly was softly curved. Everything about her seemed to scream sex. He moved so that he was standing at her feet and he nudged them with one of his own. "Spread your thighs so I can look at you."

She stared up at him, her face red. Mike cocked a brow at her. "I'm going to go down on you again in a minute and then I'm going to fuck you until you can't see straight. If you're okay with that, then you should be okay with me looking at that pink pussy."

She sucked in a harsh breath of air, her breasts rising and falling. But she slowly spread her legs. Not wide enough, but it was a start. He knelt between her thighs and pushed them wider. "Like that," he muttered. "So I can see how wet you are." As he spoke, he slid one finger through the glistening wet folds. He looked at her face as he slipped his finger between his lips. "You taste good."

She bucked as he touched her again and Mike laid a hand on

her belly. "Be still, Lori." He lay between her thighs, using his shoulders to wedge them farther apart. "Don't come before I tell you to."

"Damn it, I'm about to come *now*."

Mike slid one hand down the outside of her thigh until he could stroke the outer curve of her rump. "If you come before I say you can, I'm going to spank you." He smacked his hand lightly against her flesh and smiled as she stiffened.

He stared into her eyes while he lowered his mouth to her mound. Circling his tongue around her clit, Mike slid his other hand along the inside of her thigh. When he pushed two fingers inside her, she was already tight and hot, clenching around him. He stroked them in and out, and as he began the fourth stroke, she started making a low keening sound in her throat.

Mike lifted up and stared at her, cocking a brow. "Don't come."

"Then stop touching me!"

Mike smiled at her and twisted his fingers, screwing them in and out. Lori gasped. He lowered his mouth back to her sex, and as he stroked her clit, she erupted. Mike continued to stroke her through the climax and when her eyes opened up, he lifted her up against him. "You came."

"You made me."

"I told you that if you came before I told you to, I'd spank you."

Her eyes narrowed. "You did it on purpose."

Mike bent down and murmured into her ear, "I know." Mike stood and lifted her into his arms. He carried her over to the sofa. One end of the sofa was more of a chaise longue and he chose that end and sat, stretching his legs out. He stroked a hand up her thigh and murmured, "Turn over."

"I don't think so."

Mike fisted a hand in her hair, drew her head back and took her mouth. He kissed her until she was arching and straining against him. Then he pulled away. "Turn over."

Lori crossed her arms over her chest. Mike smiled. "Last chance."

"And what are you going to do, make me?"

"Yeah." He cupped her in his hand, pushing one finger inside her. Her sheath was hot and swollen, resisting his entry. "You ever been so close to coming, that all it would take was one more touch?" As he spoke, he nuzzled her neck.

Lori shivered against him and arched into his hand, rocking her hips faster against his palm. "Mike . . . "

"That's where I'm going to take you, so close that all you need is one more touch and you'll explode. And I won't give it to you."

That was exactly what he did. Over and over, Mike worked her to the edge of orgasm. Her body was covered with a fine sheen of sweat and she was panting, straining and arching, begging him to let her come. Mike stopped touching her. He cupped her in his hand and lowered his head, murmuring in her ear. "Turn over."

Her eyes were glassy and she obeyed blindly. Mike stared down at her rump and stroked the taut curves for a moment. She jerked at the first light slap. With the second one, she moaned. The third one, she screamed. Mike nudged her thighs apart and pushed his fingers inside her. The climax ripped through her with violent intensity.

He didn't wait until the tremors passed this time. He surged upward, spilling her onto her back. They took up most of the narrow couch but Mike didn't have time to carry her to the bed, or even move to the floor. His cock was so damn swollen, so damn sore, he was certain he would erupt like a geyser any second.

And he wanted to be inside her when it happened. He dug a rubber out of his back pocket and tore it open with hands gone clumsy. He jerked his jeans open and hissed out a breath as he rolled it down his aching length. He shoved her thighs apart and levered his weight up over her. "Look at me," he ordered.

Their eyes met and held as he pushed inside. She was tight around him and he could feel the slick tissues rippling to accommodate him. He gritted his teeth and lashed down the urge to come into her hard and fast, over and over, until he exploded. Instead, he let her body adjust to his slowly, sinking into her one inch at a time.

Once he had completely buried his length inside, he sank down against her, pressing his body to hers. He could feel every last silken inch of her naked body pressed against his. Mike slid his hands down, capturing first one wrist then the other and pinning them over her head. "You going to let me tie you down, Lori? Just how far are you willing to let me take you?" he murmured against her ear.

"However far you want, Mike." She arched under him and whimpered, rotating her hips against his. She moaned a hungry little kittenish sound and when he pulled out and slammed back inside her, the kitten turned into a tigress, arching up and purring.

"You sure about that?" He shifted so that he held both wrists in one hand and reached down with his free hand, catching her thigh and dragging it up so that she was open and exposed. "What if I pull out and tell you to turn around and bend over so I can fuck your ass? You going to let me do that?"

She clenched around him and came with sudden, violent intensity. As the walls of her sheath rhythmically gripped his cock, he lowered his mouth to her and muttered, "I'll take that as a yes."

Lori was still floating back down to Earth as he caressed her buttocks, his fingers sliding between to tease the sensitive opening there. He waited until her eyes cleared a little before he pressed the tip of his finger against her anus. "You're tight. You've never done anal before, have you?"

Her eyes were wide and dark. Mike had a feeling she was both excited and terrified. Just the way he'd prefer it. She licked her lips and shook her head, still staring at him. When he pushed the tip of his finger inside her, she shrieked and shuddered in his hands. "Relax," he murmured. "Don't tense up so much. It will just make it hurt."

"It already hurts." Her voice broke a little on the last word and Mike lowered his lips to hers, kissing her and teasing her back to fever pitch.

"It's supposed to hurt some. It's not going to feel like it would if I was fucking your pussy, Lori. Otherwise, what's the point?" He wiggled his finger a little, stretching the sensitive opening and waiting until she relaxed a little more before pushing deeper. "We won't do any more tonight, but if you aren't careful, the next time I take you, it's going to be here. And I won't stop until you beg me to."

Lori's eyes stared into his, panicked and aroused. Mike laughed, rotating his hips against hers, driving his cock deep and fast, then retreating in a slow, teasing glide. "You look ready to beg me now, Lori." He dipped his head and circled his tongue around the edge of her lips, tracing the seam between and slipping inside her mouth for just a ghost of a second before he lifted his head.

Then he moved to her breasts, taking one nipple in his mouth, caressing it with his tongue, teasing it until every touch was a toss-up between excruciating pleasure and excruciating pain. Then he went to the other nipple and did the same thing.

By the time he lifted his head to look down at her, she was panting and flushed and he knew just one more touch in the right spot would send her screaming into climax. "You willing to beg, Lori?"

Her eyes narrowed, the fog clearing for just a second. "Hell, no."

"I'll take that as a dare." Their gazes locked and held as he slowly started shafting her. Mike shifted his position so that he wasn't rubbing against her clit and every time she lifted against him, trying to get closer, he moved away. He slowed his thrusts, shortening each one until he was only sinking halfway inside before pulling out.

He kept to that rhythm until she was sweating and straining under him. Each slick curve was dewed with sweat and her eyes were dark and blind, staring up at him with desperation. Against his chest, he could feel the tight little buds of her nipples. Everything inside her was reaching for climax.

"You ready to beg?" he teased. Mike slid his hand down her

side, cupped his hand over her hip and lifted her slightly. He squeezed the taut flesh of her ass and murmured, "Beg me and maybe I'll be easy on you when I help myself to your sweet little ass."

"I don't want easy," Lori gasped. Her arms tensed, straining against the grip he had on her wrists.

"You want to come?"

"Hell, yes."

"Then beg me . . . just say *please, Mike* . . . that's all I need to hear." He pulled out and hoped she'd say it soon. As he sank back inside her, he thought his dick would explode.

She held out another three minutes. Then, as he rolled them onto their sides and lightly spanked her butt, she lost control. He let go of her hands and she closed them over his shoulders, her nails tearing into his flesh. "Please, Mike . . . damn it, I can't stand it anymore."

Hell. Me neither. Mike groaned in gratitude and rolled her onto her back again, hooking his arms under hers and gripping her shoulders. With her body braced, he started to plunge into her with hard, deep strokes. On the third stroke, they arched against each other and exploded. Mike swallowed her scream and rode her through the climax until her body went limp, collapsing into the narrow cushions of the couch.

A few minutes passed before either of them made a sound. At Lori's mumbled "Mmmph" Mike raised his head and said, "Huh?"

She smiled at him, her eyes closed. "I thought you said it was supposed to get worse."

"Ahhh. Well, I figured I should take it easy on you at first. I won't hold anything back next time." He shifted down and rested his head between her breasts, cupping his hand over one. He rubbed his thumb back and forth over a pink nipple and watched it pucker and draw tight.

"Promises, promises," she teased. Then she looped her arms around his neck and sighed. "Wake me in a week."

MIKE DIDN'T GIVE HER A WEEK, but he did give her a couple of hours. They lay on her bed, Lori curled up against his side, Mike stroking his hand through the wealth of thick curls. Her breathing was slow and even, her entire body relaxed, and Mike was burning with the need to roll her onto her back and push inside her.

Literally burning. She shifted against him and he could feel the damp heat between her legs. Her right thigh was draped over his and every time she moved, he could feel her. She was still slick and wet from earlier. Wouldn't take much to pull her atop him and push inside her. She'd take him a little easier this time and he could watch her wake up as she rode him.

Sounded like bliss.

Only problem was that the rubbers were on the damn bedside table to his right and he couldn't reach them without moving her.

"You're awake." She mumbled it against his flesh and reached down, closing her fingers around his erection.

Her hand felt soft and cool. Lori stroked him from base to tip and Mike groaned, arching into her touch. "Shit."

Her hand fell away and she sat up, staring at him with big

sleepy blue eyes. Her curly hair tumbled into her face and she reached up and shoved it back. Mike tugged down the sheet she had pulled over her breasts and stared at her. She looked like a wet dream come true—big blue eyes, sun-streaked blonde hair and ripe round breasts.

He stared into her eyes as he rubbed the back of his hand across one nipple, watching the flesh pebble under that light touch. She leaned into his touch but instead of taking advantage of it, Mike sat up, keeping his back against the smooth wooden headboard. Now that his arms were free, he could reach the rubbers he'd dumped on her bedside table and he grabbed one, tearing it open and rolling it down over his cock without ever looking away from her.

"Straddle me."

Lori touched the tip of her tongue to her lips and squirmed a little. "I uh . . . I think I should take a shower. Brush my teeth."

"Later." He reached out, caught her wrist and pulled her to him.

She came slowly, shifting so that she could plant a knee on either side of his hips. His erection throbbed, pressed between their bodies. "Take me inside you now."

She did, slowly, her nails biting into his shoulders. Once she had taken him completely inside her, she moaned and arched. Her breasts lifted and he stared at them, his mouth watering. Her nipples were small, tight and pink. He pushed up onto his elbows and, catching one between his lips, sucked it into his mouth.

Lori moaned, her hips jerking, and the snug walls of her sex clenched around his cock in a milking caress. He shifted to the other nipple, using his teeth and his tongue ruthlessly. She pumped her hips and Mike reached up, cupped her ass in his hands and held her tight against him to keep her from moving.

Mike pulled away and stared up at her with a smile. "Slow down," he murmured. "You're always in such a hurry."

She mewled and leaned down, pressing against him. "You get off on teasing people?"

"Absolutely." He fisted a hand in her hair and drew it aside, baring the long, slender expanse of her neck. Then he leaned forward and raked the sensitive skin with his teeth. In his arms, Lori shivered.

With a smile, Mike did it again, this time biting down lightly in the spot where her neck and shoulder joined. He smoothed his hands down her sides and gripped her hips, pulling her against him as he arched into her. He could feel her heat through the thin latex shield but he hated the barrier. He couldn't feel how wet she was and he wanted to. He wanted to be skin to skin. Badly enough that he almost lifted her away so he could strip off the rubber. Common sense won out but he had to have more than this.

Wrapping his arms around her, Mike shifted, rising to his knees and taking her onto her back. He withdrew until just the head of his cock was inside her and then he plunged deep. Buried inside her, he circled his hips and then withdrew. Lori's nails gouged his flesh and he turned his head and pressed a kiss to the back of one hand. Lori bucked under him and her sheath convulsed around his cock, a series of rippling little caresses, each one gripping him tighter than the last. Mike gritted his teeth and held still, waiting until the urge to come had passed. Or at least eased a little.

"Hold on to me," he whispered. Her arms looped around his neck and held him tightly.

Moving higher on her body, he started to pump inside her again. Slow, deep strokes—teasing strokes. Lori mewled, circling her hips against his. Mike stopped her by simply pressing down against her, pinning her lower body until she fell still. Then he started all over. He pushed up onto his hands and stared down between them, watching as he entered her. She stretched around him, all pink, wet and tight.

She jolted under him and he looked up to find her watching as well. She clenched around him and Mike hissed out a breath. She did it a second time, this time with a little smile on her lips. "Don't do that," Mike said.

Her lids drifted low and a husky laugh escaped her. "Do what? This?" She did it again.

Mike growled and dropped his weight down on her. He started driving into her, hard and fast. A startled scream escaped Lori's lips and Mike swooped down, taking her mouth in a demanding kiss. He nipped at her lower lip. She bit his tongue. Mike fisted one hand in her hair to hold her still.

His other hand cupped a plump, warm breast and he tweaked her nipple, squeezing until he knew she'd be hovering between pleasure and pain. Lori screamed into his mouth and came. Her sex tightened around his dick until it almost hurt.

Hard and fast, he rode her. When he felt his climax approaching this time, he let it.

She was still convulsing around him as Mike lay sprawled atop her, completely spent. After the milking little caresses in her sex eased, he forced himself to roll off her, but he kept an arm around her waist so that she ended up on top of him.

"I'm still waiting for it to get worse," Lori mumbled.

Mike laughed weakly. "You're trying to kill me."

"DAMN IT, WHAT ARE YOU TRYING to do, kill me?" Lori tugged away from his hand and climbed out of bed. Her legs were so damn weak and wobbly that she could barely stand up. Her stomach was an aching, empty pit and if she didn't get caffeine soon, she knew things were going to get ugly.

Mike's hand finally fell away from her wrist, and as she dug a T-shirt out of her drawer, she looked back at him. Her heart skipped a beat at the sight of him. He sat with his back against the headboard, tan skin gleaming against the soft baby blue of her sheets. A wicked smile curved his lips and his eyes had that heavy-lidded sleepy look. Damn, he was sexy.

He'd pulled the sheet over his lap but as she stared at him, he fisted his hand in the sheet and tugged it away. Then he brought his hand to his cock, wrapped his fingers around the thick, swollen flesh and stroked upward. As his fist swallowed the rounded head, Lori realized her mouth was watering. "You're evil."

She spun away from him and dug out a pair of panties, listening to him laugh. "You asked for it, doll."

Lori snorted. "You're right. I just now realized that my going to Exposé was an invitation for you to jump my bones and tease me senseless."

She didn't hear him move. But he was there, behind her, brushing her hair aside and pressing a hot, openmouthed kiss to her neck. His arms wrapped around her waist and he murmured, "I kept warning you. Not my fault you didn't pay attention to me."

Against her butt, she could feel the hard, thick length of his cock. After the past few hours, she shouldn't be the least bit interested. But her heart skipped a beat and her breathing got all shaky and shallow. Still, if she didn't eat something soon, she wouldn't be able to see straight. Or walk.

Well, walking was going to be interesting for the next little bit anyway. Every muscle in her legs screamed, and between her thighs, Lori felt sore and achy.

"Food. Okay?" She tugged against his hands and turned to press a kiss to his mouth. "I need food and a shower."

"Spoilsport," he murmured. But he let go, his hands falling away. His hand came up and, cupping her chin, lifted her face. He brushed a kiss against her lips. "I'm going home to grab some clothes. I'll be back."

Lori pushed up onto her toes and kissed him back. Before she pulled away, she nipped his lower lip. "You do that."

SIX

MIKE HAD NO MORE THAN grabbed a clean shirt from the dryer when he heard the front door open.

At the sound of Alex's deep voice, he swore. He headed out into the living room, about to tell Alex to get lost but then he saw his baby sister standing behind him.

Crossing over to her, he brushed a kiss against the top of her head and said, "Hey. What are you all up to?"

From the corner of his eye, he could see Alex studying him. Mike had grabbed a box of condoms from his bathroom and they were on the coffee table where he wouldn't forget them. And right where Alex could see them. Allie, too, if she ever stopped staring at her feet.

"We're going to catch a movie. I ran into Allie at the bookstore and as always, she'd planned on spending the evening with her nose in a book. So I talked her into grabbing a bite to eat and a movie. We thought you might want to come," Alex said. A wicked grin lit his face. "But if you're busy . . . "

"Ah . . . sort of."

"Anybody I know?" His gaze drifted to the box of rubbers and Mike could feel blood rushing to his cheeks.

Casually, he dropped his clean shirt on the table, covering the black box just before Allie headed over to sit down on the couch. "If you've got plans, Mike, it's not a problem."

Mike narrowed his eyes at Alex, but before he could try to think of a polite way to get Allie and Alex to leave, the back door opened. "Hey, Mike. Do you want to . . . oh. Sorry." Lori stood in the doorway, her hair hanging in wet ringlets around her face. She wore a pair of brief white shorts and red T-shirt. Braless. Mike could see her nipples pressing against the cotton.

She stopped in her tracks when she saw Alex. Her cheeks flushed red. Mike wouldn't have been surprised if she turned tail and ran back to her house, but instead, she squared her shoulders and continued on inside. "Hi, Allie."

Allie smiled and went back to studying her short nails. "Hello, Lori."

Lori crossed the room and sat down beside Allie, casually drawing her knees to her chest. "How is nursing school going?"

Allie shrugged. "Two more years and I'll have my bachelor's."

"Still working at the nursing home?"

Finally, Allie looked up, a wry grin on her narrow face. "Where else?"

"Haven't seen you in a while, Lori." Alex stepped up, a devilish smile on his mouth. "Sorry if we interrupted something. I didn't know Mike had plans for the weekend. We were going to grab a movie. Why don't you all come with us?"

Mike tried to catch her eye but she wasn't looking at him.

Shit.

"NO WONDER YOU'VE BEEN keeping her to yourself."

Mike ignored Alex.

"So how serious is this?"

Mike finally turned to Alex and gave him a humorless smile. "Get a grip, Alex. I think we've had this discussion before. I'm not looking for long-term, pal. Not in the cards for me."

"Maybe you picked up a new game without realizing it," Alex drawled as he shuffled a little closer to the counter.

Mike just snorted. "Shit, Alex. Lori is a nice girl. With a capital *N*. I don't do nice. I don't even know how to handle nice. Hell, look at Allie. She's my kid sister and I can't be around her more than a few hours without pissing her off or saying something that hurts her."

Laughing, Alex replied, "You've been friends with Lori for four years. Hell, she's one of your best friends. I think you handle nice better than you think. Until you start letting it scare you."

"Scared. Scared of *what*? Allie? Lori?"

"Hell. You're scared of anything serious. You won't try for your lieutenant shield. You don't know how to handle your sister because you don't *want* to. She sees too much in you and you can't stand it. So yeah. Scared."

It made something twitch deep inside his gut, thinking about it. It was bullshit though. Plain bullshit. "You been watching *Dr. Phil* or something, Alex? That's the biggest load of crap I've heard all week."

For a minute, Alex just studied him, smiling a little. "So you're telling me there's not much going on between you two. She's not the reason you've been in a shitty mood for the past month."

"I've been in a shitty mood because we've had several cases go straight to hell and because it's been a shitty summer. I've been bored out of my mind, I'm tired and I'm sick of the same old shit all the time. It has nothing to do with Lori," Mike snapped. Of course, he knew he was lying. Still didn't change the fact that he wasn't interested in long-term. This thing with Lori was just that. A *thing*.

It would end. Things would be like they used to be and—

"Well, if that's how it is, then, cool. I gotta admit, I've been dying to get my hands on her. She's got an amazing ass. Tell me—"

Mike whirled on Alex and grabbed him by the front of his shirt, spinning them around and driving Alex back up against a black-and-white painted column. "Shut the hell up."

Alex was grinning, an amused little smirk that made Mike feel about as intelligent as an amoeba. Alex had been baiting him. Aware that people were staring at them, Mike slowly uncurled his fingers from Alex's shirt and backed off. "You're a twisted bastard, Alex. You know that?"

Instead of waiting for a reply, he fell back into line.

Alex joined him, still grinning like a fool. "You be sure to let me know when and if you feel like letting me join in. I wasn't kidding about her ass."

AS LORI WALKED OFF TO THE BATHROOM, Alex stood up and said, "I'm going to grab a smoke."

Allie gave him a stare before looking down at the floor. "Thought you were quitting."

He reached out and tugged on a lock of brown hair. "I'm working on quitting, Allie-cat. Right now, it's just in the planning-on-quitting-someday-soon stage."

"Someday." Allie snorted. "You know, if you keep putting it off, by the time someday rolls around, your taste buds are going to be shot and your teeth all yucky and yellow."

Mike smiled a little. It was weird hearing that dry, sardonic tone in her voice, even odder to see her look at Alex dead-on. She spent so much time staring at the ground, or beyond somebody's shoulder. Rarely dead-on. It was amazing that somebody who refused to really look at *anybody* could see so much.

Alex smiled. "Everybody has to have a hobby. Mine is procrastination." He headed outside and Mike shifted a little on the seat, hoping Lori would be out soon.

"I like her."

Mike glanced at Allie. "Who?"

Allie shrugged her thin shoulders and said, "Lori. She doesn't look at you like she's sizing you up and she doesn't treat me like some sort of reject."

"You're not a reject," Mike said automatically. Then he looked at her, wondering if he'd ever made her feel that way.

"I know that, Mike. But Lori is the only lady you've ever brought to your house for more than a few hours. And all your girlfriends? They acted like I was some sort of leper."

Mike winced. Okay, now, that was true. They hadn't exactly been girlfriends, but there had been a few women who ended up getting dropped like yesterday's news because they treated Allie like crap.

"She's not my girlfriend, Allie. We're just . . . "

Allie grinned. It was a quick one, almost gone before it appeared. "Friends, huh. And that's why you keep giving Alex a 'drop dead' glare every time he gets a little too close."

Seven

"ARE YOU OKAY?"

Mike lay sprawled on his belly, his face buried in Lori's scented sheets. They smelled of cherry blossoms and vanilla. The same scent he caught from her skin. It had been all over his body when he'd left her house earlier.

"I'm fine," he muttered.

Lori smoothed a hand down his back. She pressed her lips to his shoulder and pushed up onto her elbow. He could feel the ends of her hair brushing his skin. Part of him felt like he could lie there all night, just enjoying the touch of her hands on his back.

"You're awfully quiet."

But the soft, concerned sound of her voice kept intruding on his attempts to avoid thinking. Mike flipped onto his back and sat up, reaching down to cup his hand over her sex. She was still wet from him. He held her gaze as he pushed his finger inside. The slick wet walls of her sex clasped him tightly.

"I'm horny," he muttered, leaning in and pressing a rough kiss to her lips. With his hands on her shoulders, he urged her onto her back and ordered, "Flip over."

The minute she did, Mike slid his hands under her hips and pulled her up. He pushed into her without hesitation, groaning at the satin-slick feel of her pussy. He hadn't put on a rubber. He wasn't going to.

Lori didn't know it, but this was going to be their last time and he was going to feel her when she came. Feel *all* of her. "Mike . . ."

"I don't want to talk. I just want to fuck you."

He fell forward onto his hands, crushing her body into the mattress. He bit her shoulder and caught her hands in his, then drew them over her head. Blindly, he reached over and caught one of the scarves that Lori had draped around her bedpost. Tugging one free, he used it to tie her hand to one of the slats in the headboard. He tugged it to make sure it wasn't too tight. Then he grabbed another scarf and tied her other hand.

"Not exactly the black leather you're probably looking for, but this works," he whispered, trailing his fingers down her back.

Lori tugged on the scarves and then lifted her head, looking over her shoulder at him. Her eyes were big and dark, just a little nervous.

"Don't worry, baby. I promised I'd take it easy the first time," he said, forcing a smile that he didn't really feel inside. "Put your head down."

She did, hiding those soft blue eyes. Guilt knotted his belly and he almost pulled away. He couldn't though—proving just what a jackass he was. He was going to walk away, he knew it, but he was going to have her one more time.

And he did, hard and fast, dragging climax after climax from her. She felt so silky hot, the swollen tissues of her pussy clutching at his cock, tighter than a fist.

She came again and Mike gritted his teeth, desperately holding on to his control. As she collapsed limply onto the mattress, Mike pulled away. The brightly colored scarves were still tied to her wrists, securing her to the headboard.

"Not yet," he muttered as he again flipped her onto her back.

He crouched between her thighs, staring at her, etching the way she looked into his memory. Her mouth was parted, swollen and pink. Her breasts lifted and fell in a rapid rhythm as she tried to catch her breath. Her arms were stretched overhead, her wrists crossed now, the silky scarves tangled around her hands.

"You're beautiful, Lori." She was, so damn beautiful she made his heart ache. So damn sweet. Definitely not what he needed, and he sure as hell wasn't what she needed or deserved.

He shoved the thoughts out of his mind. There'd be enough time to think about regrets and guilt later.

With focused intent, Mike sprawled between her thighs. He pushed them wide and lowered his mouth to her sex. He growled against her flesh and ordered, "Look at me."

Her lids lifted just barely and she stared at him as he pushed his tongue inside her snug, swollen folds. She shivered against him. He did it again and then he shifted his aim and licked her clitoris. Slowly circling his tongue around the hard little nub. At the same time, he pushed two fingers inside her. She clenched down around him and screamed out his name.

She climaxed against his mouth and he pulled away. He angled her hips up with one hand and with the other he caught her behind her knee and pushed it to her chest. He thrust inside her, burrowing deep, until he could go no deeper. Turning his face to hers, he sought her mouth and kissed her, tangling his tongue with hers, trying to get as much of her taste as he could.

Sweat dripped from their bodies as he planted his palms on either side of her shoulders and pushed up. "Come for me," he whispered. He circled his hips in the cradle of hers, then pulled out. A slow, shallow thrust then retreat, then a deep, hard thrust. He kept teasing her like that until she was panting and pleading with him.

He sank his weight back down atop her and eased his length completely inside, one inch at a time. "Come for me," he repeated. Then he started to shaft her, burying his cock completely before pulling back until he had nearly withdrawn. Two, three, four strokes.

On the fifth one, she exploded under him, her hips jerking convulsively. As she climaxed around him, he sank his teeth into her shoulder, biting down. As he exploded into her, she screamed and bucked under him.

Lori was so exhausted that she couldn't see straight. She could hardly move her legs, and her eyelids felt ridiculously heavy.

She wanted nothing more than to curl up against him and go to sleep, but Mike wasn't done. When he pulled away, she started to reach for him, but the scarves binding her wrists kept her from doing it.

"Untie me, Mike."

He stared at her, his eyes remote. He just shook his head silently and stood up. Her mouth was dry, but she wasn't sure if she was thirsty or nervous. He walked into the bathroom and

Lori's eyes dropped to his ass. The hard, muscled curve had caught her eyes before and she wanted to touch him.

And she was going to, as soon as he untied her.

But the thought of what she wanted to do evaporated along with all other thoughts when he came out of the bathroom.

He had a little glass bottle in his hand. It was massage oil. Lori had a weird feeling he wasn't planning on giving her a back rub with it.

"Roll over."

"Mike—"

He didn't let her finish. He covered her mouth with his, his tongue pushing inside. When he pulled away, she was breathless. By the time she caught her breath, Mike had rolled her onto her belly. Automatically, she pushed up on her knees, but with her wrists still trapped by the scarves, all she managed to do was stick her ass in the air.

Her face flamed and she started to roll back over, but Mike's hands caught her hips. "You said anything, Lori. Remember?" His voice was a husky whisper against her nape. He trailed his fingers down between her buttocks and pressed against the small opening there, a light, teasing touch.

"Remember?" he prodded again.

"Yes." Her voice came out in a terrified squeak as he touched her again. This time, his fingers were slick and wet with the oil. It was cool at first, but as he pushed inside, the oil warmed.

Warmed, hell. She felt like it was scalding her—like he was scalding her. Stretching her. He pumped his fingers in and out, working more of the oil inside her with each caress.

"Are you ready?"

She felt him pressing against her, the head of his cock rounded and a hell of a lot bigger than his fingers. "No."

Mike just laughed a little. "Yeah, you are. You're so hot, you practically burn my hands." He smoothed one hand down her hip and held her still as he pushed against her.

Lori tried to pull away—pain speared through her as he pushed the head of his shaft inside, past the tight ring of muscle. "Don't pull away," he muttered. "That won't help. Push down on me."

Lori shook her head. She bit her lip to keep from crying out and wondered what in hell she had been thinking—damn it, women actually *liked* this?

His hand lifted and she thought for a second he would let her go. Instead, he slapped her ass. It was a hard, stinging smack and she jerked. "Push down!" His voice was commanding and instinctively she did as he said and pushed down.

As she did, he pushed inside. The pain didn't go away—it exploded into something else. Something caught between pleasure and pain, between heaven and hell. He pulled back and pushed inside again.

And again—each stroke made her burn a little hotter. He was stretching her, his cock thick and hard, carving through her tightness.

He slapped her again and Lori screamed out his name. He gripped both her hips now, holding her body still as he pulled out and thrust back inside her. Lori whimpered and shook underneath him.

She could feel the orgasm building inside her, something bigger, more exhilarating, more terrifying than anything she'd ever felt before. She shied away, squirming forward, trying to move away from him and the climax.

Mike wouldn't let her though. He slid one hand around, his fingers sliding over the slick, swollen flesh of her sex.

When he pressed down on her clit, the orgasm exploded through her, taking her under like some big Goliath swallowing her whole.

As she bucked, shuddered and screamed her way through it, Mike came, his cock jerking inside her. She felt him come in a series of hot, wet pulses.

Blackness hovered around her, her vision graying out for just a second. She felt him moving both his body and hers. Felt the tension around her wrists go free as he untied the scarves.

When she lifted her head, her vision had cleared. She turned to look at Mike, staring at him as he lay down beside her and took her in his arms.

"Go to sleep, Lori."

She tried to resist—she wanted to talk him. Ask him what was wrong. Wanted to ask . . .

But before she could say anything, sleep rushed up and claimed her.

LORI WOKE UP ALONE.

It was Monday morning and she had to be at school in an hour. The students weren't due back for two weeks but Lori had a million things to do to get ready for the school year.

She couldn't force her body to move though.

Something had been wrong last night.

She'd known it when he rolled on top of her. She'd been uneasy even when he pushed inside her, but the feel of him, so thick, so hot, had distracted her. She was wet between her thighs, wet from herself and from him. He hadn't worn a rubber.

The only time all weekend.

She reached up and pushed her hair aside. Then she paused, staring at her wrist. There was a faint red mark on it. And on her other wrist. He hadn't tied her tightly, but she had jerked against the scarves hard enough, often enough, that she had faint little red marks on each wrist.

She would have smiled if she hadn't been so disturbed.

What had been wrong with Mike last night?

Finally, she sat up and headed into the shower. She turned her back to the spray and let it beat down on the tense muscles in her back. As she stood there, soaking up the steam, she brooded. Then she kicked herself about brooding.

So he'd been quiet last night. Big deal.

It wasn't like he was always a chatterbox.

Even as she worked herself around to not being so worried about it, she asked herself what *it* was. There was no relationship between them, right?

Maybe she had thought she'd felt a connection. Didn't mean Mike felt it. He hadn't implied anything like that and she had no reason to get her hopes up. The bad thing about sleeping with your best friend—you *knew* the person you were sleeping with. Like *really* knew him. She knew that Mike had absolutely no interest in long-term relationships, and marriage appealed to him about as much as getting an ice pick jabbed into his eye.

Unable to stop herself, Lori stood there analyzing every little thing that had happened since he'd left her house yesterday to change. That was when he'd started acting a little odd. A little more standoffish.

She snapped out of her daze and realized she was freezing. The water had gone cold and she hadn't even washed her hair. Shivering, she hurried through her shower and told herself to quit worrying. It had been an amazing weekend and even if that one weekend was all she got, that was fine.

He hadn't made any promises and Lori hadn't been looking for any.

Still, as she headed into her closet to find some clothes, she couldn't shake the vague sense of uneasiness.

IT ONLY GOT WORSE.

She saw Mike twice during the days that followed. He was avoiding her. There was no question about it. Each time was toward evening when he was heading home. The first time he headed inside without saying anything. The second time, she caught him as he was getting out of the car and he'd stood there for a few seconds and then given her some lame-ass excuse that he'd forgotten to do some paperwork.

She was rapidly approaching pissed by the time Friday rolled around. She wasn't sure who she was angry with though. Herself or Mike.

No, she really hadn't expected anything to come of the weekend they'd spent together, but she sure as hell hadn't expected him to start treating her like a pariah either.

It was seven o'clock and Mike's driveway was empty. She tried to tell herself that it didn't matter. But there was an odd ache in her chest. Climbing from her car, she walked over to the picket fence that separated the properties. Lori wrapped her hands around two pickets and stood there, staring into nothingness as the ache in her chest spread.

"You screwed up, Lori," she told herself. She'd been attracted to Mike for a while, but she wasn't his type. He hadn't ever told her what type he did like, but Lori knew it wasn't her. She'd been okay with that because of their friendship.

Messing up that friendship was the last thing she had wanted. But it looked like that was exactly what had happened. Sex changed things. Even when the parties involved weren't looking for anything more.

"Yeah, but you were looking," Lori muttered and made herself deal with it. As much as she hated it, she had to be honest with herself. Yeah, part of her had been hoping for something more. And judging by the gaping, empty hole in her chest, it had been a *big* part.

"SOMETHING WRONG?"

Alex glanced at the petite brunette across from him and just shook his head. "Just saw somebody I know." And it wasn't somebody he would have expected to see there either.

Of course, she looked damn good. Good enough to eat, in fact, and Alex found himself wondering if he could talk Mike into sharing.

Lori Whitmore strolled along the outer edge of the dance

floor, looking into the crowd, completely unaware of him. Which gave him the chance to admire the view. She wore a top made of teal blue leather. It laced up between her breasts so that about an inch of skin showed between the lacings. It was short, ending just a few inches below her breasts, well above the waistband of the low-slung, wide-legged black pants. She wore a necklace of hammered silver and had pulled her butter yellow curls into a high, loose ponytail.

"You know Lori?"

Alex looked at Grace with an arched brow. "How do you know her?"

Grace grinned. "We both work at Braxton Elementary."

With a chuckle, Alex said, "I wonder if the parents of this community have any idea the kind of perverts who are teaching their kids." He took a sip of his Coke, looking back at Lori. "She lives next door to my partner, Mike."

"Mike Ryan?" Grace had an odd tone in her voice as she looked at Lori. Her eyes were dark and she looked a little worried.

"Yeah. Mike won't admit it, but he's gone over on her."

Grace leaned back in her chair. "Apparently not too much. He's out in the maze."

Alex swore. Lori disappeared into the crowd and he stood up, craning his neck to see. And he did, just in time to watch her slip out the back door.

SHE'D COME HERE FOR A DISTRACTION, but it wasn't working.

In a desperate attempt to try to stop thinking about Mike for just a few minutes, she headed out into the maze. Part of her had been hoping to find Grace so she could maybe unload a little. Grace hadn't been at the bar or on the dance floor though.

For some reason, Lori didn't expect she'd find her out in the maze—and if she did, she hoped she wouldn't die of embarrassment. She walked along the path, staring down at the stones or straight ahead. She didn't have to look to know what she wasn't seeing.

The breathy sighs and moans, the occasional bit of conversation. If you could call it that. Her face was red with embarrassment and Lori turned around. She was leaving. Maybe she'd go catch a movie or—

Not.

The first few seconds of what she saw didn't make any sense. She couldn't see anything of the woman except long legs wrapped in leather, a half-naked back and yards of black curls. She was facedown, literally, her face buried in Mike's crotch. As Lori watched, she lifted up and then slid back down.

Lori couldn't actually see what the bitch was doing, but she didn't have to.

She swallowed, feeling like somebody had dropped an anvil on her chest. She looked up at Mike's face and met his dark green eyes for the quickest of seconds. He stared at her with no expression on his face.

Without saying a word, she spun away and headed back toward the club as fast as she could.

It was a hell of a time to realize that she was a lot more involved in the thing with Mike than she'd realized.

She was in love with the son of a bitch.

Turning the corner, she plowed straight into a wide chest covered with plain white cotton. "Excuse me," she mumbled and tried to go around.

Big, hard hands came up and closed gently over her upper arms. "Hi, Lori."

Numb, she looked up and saw that it was Alex. Lamely, she replied, "Hi." Then she pulled away and went around him. He said her name, but she just kept walking.

Home. She wanted to go home.

"WHAT IN HELL ARE YOU DOING?"

Braced against the high, curved back of the stone bench, Mike looked up at Alex. "Do you mind? I'm busy." He looked back down at the woman kneeling in front of him and tried to remember her name. Buffy. Bambi. Something like that . . . he thought. The inky black of her curls spilled over her shoulders as she bobbed up and down.

Unless she had her mouth full, she annoyed the hell out of him. Called him "Master" and kept wanting him to call her "Slave." But as long as she kept her mouth full . . .

Alex didn't walk away so Mike looked up at him. He ran a hand down what's-her-name's curls and fisted his hand at her nape, guiding her into a slower rhythm. "I'm not up for double play tonight, Alex. Go away."

"Apparently the only thing you're in the mood for is being an ass." He glared at the woman but she continued on, seemingly unaware.

But Mike couldn't focus on her very talented mouth when Alex continued to stand right there, glaring at him. He tugged on her curls, slowing her to a halt. She didn't pull away at first and Mike said, "Enough." He searched his brain for her name and finally remembered. "Kiki. Enough, Kiki. I need to talk to my buddy here."

She lifted her head and stared at him with neon blue eyes. She had to be wearing contacts. The blue looked too unnatural against her deep olive-toned skin to be real. She batted heavily mascaraed lashes at him and then lowered her face to rub her cheek against his thigh. "I do not mind waiting, Master. Perhaps the two of you . . . " Her voice trailed off but he got the message.

Alex chuckled. "Master? Honey, go inside and find yourself somebody who'll appreciate you a little more."

She looked back at Mike but she wasn't going to find whatever she was looking for from him. "Go on inside, Kiki. Maybe some other time."

As she left, he stood up and adjusted himself, tugging up his zipper and buttoning his shirt before he sat back down. "Say whatever it is you want to say and then leave me the hell alone. I need a drink." Or five. Ten. However many it took to forget the wounded look he'd seen in Lori's eyes as she stood there staring at him.

Alex didn't waste any time. "What kind of idiot are you?"

"The thirsty kind. Anything else?" Mike replied.

"Lori was just out here. Please, tell me she didn't see you."

Mike shrugged. "She knows what happens out here. She doesn't want to see it, then she shouldn't come out here."

"But did she know she was going to see *you* out here? And what in hell are you doing out here anyway? Did you two have a fight? I mean, even if you did, this definitely isn't the place to come. What in hell—"

Interrupting him, Mike snapped, "Damn it, what in hell are you, my mom? No, we didn't have a fight, but you're still assuming there's something going on between us and there's not. We spent one weekend together. We had sex. End of story."

"Except you don't turn into a mean bastard after a weekend of sex, pal. You've been a dick all week, but now I know why. You really *are* scared."

Mike rolled his eyes and stood up. "Don't start that shit again, Alex. I'm not relationship shy and I don't have any kind of commitment issues. Lori just isn't my type." He started to push past Alex but his partner lifted an arm, barring his way.

"She's not a type." Alex said it quietly. "She's a sweet lady."

Mike stilled. "I know that. She's a very sweet lady. She's a good girl and she expects the things out of life that good girls deserve. A husband, a family, a dog in the backyard. I can't give her that."

"Bullshit. You just don't want to try. Why are you so certain you can't have it? I mean, shit, look at what you came from. Your parents were so in love with each other, it gave people cavities. If they hadn't died in the accident, they'd still be making moon eyes at each other."

Turning away, Mike rubbed his chest. It felt empty inside, hollow. Just like it did every time he thought of his folks. They'd been killed by a drunk driver years ago but it still felt like yesterday. He and Allie, they'd been lucky. Not only had they had two parents who loved them, their parents had loved each other as well.

But it had spoiled things for Mike a little. He didn't want to fall in love because he didn't want any less than his parents had had. And these days, that kind of relationship wasn't just rare, it was almost nonexistent.

"I know that, Alex. You think I wouldn't like to have what they had?"

"Most people would. You're not stupid, even if you have been acting it lately. I don't get it, Mike. This is your chance and you're throwing it away. You think you're going to have anything lasting with somebody like Bambi?"

"It's Kiki," Mike corrected absently. Then he shook his head. "No. I know that's not the kind of thing that lasts. That's why it's how I prefer things. Marriage, kids, the whole nine yards—can you see that working out for me? I'm a homicide detective and I spend my nights at a sex club. I don't see it."

"You're more than just a cop, buddy. That's why you're good at it. And you hardly ever come here anymore. You admitted it yourself, you're getting bored with it. So what's stopping you from going after Lori?"

"Just let it go." Mike shook his head and headed out of the alcove.

Alex caught his arm. "Not until I get an answer. I'm tired of you acting like an ass and—" His words ended abruptly and he just stood there, glaring at Mike.

"And what?"

Alex let go and turned away. Reaching, he rubbed at the back of his neck. Under the plain white T-shirt, his shoulders were stiff with tension.

"Alex, either say what you got to say or go away. I want a drink and I want it now," Mike snarled.

Alex turned around, his eyes dark and glittering. Unless Mike was mistaken, his face looked a little red too. Kind of flushed.

He realized why a few seconds later.

Alex was blushing. "You're my best friend, Mike. We've known each other our whole lives. I just want you to be happy." He gestured toward the club. "This . . . hell, this is just fun for us. It's not our lifestyle. You don't want some babe calling you Master and asking permission to go to the bathroom any more than I do."

Mike closed his eyes. No. That wasn't what he wanted. Up until a few weeks ago, Mike hadn't been sure what it was that he did want. He had a bad feeling, though, that he knew now.

He knew what. He knew who.

"Come on, man. This is your chance. Why are you trying to screw it up?"

Mike looked Alex square in the eye and said, "There's no trying to it. I already have screwed it up. I just . . . hell."

Alex had been right.

Mike was scared. That's all there was to it. "Shit." He looked at Alex. "I think I really fucked things up."

Alex just shrugged a broad shoulder. "I dunno. Something tells me that Lori just might let this go, after she makes you crawl a little." A wide grin spread across his face. "Can I watch?"

Mike flipped him off and headed for the club.

Behind him, Alex asked, "Aren't you even going to say thank you?"

He spun around but kept walking. "Thanks."

Alex wagged his eyebrows. "I was thinking something a little more tangible than that. Like maybe let me have a taste of the pretty blonde thing . . . after awhile. When she's done making you crawl and beg. See if she'd be willing to let me come play a little."

Mike just snarled at him.

As he spun back toward the club, he could hear Alex laughing behind him.

LORI WAS SCARED. Hell, screw scared. She was terrified.

She'd changed the locks after she'd kicked Dirk out, but that hadn't kept him out. The shattered glass and the rock on the kitchen floor made it pretty clear how he had gotten inside too.

He stared at her with a wild, half-manic look in his gray eyes and something about that look made her skin crawl. He didn't look like he had shaved in a week and his clothes were wrinkled, his hair a mess. Considering that Dirk was the ultimate metrosexual, it wasn't just surprising to see him that way.

It was downright disturbing.

"I saw you."

When he spoke, his voice was soft, almost whisper quiet. No reason for it to terrify her. But it did.

"Saw me where, Dirk?" Her cell phone was in her purse. If she could get to it . . .

He laughed and took a step toward her, then another. She started to back away but he didn't move any closer. Instead, he started circling her. "With him. I've been watching you. You've been going to that club." He nodded a little. "That's my fault. I should have listened when you said you wanted to go. You want to get fucked and let other people watch, hey, why not? But you had to fuck *him*?"

Dread curdled in her belly. He had been watching her? And he'd seen her with Mike. It hadn't occurred to her that Dirk would go all stalker crazy on her, but apparently that was exactly what had happened. And if he had gone and gotten obsessive, seeing her with Mike was *not* a good thing.

Dirk couldn't stand Mike. Lori had always suspected that Mike intimidated the hell out of Dirk, made him feel inadequate.

He stopped in his tracks, staring out the bay window. It faced toward the back, .but the angled side windows let her see the back half of Mike's house and that was where Dirk was looking. "Of all the guys, you had to pick him."

While he had his back to her, Lori carefully slid her hand in her purse and grabbed her phone. He turned to her and she tucked her hand behind her back, hiding the phone from his view.

"Why him, Lori?" he asked, his voice soft and silky. "Of all the guys, you had to sleep with Mike. Had to let him touch you. Why did you do that?"

She lied. What the hell else could she do? Dirk had gone off the deep end and Lori wasn't planning on letting him take her with him. "I'm sorry, Dirk. I wasn't thinking," she said. It wasn't too hard to sound upset, considering she was absolutely terrified.

He didn't need to know it was fear making her voice so shaky, right? "I was just so hurt. So lonely . . . "

Dirk nodded like he understood. "Were you missing me, baby?" he murmured, moving a little closer.

As he did, Lori realized it wasn't only shaving he had been neglecting. He smelled like he hadn't taken a bath in a week. She started to breathe shallowly through her mouth so she wouldn't take in so much of the sour scent of his body.

"Did you miss me?" he asked again.

"Every day." Okay, squeezing that lie out hadn't been easy. When he stepped even closer, warning sirens started to screech in her head. Lori spun away from him and went to the table. She'd never been the best actress but she sat down and buried her face in her arms and started to wail. "I just missed you so much. But after what you did . . . "

He made shushing sounds and she flipped open the phone, hoping she had it hidden well enough. With her hair falling in her face and her other arm up, she just might . . .

"So that's why you went to Mike."

Lori wailed a little louder and hoped it covered the sounds as she keyed in 911. His hand touched her between the shoulder blades and he rubbed her back in soothing, slow strokes. "I knew you were just trying to punish me." He moved away and she heard a cabinet open, heard the water running.

She breathed out a sigh and carefully sat up, keeping the phone in her hand. From the corner of her eye, she could see him filling a glass with water and she tucked her hand under the table. She tried to muffle the sound with her hand, but the tinny "Nine-one-one. What is your emergency . . . " was loud and clear.

Dirk turned around and stared at her, his eyes narrowed down to slits. As he lunged for her, she jumped up from the table and put it between them. "Stupid bitch! Lying whore!"

"You don't really think I'd take you back, do you?" she said, sneering at him. "You're pathetic."

"Shut *up*!" he bellowed. He feinted to the left and Lori moved with him, keeping the table between them, not letting him force her to move anywhere she didn't want.

She could still hear the operator's voice coming from the phone in her hand. Keeping Dirk in her sights, she lifted it up and said, "I've got an intruder." She barely managed to recite her address before he came over the table at her. She backpedaled and slammed into the island. He caught her there and pinned her up against it.

"You're going to pay for that, Lori," he panted, struggling to pin her hands. Lori fought back, fighting to get just a little bit of leverage. She brought her foot up and slammed the heel of her boot onto his foot, grinding down. He yelped and one hand loosened enough that she was able to jerk her arm free. Stiffening her fingers, she jabbed them into his throat.

He fell back, choking for air, and Lori scrambled away. She nearly made it to the front door when he caught her. She went down struggling and as he flipped her over, she jerked her knee up, catching him square in the balls. "The police are coming, Dirk. You need to get lost."

His eyes were wild. His face was pale and he could hardly breathe, but he pinned her down, his knees pressing into her upper arms to keep her trapped against the floor. He reached down and closed his hands around her throat. "You're mine, Lori. If I can't have you . . . "

She struggled to breathe as pain exploded through her. His fingers got tighter and tighter and she kicked, but he had her pinned a little too well. She could feel the strength draining out of her, the blackness growing. Her lungs threatened to burst from the pressure and still she couldn't get a breath in.

As everything went completely black, she heard a crash.

EIGHT

FOR THE REST OF HIS LIFE, he was going to see it. Dirk on top of Lori, his hands choking the life out of her.

When the 911 call had come through, he had been almost home. Terror had turned his blood to ice and he had put the gas pedal to the floor, keeping it there until he pulled into Lori's yard. Literally. He had taken out the white picket fence and destroyed several of her flower beds as he practically drove his car through the front of her house.

He'd buy her new flowers. Hell, he'd buy her an entire warehouse of them, so long as she lived.

Alex had shown up at the hospital just as the security guards were trying to drag Mike from the treatment room. How the hell Alex knew already, Mike didn't know. Didn't care. He'd almost popped Alex in the mouth because he was helping the security guards drag him away.

"Come on, Mike. Let them help her . . . " Those words finally penetrated and Mike had let Alex guide him out. That had been nearly thirty minutes ago. Although nurses came and went from the curtained-off room, not one of them had approached.

Finally, the curtain was pushed back and Mike stood up. His legs felt leaden and he was pretty damn sure he was going to choke if he had to say anything. The knot in his chest was so damn huge, he could hardly breathe.

Fortunately, he didn't have to say anything.

The doctor was young, pretty and looked entirely too perky for Mike's peace of mind, and she smiled at him. "She's going to be fine. There's been some trauma to her throat and she was without oxygen for a few minutes . . ."

Mike knew that. He had been doing CPR when the ambulance got there. She hadn't been breathing . . .

"We're going to have to keep her overnight. I think she's got a few broken ribs, either from the attack or the emergency CPR, I'm not sure. We're going to X-ray . . ."

Nothing else she said made sense. Mike stopped listening. He moved past the doctor, aware that she was following him, that she was still speaking, but none of it mattered.

What mattered lay in the bed in front of him. Her face was pale, but unmarked. Apparently, Dirk hadn't been interested in beating on her, just killing her. The evidence of that lay in hideous, ugly red bruises that ringed her pale throat.

As he sat down on the stool beside her bed, her eyes opened. She opened her mouth to talk but all that came out was a weird garbled sound. He reached up and touched her lips. "Don't try to talk. Your throat's going to hurt for a little while."

She stared at him for a moment and then her lids drooped. Within a few seconds, she was fast asleep.

"We gave her some pain medicine. There's no head trauma, no cuts, no lacerations. Really, she's incredibly lucky. Aside from her ribs and the trauma to her throat, she's unharmed."

Mike looked over his shoulder at her and rasped, "You call this lucky?"

The doctor gave him a sad little smile and suddenly she didn't look so young and perky. Her hazel eyes looked incredibly old as she murmured, "Yes. She's alive. All of her injuries will heal. You all got to her before he . . . " Her voice trailed off but Mike knew what it was that went unsaid.

Before Morrigan could have killed her, raped her, or both.

She turned and left but before the curtain swung back into place, a dark hand caught it. Alex stepped inside. He looked at Lori for a second and then looked at Mike.

"You okay, man?"

"No." Mike lowered his head to the bed. He reached up with one hand and sought Lori's, linking their fingers and pressing his palm to hers. "No, I'm not."

SHE WOKE UP SURROUNDED BY FLOWERS.

On the table nearest her bed, there was a huge crystal vase. It sparkled in the light filtering through the blinds. It held roses, dozens of them. Each one a deep, perfect shade of red.

She reached up and touched her fingers to one of the petals.

"You're awake."

Lori rolled her head on the pillow, too damn tired to lift it. She found herself practically nose-to-nose with Mike. He had huge bags under his eyes, his hair was standing on end and he looked like he had aged ten years.

"You look awful," she said baldly. Her throat hurt like fire when she spoke and she reached up and touched it with her fingers. Even that light touch hurt.

"Don't try to talk," he murmured. He reached up, caught her hand and drew it away from her throat. "It's going to be a day or two before you can speak without it hurting so much."

Mike stared at her, his eyes focused, intent. "God, I'm so sorry." His eyes dropped down and she knew he was staring at her throat.

Ignoring his order that she not speak, she asked, "How bad is it?"

He cocked a brow. "Don't talk." Then he reached up and gently touched one finger to her neck. "Bruised. Very ugly and bruised. But it will be okay. Do you remember?"

Lori nodded silently. She wanted to say something. But she wasn't sure what. *It's a good thing I didn't marry him. How did I get out of there alive?* Those were the things she *should* be saying.

Instead, she found herself wanting to yell at him about the bimbo brunette who had been giving him a blow job. She wanted to gouge the woman's eyes out. And then either slap Mike or jump him.

Not very normal reactions for somebody who had been nearly choked to death, she was sure.

So she focused on one thing she really did need to know. "Dirk?"

His eyes fell away. "He's dead."

Her eyes widened. "How?"

"Later. When you feel better. Now, will you stop talking?" he asked with a pained expression. "The sound of your voice makes *my* throat hurt."

Lori nodded. "After you tell me one thing."

Mike scowled a little. "What?"

"If you were going to start pretending I didn't exist after . . . " Her voice trailed off. *After a weekend of wonderful sex.* Lamely, she just left it at that. "Why did you even bother? We were friends."

"Lori, this isn't a good time to talk about it." His eyes were flat and unreadable. "You don't know how badly you were hurt."

"Mike—"

His voice rose. "Didn't you hear me? You weren't breathing!" He was shouting by the time he finished, his face tight with fury. He closed his eyes and she watched him battle the rage. His voice was a little softer when he continued, "You weren't breathing. Do you have any idea how much that scared me, seeing you there like that?"

"Seeing me . . . You found me?"

He nodded curtly. "I had left the club to come and find you when I heard the 911 call on my radio. I was nearly home. And still almost didn't make it in time. You were lying on the floor and he . . . "

He closed his eyes and rubbed them as if he could wipe away the memories. "He was choking you. He pulled a knife. He must have grabbed it out of your kitchen. If he had used it instead of his hands, you wouldn't be here."

"Oh God." Nausea roiled in her belly and she clapped a hand over her mouth. If she threw up . . .

Mike was there, rubbing her back with a gentle hand. "You don't need to hear about this right now," he said.

Lori leaned into him, her mind whirling as it pieced things together. He hadn't said it, but Lori knew. Mike had killed Dirk. She had been engaged to the man for nearly a year, with him for three. But all she felt was relief and some distant sort of regret. She wasn't really even angry, although she suspected she would be eventually.

"Why were you coming to look for me?" she asked. Every word felt like she was pushing raw glass through her throat, but she had to know.

Mike sighed. "You must enjoy having your throat hurt like that."

"I just need to know."

He shifted around, turning so that he sat on the edge of the bed, facing her. "To tell you I was sorry. I knew you were in the maze. And I'm sorry. But also, for the past week. I've been a bastard."

"Why? I mean, it's not like I was expecting rose petals and a diamond ring."

She stared at him as he reached down and took her hand, rubbing the back with his thumb. "I know. The problem is, part of me wanted just that."

Her jaw dropped open. She probably looked like an idiot, lying there staring at Mike with her mouth hanging open but she just couldn't help it. He reached up and pressed his finger against her chin, closing her mouth. "Don't look at me like that."

"What are you talking about?"

Instead of answering right away, Mike leaned over and pulled one of the roses from the vase. He stared at it intently as he started to pluck the satiny petals off. He dropped each one on the sheets that covered her lap. "I'm not much into romance. Never have been. That probably won't change. But you're the only woman I've ever met who made me want to give her roses, Lori. You're the only one who's ever made me want a little something more. And it scares the hell out of me. I don't react well to being scared." His gaze lifted and Lori felt her heart stutter to a stop at the emotions she saw there. "If last weekend was just a thing for you, that's fine. I'll deal with it. But if . . . Well, maybe it meant a little more and maybe, well . . . I mean, if I haven't totally fucked it up with what happened at Exposé, maybe we could . . ."

How cute. A smile spread across her face and if it wouldn't have hurt so much, she would have laughed. As he fumbled for the words, she couldn't help but think how damn cute it was, seeing him look so damn awkward.

Finally, though, she leaned in and pressed her lips to his. It was either kiss him or let him try to explain for the next thirty minutes. She'd rather kiss him.

Pulling back, Lori reached up and cupped his cheek. "Yeah. Maybe we could . . ."

IRRESISTIBLE

BEVERLY HAVLIR

Prologue

BUTTERFLIES DANCED in Madison Cahill's stomach as she waited for the hotel elevator. She couldn't stop smiling, excitement bringing her nerve endings alive. The man next to her gave her a curious glance. She lowered her face, hiding the blush spreading on her cheeks. As she did, she glimpsed her wedding ring. *Mrs. Cahill.* She still couldn't believe that it had been two months since she and Gavin had been married in a quiet, intimate ceremony. But shortly afterward Gavin had to leave on a national book tour, and it'd been close to two weeks since she'd last seen him. Unable to wait any longer, she'd decided to surprise him. He had no idea she was coming. She glanced at her watch. From the time her flight got in to the ride here to the hotel from the airport, she'd timed everything perfectly. It was just a little bit before seven o'clock in the morning.

Gavin was going to have the surprise of his life.

Madison grinned as she stepped into the elevator, her pulse racing. As the doors closed, she looked at her reflection in the mirrored wall panels. Her dress was perfectly decent, a deep blue creation with simple lines and a hem that fell to her knees. But it was the body-hugging lacy lingerie she'd donned underneath that was the real treat for her husband. It was red and barely there, revealing the naughty smoothness between her thighs. Her hair hung loose, the curls trailing to the middle of her back, just the way he liked it. She'd even worn the sexy "fuck me" shoes that her friends assured her were foolproof. Hot anticipation slid down her spine. Gavin wouldn't know what hit him.

A giggle bubbled up in her throat, earning her another curious look from the man who rode in the elevator with her. Biting her lip, she clutched her purse and the small case that held a change of clothes, resisting the urge to tap her toes in impatience. When Gavin had called last night, he'd confessed that he missed her and couldn't wait to get back home. Madison had decided to fly out on the spur of the moment and visit him. She'd booked a flight, packed a bag and taken a cab to the airport with plenty of time to catch the red-eye to Chicago. Even a few hours spent with Gavin were worth it.

The elevator pinged and stopped on Gavin's floor. Madison got off and walked down the deserted hallway. She quickened her pace, and she'd given up suppressing her silly grin. She couldn't wait to see her husband.

Her smile froze as she turned the corner.

Gavin stood by the door, his hair tousled, naked except for a pair of boxer shorts. He was kissing a sexily dressed blonde woman in the hallway, in plain view of anyone who happened to walk by. Madison gasped, reeling from shock. It was Kimberly, his publicist.

Gavin looked up. "Maddie!" he exclaimed, the stunned astonishment on his face quickly followed by guilt. Kimberly wore a smug expression, her heavily made-up eyes glinting with triumph.

A horrible silence ensued. Madison couldn't move, and stood there clutching her purse like it was an anchor. *Oh God, oh God, oh God.* Gavin was *kissing* another woman. She trembled in disbelief and tried to speak, but no words came out. All she could feel was the searing pain of betrayal. She was instantly catapulted back to the worst nightmare of her childhood, the rainy afternoon when she'd come home with her mother and they'd caught her father in bed with somebody else. Madison choked on a sob. She was her mother all over again, married to an unfaithful man.

Somehow she got her legs to move and she fled back the way she came.

"Maddie, wait. *Goddammit!*"

She ignored Gavin's call to stop, bypassing the elevator, shooting instead for the stairwell. Scalding tears streamed down her face, blurring her vision. Madison stumbled on the steps, her anguished cry echoing in the silence when her case flew from her hand. Hastily retrieving it, she gripped the banister tightly as she navigated the stairs once more. The tightness in her chest didn't diminish, even when she finally emerged into the lobby and ran out the ornate doors of the hotel where she hailed a taxi and quickly got in.

"The airport, please." As soon as she wiped away her tears, more fell down her cheeks. She gazed blindly at the passing scenery. Her mind was filled with the heart-wrenching image of a barely dressed Gavin kissing another woman, looking like he'd just gotten out of bed. It was akin to a knife sinking into her heart over and over, stabbing into the same spot, wounding her again and again.

"Everything all right, miss?" the driver asked, looking at her through the rearview mirror.

"No," she whispered.

The elderly man shook his head, his dark eyes filled with compassion. "Sometimes things are not as bad as we think they are."

Yes, they are. Madison felt sick, hollow and empty inside, desperate to get as far away from Gavin as possible. The taxi had barely pulled to a stop at the busy departure area of the airport before she scrambled out of the car, pausing briefly to toss some bills on the front seat before running inside the terminal with her case.

"Miss, this is too much—" The automatic doors closed, cutting off the rest of the cab driver's words.

Madison wiped away more tears while she booked a seat on the next flight back to L.A., which was scheduled to leave shortly. Ignoring the speculative light in the airline employee's gaze, she paid for the ticket and sought a deserted corner against the plateglass window. As she waited to board, she called her friend Amanda. "It's me." Madison smothered a soft sob. *Damn it. Why couldn't she stop crying?* "I-I'm on my way back. Can you pick me up from the airport?" She rattled off her flight number and arrival time.

"You're coming back already? What's wrong, Maddie?" Amanda asked, concern in her voice.

She gulped hard. "I-I can't talk right now. Just be there, okay? And . . . if Gavin calls you, tell him you don't know where I am."

She hung up, clutching the cell phone tightly. It rang immediately. A glance at the screen revealed the caller. *Gavin.* She ignored it, letting it go to voice mail. A few moments later, it rang again. Unable to stand the incessant ringing, she turned it off and pushed it to the bottom of her purse.

When Madison arrived back in Los Angeles, her two best friends, Amanda and Kylie, were waiting for her at the airport. They took one look at her tear-streaked face and bundled her in the car and drove her to Amanda's apartment.

"What happened, Maddie?" Kylie asked.

The question triggered more of the tears she'd thought were finally under control. Pain hit her anew when she told them what happened. "I was so stupid. I trusted him." Madison gave a choked, self-deprecating laugh. "Before we were married, the only thing I asked of Gavin was fidelity. I trusted him not to hurt me that way." She wrung her hands tightly. "He said he would never hurt me. He lied."

Amanda rubbed her back soothingly. "Have you talked to him?"

Madison shook her head. "What I saw was clear enough."

"He's your husband, Maddie," Kylie countered quietly. "Don't you think he deserves the chance to explain?"

"Explain what? Explain how he came to be standing half naked at his hotel door kissing another woman?"

"Maybe things aren't what they seem." Amanda sighed. "Talk to him. He called us both several times looking for you."

"Did you tell him I was coming here?" Madison asked sharply.

Amanda shook her head. "Of course not. You expressly forbade me from letting him know you were here."

"I still think you should talk to Gavin, Maddie," Kylie urged in gentle tones. "You need to clear things up."

Madison stood by the window, blind to the beauty of the clear Southern California day or the white-capped waves that hit the shore. "I can't," she whispered brokenly. "You both know my father cheated on my mom time and time again. And each time was more painful than the last. I don't want to live that life again."

"What if you're wrong?" Kylie went over to Madison and put an arm around her shoulder. "I think you should give him a chance to explain."

An incredible sense of loss weighed her down. "It's over."

"Just like that?" Amanda asked gently. "Is it that easy to let Gavin go?"

God no. It was tearing her apart. "I have to." Madison wrapped her arms around her middle, feeling cold and empty. The fear that she'd carried with her all her life rose up to her throat, threatening to suffocate her. "I don't want to end up like my mother. I just can't."

"Gavin sounds miserable. He's going crazy looking for you all over the place. Would you please just talk to him?" Kylie entreated.

Unlike her mother, Madison knew when to cut her losses and wipe the slate clean. She wouldn't cling to a marriage hoping that things would turn around. As a young girl, she'd once overheard her grandmother tearing into her mom, her contemptuous words echoing in the silent house. *"You're a fool, Janice, to stick around waiting for Peter to change his philandering ways. Once a cheater, always a cheater. You're a damn fool!"*

Those harsh, unforgiving words had stuck with Madison.

They carved a place in her young heart, planting the fear that she'd someday end up like her mother, clinging to a husband who broke her trust over and over again. The determination to avoid the same bitter fate had been rooted in her mind from that day on. Leaving Gavin was the right thing to do.

"Maddie?" Amanda prompted softly.

Sadness overwhelmed her. "My marriage is over." She absorbed the pain that sliced into her with those words. "It's over."

ONE

A WEEK LATER, after making sure Gavin was nowhere around, Madison went back to the house they'd shared and gathered her few belongings. She left her rings—left *everything* he'd ever given her—and only took what was hers to begin with. Gavin had been searching for her, calling her friends, hanging out at the coffee shop. She'd moved in with Amanda, needing the time away. She couldn't hide from Gavin forever, but she wasn't ready to face him yet.

Later on that day, with some help from her friends, Madison converted the empty apartment space above her coffee shop into her new home. "It's a little small, but it'll do."

Amanda dropped down on the love seat by the window, putting her feet up on the dark cherry coffee table in front of her. "You need to get a *real* apartment, not this dinky one above the shop. You'll never get away from work."

Madison popped open a soda. "This will do just fine. I don't even have to drive to work. All I need to do is go down a flight of stairs and, voilà, I'm there." She looked at Amanda and Kylie. "Thanks for helping me fix the place up."

Amanda grinned. "Thank Kylie's flirting, you mean. The delivery guys brought up not only your new bed but also all the other furniture that we'd have had to carry up the stairs."

Kylie laughed, tossing her hair over her shoulder. "It was nothing. A little wink, a little swing of my ass, and they were putty in my hands."

Madison chuckled. With her strawberry blonde hair and sparkling blue eyes, Kylie had always drawn attention. "You're incorrigible."

Her friend shrugged. "It was no big deal. The dark-haired guy was kinda cute too."

"Not again." Amanda groaned. "What happened to last week's eye candy?"

"Derek is *so* five minutes ago. Time to move on, ladies. Speaking of moving on," Kylie said, raising an eyebrow in Madison's direction. "Are you one hundred percent sure about what you're doing?"

She pasted a smile on her face. "Absolutely."

"He'll show up here. You know that, right?" Amanda pointed out.

"I can't put it off any longer. I'm ready to face him." Madison mentally crossed her fingers, hoping that when that time came, she'd be able to handle it.

"He won't give up," Kylie added.

"Our marriage is over."

"If it was somebody else, I'd believe it," Kylie countered dryly. "But you, Maddie? You're not the type to bounce back easily from this."

"I'm not one of your patients, Kylie." Madison winced as her voice cracked midsentence. She covered it up with a brief laugh. "Please don't analyze me."

"I'm just concerned about you. I know how much you loved Gavin." Kylie put an arm around Madison's shoulders. "If you ever need anybody to talk to, just let me know. The first session's on me." Despite the teasing tone, Madison knew the offer was genuine.

"Are you *sure* you'll be fine, Maddie?" Amanda asked quietly.

Their concern was touching and it nearly drove Madison to tears. *Again*. It seemed these days she cried at the smallest things. "I'll be fine. Don't worry about me. I have the coffee shop to keep me busy, and now I have my own place, instead of having to crash at Amanda's apartment." She infused her tone with a lightness she was far from feeling. "It's a brand-new start, girls. The start of a new life."

Madison uttered those words again later that evening when she was finally alone. Her clothes now hung in the closet and she'd put her computer and desk in one corner, along with all her files and accounting books for the coffee shop. She was doing fine until she plugged in a new answering machine and recorded a message.

"You've reached Madison. I'm not here to take your call, but please leave a—" And just like that, she couldn't go on. Her finger shook on the record button. The realization that she was alone hit her with the force of a hurricane. Gavin was gone from her life.

Madison sobbed as she dropped into her chair. Pain once again cut through her, inflicting new wounds, opening old ones. Tears fell on some papers spread out on her desk. Her gaze landed on the change of address form she'd planned to take to the post office tomorrow. Inexplicably, it made her cry more. Everywhere she looked, there were stark reminders that Gavin was no longer a part of her life. He wouldn't be there to cuddle her at night, would no longer wake her up with kisses and fresh-brewed coffee.

Gavin had broken her heart and for that, she could never forgive him.

A knock sounded on the door. Wiping away her tears, she looked through the peephole. Her stomach sank as she pulled open the door. "Mom."

Janice Price swept into the room without waiting for an invitation. "I won't say I told you so. I'm sure you've said that to yourself over and over."

Madison closed the door, trying to hold back her sniffles. "I'm really not in the mood for this right now, Mom. I'm tired and—"

"Were you even going to tell me you'd left him?" Janice demanded. "I found out from Stacy, your waitress downstairs, when I stopped by for coffee tonight!"

"You had no right to do that. My personal life is nobody's business but mine."

"That's the only way I find out anything about you, Madison." Her mother's tone was accusatory. "Ever since you married Gavin, you've kept me out of your life."

Maddie closed her eyes and rubbed her forehead, wishing she hadn't answered the door. "Can you blame me? You never liked him. You couldn't even wait until after the wedding before you predicted that my marriage wouldn't last."

Janice lifted her chin, not the least bit apologetic. "Was I wrong?"

"Does it make you happy that you were right, Mom?" Madison asked, resigned to her mother's venomous bitterness.

Janice had the grace to flush. "Of course not. I just wished you'd listened to me. I mean, you hardly knew Gavin before you up and married him. Marry in haste, repent at leisure and all that."

Madison winced, tempted to give in to the urge to cover her ears and drown out her mother's words.

"Besides, I knew right away what kind of man Gavin was. He's not the type to be satisfied with just one woman."

The words shot straight to Madison's heart. Her mother just couldn't resist pointing that out. It was like rubbing salt into an already festering wound. "I'm tired, Mom."

"I just want you to know that I think you're doing the right thing. Cut your ties with him now while you can. Don't be like me, Madison. Don't wait until it's too late," she said firmly.

Madison lowered her eyes, not bothering to respond. Her mother was a disillusioned, unhappy woman who harbored a deep distrust of men because of what she'd endured in her marriage.

"Is there anything I can do?" Janice asked. "Do you need anything?"

Yeah, a new heart. "I just need time to be alone."

"I care about you, Madison." Her mother's voice softened. "You may not agree with everything I say or do, but you're my daughter and I love you." She marched to the door. "Trust me, honey. It's better to suffer now and get it over with, rather than prolong the pain and suffer for the rest of your life. Don't be like me." With that final comment, she left.

With her mother's words still ringing in her ears, Madison lay down on her new bed. She pulled a pillow close to her and buried her face in the soft folds, once again letting her tears flow, hoping it would ease the pain in her heart. Somehow, she doubted it.

GAVIN SHOWED UP THE NEXT DAY.

Madison's knees nearly buckled and she gripped the door for support. "W-what are you doing here?"

"I'm here to take you home."

"I'm not coming back."

Gavin raked a hand through his thick, dark hair. "Maddie, don't do this. I can't lose you."

She flinched at the deep voice she'd once loved to hear. How many times had she lain on his chest, simply listening to him talk? "It's too late. You should've thought of that before you cheated on me."

His nostrils flared. "I didn't cheat on you."

"You were kissing her right outside your hotel room, Gavin." The memory brought forth more anguish. She was *not* going to cry. "You were nearly naked."

"I just woke up," he bit out tightly. A muscle at his jaw ticked and he pulled in a deep breath. "I sleep naked. You *know* that."

Madison quivered in anger as she scoffed at his statement. "And the kissing part?"

"Maddie, *she* kissed *me*. Not the other way around."

She turned away, rubbing a hand over her heart, trying to stem the tide of pain that was threatening to consume her. "And even though you outweigh her by over a hundred pounds, you just couldn't stop her, right?" She squeezed her eyes shut. "Just stop it, Gavin. I don't want to hear any more of your lies."

"What do I have to do to make you believe me?" he growled in frustration. He stood right behind her, so close that she could feel the heat emanating from his body. "I have *no* reason to stray from your bed."

Madison whirled around and confronted him. *"I know,* Gavin. I know because I did everything you wanted me to do in that bedroom. *Everything*." She blinked back the tears. "I gave you my heart."

"Then why would I turn to another woman, Maddie?"

"I don't know." Her voice broke. "You tell me."

Gavin looked at her earnestly, taking her hands in his. "This is all just a misunderstanding. Come home, babe. We can work this out."

She pulled away. "You hurt me."

"You think I'm not hurting right now?" he countered gruffly. "You don't think it hurts to come home and find you gone? That you trust me so little you won't believe me when I tell you I'm not lying?"

Madison was too steeped in her pain to listen. "I told you that infidelity was the one thing guaranteed to drive me away, Gavin."

"Damn it, Maddie—"

"I want a divorce." The words hung in the thick atmosphere.

Gavin paled. *"What?"*

"I want a divorce," she repeated dully.

"No!"

"I-I can't trust you anymore. I should have listened when people told me we didn't know each other well enough to get married."

"Who said that? Your mother? She never liked me, Maddie."

"But she turned out to be right." Madison tried to keep the bitterness from her voice, but she couldn't. "Look at what happened to us."

Gavin held her tight. "I'm your husband. You should believe *me*."

Misery engulfed her. "It was a mistake to get married."

"Not for me. I knew I wanted to marry you the moment I saw you." His voice rang with conviction.

"You wanted to sleep with me, you mean."

"You felt the same way." He pulled her close, ignoring her resistance, wrapping his arms tight around her. "There's more than just lust between us, Maddie. We both know that."

She wiggled out of his arms. It hurt too much to let him hold her, knowing that he'd gone to another woman. "It's too late. I want a divorce, Gavin."

A muscle in his jaw ticked. "No fucking way."

"You don't have a choice."

His eyes flashed angrily. "I didn't cheat on you."

Madison trembled, close to the breaking point. "Please, stop. Just . . . stop."

"I'm not lying," he growled. "Don't you care enough about us to want to know the truth?"

Madison turned away. When she'd met Gavin, she had a small inkling of the kind of life he led. Successful and handsome, his social life had been featured in multiple magazines. What had made her think she could keep him satisfied when there were a number of women ready and willing to please him? She was just a simple coffee shop owner, not a glamorous social butterfly who would willingly look the other way while her husband played around. Marrying Gavin had been a dream, a temporary one. The words her mother said on her wedding day echoed in Madison's mind. *Don't be a fool. I knew from the moment I met him that Gavin is not the type who'd be satisfied with just one woman. Men like him never are.*

"Goddammit, Maddie. Don't do this."

Madison clutched at a nearby chair and forced herself to confront him. "We were never meant to be together, Gavin. Let's just accept that."

Anger emanated from every inch of his six-foot-four frame. "Bullshit. We have something, Maddie. Don't just throw it all away."

She couldn't hold back the tears anymore. "Don't you see? We don't have anything in common. We . . . we don't even know each other that well. It was too soon. We shouldn't have gotten married."

"Is that what you really think? That getting a divorce is the best thing to do?"

"Yes," she choked out. In the next moment, she gasped as he pulled her into his arms. Gavin clamped his lips over hers, thrusting his tongue inside her mouth. Madison resisted, feebly struggling against his hold, desperately holding back the response that he could arouse with little effort. The kiss turned persuasive, carnal. *No fair.* Her thoughts scattered, her mind became fuzzy. A tidal wave of hunger swept over her, wiping away all thoughts of resistance.

He ground his hips against hers. "Only you can make me feel this way, Maddie. I ache for you. I can't sleep at night." Her tank top was no obstacle to the questing fingers that pushed it out of the way. Like a starving man, Gavin suckled her nipple, pulling on her deeply.

Madison felt the jolt directly to her sex. She rubbed against him, as much a slave to the need as he was. Gavin slipped a hand under the elastic waistband of her shorts, wasting no time, plunging into the wetness of her pussy. She gasped, knowing she should stop him before it got any further. But her body refused to follow her mind's instructions. When Gavin laid her on the couch and disposed of her shorts, she remained pliant.

His eyes gleamed hotly. "You're mine, Maddie. You'll *always* be mine." Like a fine-tuned instrument, he played her body with consummate skill, arousing a need only he could assuage.

Tingles of electricity raced up and down her skin. "Th-this is wrong," she moaned. Her words were at odds with the way her thighs splayed open for his touch, primed and waiting.

He squeezed her nipples. "Come home with me."

Her eyes fluttered at the sharp pleasure and pain that reverberated in her flesh. "N-no," she managed to gasp.

"I didn't cheat on you." He licked her from the top of her slit to her ass, lingering wickedly to rim the small ring of muscles there. Madison gasped. "I didn't lie." He buried his face in her soaked folds and ate her hungrily. Within moments, she was panting, racing toward that one little place that could offer her oblivion, even if only for a short while.

"Gavin . . . " Her plea turned into shock as he abruptly stopped.

"Do you believe me, Maddie?"

Her body quivered with need. "Why are you doing this?"

"I want you to trust me. I want you to let me explain what really happened that day, and most of all, I want you to come home, Maddie. But you have to learn to trust me."

A fat tear rolled down her cheek. "What's the point, Gavin? I saw you. I was there."

"You *thought* you saw me cheating, but it's not true," he insisted, frustration ringing in his voice. "I've given you the space I thought you needed. But enough is enough. I want you to come home." His hot gaze swept over her. "We can make this marriage work."

"You broke my trust. I-I can't live with that. Can't you see?"

His face hardened into an angry mask. "So what are you telling me? It's over? Just like that? Tell me, Maddie. Tell me to my face that we're over."

Her heart splintered into a million tiny pieces. "It's over."

"What about this?" His hand swept over her. "You fell into my arms like you always do. You were as hungry for me as I was for you. Can you turn your back on that?"

"Yes." Forcing that lie from her lips was the hardest thing she'd ever done.

Gavin was silent for so long that Madison finally raised her eyes to look at him. His dark eyes were dull and lifeless. "I'm not going to beg, Maddie. I'm not going to plead that you give us another chance, that you believe me when I tell you I didn't cheat on you." The distant, icy tone underscored the cold fury etched in his handsome features. "I can't force you to do what I want. Just remember what you're throwing away here." He left, closing the door softly behind him with a decisive click.

He was gone. Alone, Madison was consumed by a gnawing emptiness inside. She rocked on the couch, wrapping her arms around her middle. Hot, unfulfilled need washed over her. She longed for his touch, ached for the release that he could give her. But at what price?

Oh Gavin. She began to weep for what could have been, for the love she still felt for him, for their life together that had been abruptly cut short. If only he hadn't cheated. *If only.*

"JESUS, WHAT THE HELL HAPPENED?"

Gavin opened his eyes and blinked, trying to focus. "Wes?"

Wesley Halverson swept empty liquor bottles out of the way before hefting him into a sitting position on the couch. "You're drunk out of your mind."

Gavin groaned and cradled his head in his hands. "*Was* drunk. Last night. What time is it?"

"It's Monday morning, nine o'clock," Wes drawled, taking the chair across from him. "What's going on, man?"

"Monday?" Gavin repeated, incredulous. "Christ."

"Judging from the number of bottles scattered around here, either you had one hell of a party and I wasn't invited or there's something going on here that you need to tell me about."

Gavin rubbed his face. His eyes felt gritty and his mouth felt like it was full of cotton. "What are you doing here?"

"I've been calling you since yesterday. When you didn't answer, I got concerned." Wesley frowned. "What the hell is going on?"

"I got drunk."

Wesley snorted. "That much is obvious."

Gavin slumped against the couch. "Maddie left me."

"Say that again?"

"She left me." Without glossing over any details, Gavin told him the whole story. "I didn't expect her to show up like that. And *damn* Kimberly for getting me into this mess in the first place."

"That woman was trouble from day one," Wesley grumbled. "All she saw were dollar signs on you."

Gavin shut his eyes tightly. He didn't give a fuck about Kimberly. "Maddie wants a divorce."

"Shit. Did you try to explain?"

"Maddie has . . . trust issues. I tried but she won't listen. She's convinced I cheated on her." Anger and frustration knotted inside his chest. "I *didn't* cheat on her, Wes. Why won't she believe me?" He clenched his fists. "I love her. I had no reason to even look at another woman. Why can't she see that?"

Wesley sighed. "I believe you. In all the years I've known you, I've never seen you act this way over a woman."

Gavin raked his fingers through his hair. Maddie was different from all the other women he'd known. From the moment they met, she'd made him feel things he'd never felt before. "This whole thing has got me so wired. I'm her husband. She *should* trust me."

"Yeah, but if she has trust issues like you said . . . well . . . it's just not easy."

"Fuck easy," Gavin bit out, furious. "She told me she wants a divorce. Just like that." He snapped his fingers. "She'll throw everything away and not even try to work things out."

"Gavin, man, anger isn't going to help you right now."

Gavin pushed off the couch and stalked to the window. "But I am angry, Wes. I married *her*. I promised to love, cherish and honor *her* for the rest of our lives. Doesn't that count for anything?" He gritted his teeth. "If Maddie thinks I'm going to beg her to come back, she's dead wrong. I'm done with this whole fucking mess."

Anger and resentment flowed through him, hardening his resolve. Gavin was sick of defending himself. He closed his eyes, the stinging pain of heartache slamming into him for the first time in his life. Madison had been the only woman who'd cut a path straight to his soul. Every fiber of his being was against letting her go. If she truly loved him, she wouldn't be so quick to resort to divorce. If it was so easy for her to throw away their marriage, then their relationship truly was over.

TWO

WESLEY STARED AT GAVIN across the length of his desk. "You look like shit."

Gavin shifted on the plush, oversize leather chair. "Gee, thanks. Nice to see you too, Wes."

"What the hell have you been doing?"

"Working," he answered curtly. Too restless to sit, Gavin stalked to the window. The view from Wesley's downtown law office was impressive, the beautiful skyline bathed in bright Southern California sunshine. But he hardly noticed it. Instead, he gazed at his reflection in the tinted glass. Wes was right. He did look like shit. In the month since Maddie had left him, he'd been plagued by insomnia and his appetite was shot. Worse, his latest manuscript was due in a month and he hadn't written anything worth a damn.

"I think you need help."

Gavin scoffed at that. He ran a hand through his hair and looked over his shoulder at the man who was his best friend as well as his lawyer. "I assume there's a reason why you wanted me to come here today? Because I assure you, I'm not in the mood for a sermon right now."

Wesley frowned. "Have you had lunch? I can have Marie get you something from the deli downstairs."

His stomach roiled at the thought of food. "No thanks."

"Are you trying to kill yourself?"

If he was, it wasn't working. "That would probably be a good idea," he muttered. "But no, as it happens, I'm not."

"This self-pity bullshit has got to stop."

Gavin narrowed his eyes. "Fuck you. I don't need this. I'm outta here." He strode to the door.

"She filed for divorce."

He froze, his mind going blank. He turned around slowly. *"What did you say?"*

Wesley exhaled loudly and stood up, jamming his hands in his pants pockets. "Maddie filed for divorce. I got the papers yesterday from her lawyer."

Cold fury welled up in Gavin's chest. *She actually went through with it. She actually filed for divorce.* Madison was really done with him, done with their marriage. He pulled in a deep breath, desperately trying to come to terms with it. He swallowed the lump in his throat and forced the word past his lips. "Fine."

"What?" Wesley asked, clearly shocked. "Just like that?"

"What do you want me to say? That I'll fight it? That I'll never give her a divorce?" Gavin shook his head. "If she wants to get out of this marriage, fine. I'll give her a fucking divorce."

"You're going to let Maddie go?"

Pain sliced into his heart. "I don't have a choice, do I?"

"Keep telling yourself that, maybe you'll believe it," Wesley muttered.

"What do you want me to do, Wes? Force myself on her? Hell no. I've never loved another woman the way I love her. If she wants to end our marriage, then so be it. I can't be with a woman who's incapable of trusting me."

"Gavin—"

He raised a hand. "I won't fight it. Give her whatever she wants."

"Alimony?"

"Yeah." God, he needed a stiff drink, even though alcohol didn't really solve anything. He could drink himself to oblivion, much like he'd been doing lately, but it only masked the pain. It never took it away. What he needed was to move on. Get on with his life.

"*Whatever* she wants?" Wesley persisted.

"Whatever she wants. Give her the fucking divorce, give her half my money. Hell, she can have all of it. I really don't care anymore."

"Is this what you really want?"

"What I want doesn't seem to matter."

"You don't want to try to talk to her again? One more time?"

He pulled in a shaky breath. "It's over."

For a moment, Wesley looked as if he would argue some more but finally he nodded. "All right. I'll arrange a meeting to iron out the details. You'll have to be present, of course."

At the thought of seeing Madison once more, his pulse jumped. It had been thirty-six days, five hours and—he glanced at his watch—twenty-eight minutes since he'd last seen Maddie, naked and splayed on the couch, trembling beneath his hands. It had taken all of his strength to walk out the door. Gavin shook his head. "No."

"No?" Wesley echoed in disbelief.

"I don't want to see her." Coming face-to-face with Maddie while they finalized the dissolution of their marriage would be the last straw. To see her and know that she wasn't his anymore would surely be the blow that finally killed him. No. It was better that they didn't see each other. Wipe the slate clean and move on. "I don't want to see her again."

WHEN THE SUN PEEKED THROUGH the early morning clouds and began to cast a warm glow over the still-quiet city, Madison gave up trying to sleep and got out of bed. Today was *the* day. At ten o'clock sharp, she, accompanied by her lawyer, was scheduled to meet with Gavin and his lawyer to discuss their divorce.

Divorce. Her heart tripped over the word. It was hard to accept that her marriage was coming to an end. Had it really been over a month since she'd left Gavin? It seemed longer.

After taking a shower and drying her hair, she applied her makeup carefully. *I'll be fine. I'll recover.* After all, she was only twenty-eight, plenty of time left to find a trustworthy man to fall in love with and have a family. It was unfortunate that Gavin wasn't that man.

Walking to her closet, Madison tried to decide what to wear. This was the first time she'd see him again after he'd left her apartment. One part of her wanted to blow him away and remind him of what he'd lost. The other part mocked her for caring. *Damn him.* He was still tying her in knots.

Deciding on an ultraconservative black suit, she pulled it out and laid it on the bed. The jacket buttoned down the front and the skirt reached exactly to her knees. It had the right tone of unapproachable formality she wanted to convey. Madison sat down in front of her dresser and ignored the quick twinge of pain in her heart. Too late for regrets.

Gathering her thick hair into a twist at her nape, she secured it with a clip and smoothed down the sides. She slipped her feet into black, chunky-heeled pumps before looking at her reflection in the mirror. The effect was severe, and not in the least sexy. Good. That's what she wanted.

The coffee shop was full but not crowded when she came down from her apartment. Madison nodded to Kelly, one of her part-time employees, and headed to a table in the back where her lawyer sat waiting for her.

"Good morning, Dana."

Dana Hightower looked up from the notes she'd spread out on the table and gave her a smile. "How are you feeling today? Ready for the meeting?"

"Ready as I'll ever be. I want to get this over with."

Dana gathered all the papers together before stuffing them into her briefcase. "I'll try to make this as painless as possible. Shall we?" Madison followed her out to the car, thinking that the woman's petite frame and pretty features were totally at odds with her reputation as a shark in the courtroom, with a long list of divorce cases she'd successfully represented.

"We have to discuss a settlement for you." Dana pulled out smoothly into traffic. "Your husband has considerable assets."

"I don't want his money," Madison enunciated carefully. "I'm not asking for anything."

"You shouldn't be so quick in making these decisions," her lawyer chided gently. "Gavin Cahill is worth a lot of money."

"I don't want anything."

"Not even the house? A nice financial settlement?"

Madison shook her head firmly. "Nothing."

"You never know when you might need it," Dana reminded her in a mild voice.

She breathed deeply. "I'm doing fine. My coffee shop is all I need."

"Then what is it you *do* want?"

"I just want a divorce so I can get on with my life." Saying the words out loud always resulted in a familiar twinge in her heart. Would the pain ever go away? With time, maybe. And she had nothing but time at this point. For her to be able to start another chapter of her life, she had to close the book on her disastrous marriage. She needed to put Gavin completely out of her life . . . forever.

Dana pulled into the underground parking garage of the high-rise building that housed Gavin's lawyer's office. They rode in silence as the elevator swiftly rose to the fortieth floor. Madison wiped her damp palms down the sides of her skirt. Her heart was starting to beat erratically.

"Remember," Dana reminded her in a low voice, "let me do the talking, okay?"

"Not a problem." Just being here tied her stomach in knots.

The law offices of Halverson & Auburn occupied the entire floor of the building. The receptionist was a stylish blonde who wore fashionable eyeglasses and a headset.

Dana approached her. "Hello. We're here to see Mr. Halverson."

The young woman pressed a button on the console, talking in low tones before she addressed them once more. "Somebody will be out to see you in a moment."

While they waited, Madison glanced around the plush reception area. She'd met Wesley on numerous occasions, but had never been to his office. She fought the urge to fidget. She tried to relax, half anticipating, half dreading seeing Gavin once more.

A woman dressed in a cream-colored suit ushered them into a large conference room furnished with a long, polished table and cushioned chairs.

Taking the seat next to Dana, Madison tried to quiet the butterflies flitting around her stomach. She pulled in a couple of deep breaths. The door opened and a man came in dressed in an impeccable gray suit with a neat tie, a thick file folder in hand. Madison schooled her face into a polite mask. Wesley Halverson was a handsome man with sun-lightened hair and a charming smile.

"Ladies," Wesley greeted them warmly. He extended a hand out to Dana. "Wesley Halverson." Then he turned to Madison. "Hello, Maddie."

Madison nodded, unable to muster a smile. "Wesley."

He put the files down on the table and sat. Dana frowned. "Where is your client, Mr. Halverson?"

"Mr. Cahill won't be able to make it today."

Madison clamped her lips together. *He couldn't even be bothered to show up.* He probably didn't want to see her. Now, why should that thought hurt? She should be relieved that she didn't have to face him today instead of being disappointed.

Her attorney was none too pleased. "I thought we agreed that all parties would be here today to discuss the dissolution of this marriage. How are we supposed to do that if your client is not here, Mr. Halverson?"

"Call me Wesley, please." His eyes sought out Madison's. "Gavin is under a very tight deadline, Maddie. There was just no way he could be here today." His eyes slid to Dana. "As to the matter of this divorce, my client is prepared to cooperate and does not intend to fight it."

He does not intend to fight it. The words swam in Madison's head. She pulled in a deep breath in an attempt to ease the tightness in her chest. That was good, right? So why did she have the sudden urge to weep?

"All right. Let's proceed." Dana opened the file in front of her and perused the papers.

Wesley spoke first. "My client is willing to pay alimony, whatever amount your client wishes."

That took Madison by surprise. Why would Gavin do that? To soothe his guilty conscience? "I don't want—"

"Madison," Dana warned softly. She nodded to Wesley. "Go on."

"Gavin is also willing to sign over the deed to the house in Pacific Palisades." As Madison sputtered in denial, Wesley looked at her directly. "He wants you taken care of."

Dana smiled. "All right, then." She picked up a pen and began to write.

"No. I won't *accept* anything from him," Madison declared firmly. "I just want a divorce." Dana looked at her in disbelief but Madison stood her ground. "Nothing else. And I won't change my mind about that."

Wesley frowned. "But Gavin wants to—"

"What he wants no longer matters here," she interrupted firmly.

"Madison, I'd like to remind you that under the laws of the state, you're entitled to half of your husband's assets." Dana's voice was mild but the message was clear. She'd be a fool not to take what Gavin was giving her.

"No, Dana. That's final."

Her lawyer pursed her lips before she relented. "Whatever you say."

As Dana and Wesley discussed the other legalities of the divorce, Madison tuned them out. Money, or the fact that Gavin had a lot of it, had never mattered to her. She'd have given everything she owned to be able to go back to the early days of their brief marriage. Their honeymoon had been beautiful and unforgettable, full of love and laughter. They'd talked about having children in the near future, maybe four, even five. Gavin had wanted a big family and she'd agreed, weaving daydreams of little children running and playing around the house.

Madison swallowed, blinking back sudden tears. It was foolish to long for those times. Soon her marriage would be dissolved forever. The anger that she'd initially felt at Gavin's betrayal was gone. In its place was pain and regret.

When the two lawyers wrapped up their discussion, Madison breathed a sigh of relief. Dana extended her hand to Wesley. "I'll send you the final papers for your client to sign."

As they shook hands, Madison made her way to the door. She needed to get out of there before she completely broke down and made a fool of herself.

"Maddie?"

"Yes?"

Wes pulled her into a hug. "Good luck."

"Thanks," she whispered, closing her eyes for a moment. Fearing she might burst into tears, she opened the door and hurried outside, past the receptionist, heading directly to the elevator. She was barely aware of Dana getting into the car with her.

"Are you all right?" Dana asked, her voice tinged with concern.

No. "Yeah, I'm okay." But even to her ears, the words rang hollow. She didn't have Gavin anymore. She was never going to be fine. Ever.

GAVIN WATCHED MADISON THROUGH the two-way mirror in Wesley's office, hungrily tracing the features of her face, lingering on the full, pouty lips that never failed to stir him. He'd tried to stay away but he couldn't. When he had shown up earlier today, Wesley had been surprised. But Gavin didn't trust himself enough to come face-to-face with Maddie. He was starving, famished for her. Up close, he might have been tempted to touch. This was safer. He just wanted to see his wife again.

Except she wouldn't be his wife for much longer.

He took in her appearance, examining the beautiful, thick hair she'd twisted into a knot at her nape. She knew damn well he didn't like it when she put up her hair like that. And that suit. He was sure she'd come here dressed in that severe schoolmarm look expressly to tick him off. It'd had the opposite effect.

The suit jacket couldn't contain those magnificent breasts of hers. Though she'd buttoned the thing up to her neck, her breasts thrust tightly against the soft material. His imagination ran riot, bringing to mind visions of her generous flesh cupped softly in a lace bra. His cock stirred to life, lengthening under the denim, making his jeans damn uncomfortable.

When she stood up, his eyes caressed her rounded hips, wishing she would turn around so he could see her ass pushing softly against her skirt. The modest skirt couldn't even begin to disguise her shapely legs. And what was up with those ugly shoes? He knew she had a preference for strappy, high-heeled, drive-a-man-crazy stilettos. Did she think if she dressed down she would be undesirable to him? She could be dressed in a burlap bag and she'd still give him a hard-on.

Madison may have broken his heart but she still could make him want her like he wanted no other woman.

Gavin clenched his fists. God, it had been too damn long since he'd held her in his arms. It was all he could do not to burst into that conference room, push her against the wall and fuck her—to hell with the spectators. His mouth watered as he followed her progress to the door until he couldn't see her anymore.

Wesley walked in. "You should have joined us."

He slipped his hands inside his pockets. "She's as beautiful as ever."

Wesley shook his head. "Man, you're still lovesick. Why the hell are you divorcing her?"

He'd asked himself that question many times. He was no closer to an answer now. "It's for the best."

"I never thought I'd see the day when you just gave up without a fight. That's not the best friend I grew up with." Wesley threw him a challenging stare. "The Gavin I knew would march over to Maddie's apartment, fuck her brains out and then tell her hell would freeze over before he'd give her a divorce."

I'd still love to fuck her brains out. At that thought, heat swirled in his belly. His wife was the hottest woman he'd ever had in his bed. "Can't beat a dead horse, Wes."

"I still think you gave up too easily." When Gavin didn't answer, Wesley shrugged. "Look, if there's truly no hope left for you and Maddie, then maybe we should go out tonight. Grab a drink or something. We could go to a bar, pick up a woman and get you laid. Maybe that's just what you need."

"Been there, done that," he muttered. He'd gone out, fully intending to bring a woman home to sink into and forget his wife, even for a little while. When that had failed, he'd called up an ex who'd always made it clear she was available to him, whenever he wanted. He'd gotten as far as kissing her, then . . . nothing. He didn't get hard. And after the same thing happened again with a different woman, he'd given up. He just couldn't muster any enthusiasm.

But one look at Maddie and his cock had snapped to attention, ready to play, eager for her pussy. Pathetic, that's what he was. *Fucking pathetic.*

Gavin straightened his shoulders, suddenly needing to get far away from everything. "I'm going up to the cabin. Just send me the papers to sign when you get them."

"How long are you gonna be there?"

"I don't know." He shrugged carelessly. "As long I need to be there, I suppose." The cabin in the mountains had always been the one place where he could go to think, where he could find peace of mind. It was also where he and Maddie had shared some of their happiest moments.

It was time to exorcise her ghost from his life.

He'd start there and work his way up, until all traces of Madison were gone and he could finally move on.

AMANDA WALKED THROUGH THE DOOR and pointedly eyed the wide array of pots and bowls littering the kitchen counter in Madison's apartment. "All right. What's the emergency, Maddie?"

Kylie, who sat on a bar stool, snickered behind the can of soda she held to her lips.

Madison glared at Kylie and kept on stirring cake batter. "What makes you think there's an emergency?"

"Because you cook and bake in massive quantities when something is bothering you," Amanda supplied dryly, running her fingertip over the rim of the bowl, swiping some of the delicious mixture.

Maddie gave a snort and swatted Amanda's hand away. "I invite you two over for a home-cooked meal and this is the thanks I get?"

Kylie grinned. "I'm glad you don't have too many of these crisis episodes, Maddie. My hips can't take it."

"I just felt like cooking, that's all."

"Uh-huh," Amanda mocked over another mouthful of batter. "Kylie, remember that time she broke up with Randy Nielsen right after the prom?"

"Yup. That was the first time she cooked us a four-course meal. There was so much food left over that I took some home and told my mom I made it to impress her."

Amanda laughed. "And remember when she didn't know how to break up with Bill? You know, the one with the tragically short tongue?"

Kylie burst out laughing. "Who could forget that? He couldn't . . . ah . . . perform certain things well because of that particular handicap." She gave a dramatic sigh. "Too bad. If not for that, he was an okay guy."

Madison rolled her eyes and checked the pot roast.

"Exactly," Amanda quipped. "Maddie baked soft and chewy chocolate-chip cookies that were to die for. Those cookies alone were responsible for the five pounds I gained that summer." She swiped some more batter and licked her finger. "And remember when Maddie left Gavin and stayed at my apartment for a couple of weeks?"

"Oh, yeah," came Kylie's reply while she sniffed the soup simmering on the stove. "That was the big one. She baked us six different kinds of cake in one day." She groaned. "I still haven't gotten over that white chocolate cake, Maddie. *Unbelievable.*"

"I know." A blissful sigh came from Amanda at the memory. "I'll never forget that one."

"All right, all right," Madison interrupted, exasperated. They knew her too well. "There *is* something."

Two pairs of interested eyes, gleaming with anticipation, swung around to look at her. Kylie narrowed her eyes. "Let me guess. You decided to stop pining for Gavin and got laid last night?"

Amanda jumped at that. "Ooh, ooh, you finally went out with John?"

"No, nothing like that." Just the thought of sleeping with someone else was . . . well, unpalatable right now. Madison sighed. "I filed for divorce."

The two women were shocked, momentarily speechless. Amanda recovered first and reached for Madison's hand. "Oh, sweetie, why didn't you tell us?"

"I don't know," she confessed. "I guess I just didn't want to talk about it. I'd planned on telling you the news after we ironed out all the details."

"Did everything go okay?" Kylie asked.

"Gavin didn't even show up." Madison couldn't keep the frustration out of her voice. "He let his lawyer take the meeting. Wesley said that he had a deadline he couldn't miss."

"Wesley, huh?" Kylie lit up with sudden interest. "I remember him. He was Gavin's best man at your wedding, right? He's cute."

Amanda frowned. "Focus, Kylie. We're talking about Maddie now." She put an arm around Madison. "Tell us what happened."

"Gavin agreed to the divorce."

"That's a good thing, right?" Kylie was puzzled. "Why do you look so sad?"

Madison's shoulders slumped. "It's just so difficult. I'd prepared for this meeting, telling myself I could see him again without feeling angry." She bit her lip. "I guess I was a little disappointed that he couldn't even be bothered to show up to discuss our divorce."

Amanda and Kylie exchanged knowing glances.

"What?" Madison asked.

"You sound disappointed that you didn't see him, Maddie," Amanda observed gently.

"I do?" she hedged. "Well, maybe I was. I just thought that . . . you know . . . I'd see him one last time."

"You miss him," Amanda commented. "That's perfectly normal. We know how hard you fell for Gavin. Something like that doesn't go away quickly. It's not easy to just completely erase somebody you love from your life."

"What you need is some form of catharsis," Kylie declared, nodding her head wisely.

"Catharsis?" Madison echoed.

"You need to purge all the hurt you feel and focus on the good times. Let go of the bitterness and the anger. That's the only way you can move on."

Amanda nodded. "Kylie's right. Bitterness warps the mind and all that."

"How do I do that?"

Kylie shrugged. "Any way you can. Find some emotional release, something that will drain the heaviness, the lingering pain from your heart."

Later that night, Madison poured herself a glass of wine. The kitchen was once again immaculate, no trace left of the cooking and baking frenzy she'd indulged in. Amanda and Kylie had long since left, sent off with carefully packed boxes of cake and cookies. She turned off the light and made her way to the darkened bedroom and sat on the bed. Her muscles felt stiff. She rolled her shoulders and neck, hoping to ease the painful tightness. The tension began to gradually seep from her body. She'd been on an emotional roller coaster from the moment she'd gotten up and dressed to go to the meeting. Thank God the day was almost over.

Madison relaxed against the pillows and sipped her wine. Her life had been doing just fine . . . until she met Gavin. What was that movie where the heroine confesses to the hero, "You had me at hello"?

Once, she'd grimaced at the clichéd dialogue. Nobody said or did those things anymore. Little did she know that was going to happen to her. Gavin had swept her off her feet, making her disregard all the precautionary measures a woman living in this day and age swore by.

Don't sleep with a man on the first date. Madison blushed at the memory. She'd slept with Gavin the night they'd met.

Don't let lust rule your head. She'd *certainly* done that. After Gavin kissed her for the first time, she'd been hopelessly lost.

And last, the rule that she learned from her very own mother. *Don't trust a man with your heart, because sooner or later, he'll break it.* It had been her mother's mantra, something she'd drilled into her daughter early on.

Madison had plunged headlong into a hot, torrid affair with Gavin Cahill, culminating a couple of months later in a small, elegant wedding. She supposed it was inevitable that they would get married. They'd been inseparable since the night they met. And the sex . . . *wow*.

She squirmed restlessly on the bed at that thought. Sex with Gavin had been incredible. In the bedroom, he had been her lover and her master. He'd taught her exactly how to please him. In return, he'd done things to her she had never even imagined. He'd known just how to use his cock—long, thick and mouthwatering—to drive her crazy. Their sex life had been rich and varied, never boring. Gavin had been perfect for her in every way.

Her nipples tightened under her shirt, rubbing against the cotton material, suddenly sensitive and painful. With shaky fingers, she pulled it over her head. The tips of her breasts were hard and tingly, made even more so by the rings she still wore. *Gavin's nipple rings*. Even after everything that had happened, she couldn't bring herself to remove them.

With the tip of a finger, she rubbed the stiff nub caught in the delicate gold circle. Heat washed over her. Her pussy clenched with need, moisture pooling between her legs. It had been so long since she'd felt his touch. She pulled at her nipple, elongating the tip, imagining it was Gavin's talented fingers working it. The slight pain only aroused her more.

Madison slipped her hand under the waistband of her shorts and through the edge of her panties, parting her legs wider. She sought and found her aching clitoris, shuddering with need. She swirled around it, tugging gently at the clit ring—another token from Gavin that she couldn't bear to remove.

Hungry for his touch, she did the next best thing. Madison undressed and lay down on the bed. She slipped her fingers inside her sheath, drenching the digits in her warm wetness and began to pleasure herself. In her mind, it was *his* strong fingers plunging in and out of her sopping vagina, gently pulling at her ring, the overwhelming pleasure drowning out the slight sting of pain. She brought her other hand up and fondled her breast, working the aching tip until she was moaning and writhing feverishly on the bed. Madison whimpered, driven by intense need. It had been so long and she needed it so bad . . .

She came, her inner muscles contracting hungrily around her fingers. "*Gavin!*" His name exploded from her lips as she crested, revealing the stark need she harbored deep in her soul.

Afterward Madison burst into tears, overcome once more by a horrible feeling of emptiness. What had just happened was a temporary solution to the hunger gnawing at the very center of her being. She hugged a pillow tightly, pressing her tear-streaked face into the soft folds. Touching herself was a feeble, ineffective replacement for what she really needed. She needed the real thing. She needed Gavin.

THREE

SIX MONTHS AFTER SIGNING the divorce papers, Madison had to admit she was a fraud. Her life was a never-ending cycle of dreaming about Gavin when she was asleep and longing for him when she was awake. In the company of others, she presented a happy front, but alone, her mask crumbled and she gave in to tears. It was a lonely existence. Too many times she'd thought of Gavin. Where was he? What was he doing? More important, *who* was he doing it with?

When his latest novel had come out, she'd immediately gone to the bookstore and bought a copy. How many times had she stared at his picture on the inside of the book jacket? And when he'd hit the bestseller list once again, she'd been tempted to pick up the phone and congratulate him. She'd scoured countless magazines and newspapers for any news of him. When he'd been snapped at a lavish gala with a stunning woman clinging to his arm, a hot stab of jealousy had lanced her heart. It tortured her to think that he was dating again. Over and over, she looked at the picture of him with the beautiful woman in the red dress. She couldn't stop herself.

Madison threw the magazine in the trash can. This had to stop. Kylie was right. What she needed was to start over completely. Gavin was getting on with his life, so should she. But how was she supposed to do that? She had absolutely no desire to date at all. The sudden ringing of the phone interrupted her pity party. It was Wesley.

"Gavin is selling the cabin in the mountains."

Madison was stunned. "B-but he loves that place."

"Believe me, I'm just as surprised as you are."

The cabin was where they'd spent their honeymoon. Why would he possibly want to do that? Unless . . . Madison drew up short. The answer was pretty obvious. *He's cutting all ties with me.* He was getting rid of everything that reminded him of their marriage.

"My instructions are to let you know in order to give you a chance to get whatever you want from the cabin," Wesley continued.

Madison swallowed. She'd left numerous pictures back at the cabin, most of which she'd taken herself. Their wedding album was also there, as well as other mementos of their time spent together.

"I'm sorry for the short notice, but Gavin would like this taken care of as soon as possible." When she didn't say anything, Wesley uttered a sigh, clearly uncomfortable. "I know this must come as a shock to you, Maddie."

"A-a little," she admitted.

"If you're not interested, he'll hire somebody to take care of it and get rid of everything."

"No!" she blurted out in a rush. "D-don't do that. I want them back." This was her chance for a much-needed catharsis, to let go of the bitterness and hurt. Going back to the place where she and Gavin had been the happiest would be an enormous release. To go there for the last time would be the cathartic event Kylie said she needed. She made a sudden decision and said, "I'll fly up there. This weekend."

"You will?" Wesley asked doubtfully.

"Yes. If that's okay with Gavin."

"Of course it is. He specifically told me to let you know so you could have the chance to get them yourself."

"I'll book a flight for Friday."

"Okay. Sounds great." Wesley paused. "I'll inform Gavin. You know, just to make sure he won't be anywhere nearby."

"Thanks," Madison managed to say before she hung up. She dropped onto the couch, her legs shaky. This was further proof that Gavin was indeed moving on. If he could do it, why couldn't she? She needed to do this, desperately. For the last time, she'd like to see the place that bore witness to the love that she and Gavin once had. Then she could finally put Gavin and their failed marriage behind her and move on. Picking up the phone, she booked a flight to Colorado.

THE ROCKIES LOOMED IN THE BACKGROUND as Madison filled up the tank of her rental car, shivering under her thick parka. There was a distinct chill in the air, and the temperature seemed to have dropped drastically. She ran inside the local convenience store, where it was blessedly warm, and bought a bottle of water. The man behind the counter recognized her. "Mrs. Cahill, right?"

She smiled, not bothering to tell him she was the ex–Mrs. Cahill. "Yes."

"You headin' up to the cabin?"

Madison nodded. "Yes, I am."

He indicated the clouds gathering in the sky. "Looks like a nasty storm brewing. Be careful."

She looked over her shoulder at the thick clouds that covered the sky. "I should make it there in good time. Thanks." But as the car ate up the miles leading away from the town of Cripple Creek, Colorado, the clouds suddenly appeared more ominous than she'd first thought. She began to feel nervous as the first snowflakes started to fall. Gripping the steering wheel tightly, she pushed on, saying a quick prayer that she'd make it to the cabin before this turned into a full-fledged storm. Her prayers went unanswered. The snow started falling harder. It was still a couple of hours until sunset, but visibility was almost zero as the snow fell thicker and faster.

Not for the first time, Madison thought about turning around. She could barely see in front of her. But she was close, she knew it. To turn around now would mean that she would spend even more time driving in this horrible weather. Apprehension filled her as she looked in vain for a mile marker or something to tell her where to turn. There was nothing but blinding white powder blanketing the countryside. *Damn it.* If she hadn't been delayed at the car rental counter at the airport, maybe she would have been safely to her destination already. A savage winter storm was suddenly raging and she was in the middle of it.

Madison adjusted the thermostat of the car heater. Along with the cold, she began to feel very real fear as she inched forward on the deserted road. The windshield wipers couldn't move fast enough to clear the view and she could barely see in front of her. Why hadn't she turned back earlier when it had been safe to do so? *Stupid, stupid, stupid.* She could only hope that she reached the turnoff soon and got to the cabin in one piece.

Her hopes quickly dimmed even further. She was essentially driving blind, following a road that she couldn't even see anymore. Her heart pounded. Beneath her gloves, her palms were damp. *God, please just let me get there in one piece.* She was trying to verbally bolster her courage by chanting "I'll get there, I'll get there" when she hit a big rut in the road and jolted to a stop. Madison shrieked in terror. The car was tilted sideways, the right front fender dipping low, hanging over something she couldn't even see.

Her heart pounded. *Okay. Calm down. Panicking will not help in this kind of situation.* Gingerly, Madison put the car in reverse, stepped on the gas and tried to turn the wheel. The tires spun uselessly. The engine groaned as she revved it, but the car didn't budge. She did it again. Nothing happened. She stayed right where she was.

A choked sob escaped her throat. *What am I going to do?* The car was stuck. Taking a deep, calming breath, she tried to peer through the windows. Where the hell was she? She couldn't see anything at all, no clue as to where exactly she was. Flipping her cell phone open, she dialed 911.

No response. Madison glanced at the screen. There was no signal. Refusing to give in to the panic threatening to suffocate her, she tried again, punching the three numbers that would send help to find her.

Again, nothing.

Don't panic. Trying again, she carefully punched the emergency number once more. When she got the same result, she pounded the steering wheel in frustration. She took a deep, steadying breath. *Think, Maddie.* Her options were limited. Going out in the storm would be sheer stupidity, since she didn't have the faintest idea where she was. Staying in the car seemed like the wise thing to do. Pulling her parka closer around her, Madison zipped it up and peered outside her window. *Please, God, let somebody come along to find me.*

She picked up her purse and checked the contents for food. All she found was a half-eaten candy bar she'd bought at the airport this morning plus the water she'd bought at the store in town. She'd have to save the candy bar for when she got really hungry. God only knows how long she was going to be stuck here.

Time slowed to a crawl. Madison huddled deeper in her thick parka, thankful she'd at least done one thing right and put on sensible clothes. Every few minutes, she'd try her cell phone again, only to get the same results. Frustration mounted along with fear, but she forced herself to stay calm. She was stuck in the middle of nowhere. It wouldn't help at all to become hysterical.

But as the snow continued to fall unabated and with ever-increasing ferocity, it was getting harder and harder not to panic. She shivered. Every few minutes, she let the engine run so she could turn on the heater. But as soon as she turned it off, the cold came back with a vengeance.

The wind howled incessantly, rocking the small car, jolting her nerves further. Darkness fell and with it, Madison's hopes of being rescued. In the inky blackness outside, she'd given up even trying to see anything. She rubbed her gloved hands together, just needing to move. In the time she'd been in the car, she'd gone from anger to self-pity to blaming herself for even wanting to come out here. Now she just felt hopeless. Tears pricked at the corners of her eyes as she reclined the seat all the way back. If she was going to die, she might as well be comfortable.

Madison eyed the empty candy wrapper on the passenger seat. No food. No more water either. At least the heater was still working, giving her some warm air. But luck wasn't on her side. At that exact moment, the engine sputtered and shook before it fell silent. She eyed the gas gauge in dismay. Empty. She shivered. Would she die of hypothermia out here? How long would it be before she was found? A few hours? Worst-case scenario, a day maybe? Several people knew where she was headed. Surely they'd send out a search party for her once they realized she'd been caught in the blizzard.

A bright light shone into the car, jolting her upright. The sudden pounding on the window elicited a small cry of terror from her lips. A gloved hand cleared the snow from the windshield, the beam from the flashlight briefly illuminating a masculine face. Madison blinked. Gavin? After fumbling with the lock, she opened the car door and all but fell into his arms.

"Of all the stupid, brainless fucking things to do," he roared, "this takes the cake, Maddie. Didn't you check the weather report?"

Fear, panic and terror were instantly wiped away, replaced by giddy euphoria at being found. She shivered in the freezing temperature, raising her voice to be heard over the howling wind. "Oh, thank God you found me." She hugged him on impulse. "It-it's so cold."

Gavin's jaw tightened dangerously as he threw another, bigger, parka over her, zipping it up quickly and tightening the hood over her head. "How do you feel?" he asked gruffly, once again shining the flashlight in her face.

She brought a hand up to shield her eyes. "I-I'm cold but okay. The heater was working until I used up the last of the gas just a few minutes ago."

"Get on the snowmobile."

"M-my stuff."

"I'll get it," he told her curtly. He reached inside the car for her purse and small case and stowed them on the trailer attached to the back of the snowmobile. "Let's go. We need to get you out of this cold."

Madison climbed behind him, sliding her arms around his waist. It felt good to hold him. She blinked back the tears of relief that threatened to fall. Gavin had found her. She wasn't going to freeze to death in the car.

He started the engine. "Hold on."

Madison hung on for dear life. Even through the thick parka he wore, she felt his shifting muscles as he maneuvered the vehicle. Snowflakes pelted her cheeks as they sped through the darkened night. Madison buried her face in his back, immediately assaulted by the smell that was uniquely Gavin. *Damn.* His body heat seeped through the layers of clothing that separated them. Even as cold as she was, her body stirred. *Don't go there.* She didn't feel that way about Gavin anymore. It was just a natural human reaction after being rescued from a potentially fatal situation.

With a sigh of relief, Madison spied faint lights flickering through the dark. Gavin covered the last hundred yards in record time before pulling to a halt right at the front steps of the cabin. Disengaging her arms, he quickly stood up and gathered her things.

Madison hurried up the steps. The lights of the cabin were blazing like a welcoming beacon in the middle of the sea. A plume of smoke rose from the chimney. *Oh, to be warm again,* she thought longingly as she followed Gavin through the front door. The delicious heat emanating from the large fireplace enveloped her instantly. She closed the door, relieved to be out of the freezing weather.

"How are you feeling?"

Madison shook the snow from her jeans and parka. "I'm fine, thanks." She winced at the breathlessness in her voice. "Damp and cold, but okay. How did you know I was caught in the storm?"

"Frank, the owner of the local store, radioed me. He said you got some gas a couple of hours back and wanted to check if you'd made it here okay. It shouldn't have taken you long to get here. I knew right away that you were lost somewhere out there. I drove up and down the road searching for any sign of your car." Gavin frowned. "You made a wrong turn and ended up on Gold Camp Road instead of Highway 67."

Madison flushed. "It was snowing so hard I really couldn't see in front of me. I would've frozen to death out there if you hadn't come along."

His dark gaze was unreadable. "What are you doing here, Maddie?"

Butterflies danced in her stomach at being this close to him again. "I-I . . . " She pulled in a deep breath. "Wesley told me you were selling the cabin. I wanted to get some things from here and . . . " she trailed off. *Get a grip, Maddie.* "You're not supposed to be here," she finished lamely.

Gavin ran a hand through his hair. "I was scheduled to leave a couple of days ago but decided to stay."

"You didn't know I was coming?"

"There's no telephone here, remember? Wesley probably left a message for me at home."

Madison flushed. "I'm sorry for showing up here unannounced." He was clearly uncomfortable with her presence. "If I'd known you'd be here . . . "

Their eyes met and held. Slow, insidious heat invaded her veins. Madison tried to ignore it, but it was impossible. There was a curious tingling in the pit of her stomach, and the significance of their situation hit her. They were alone in a secluded cabin, miles from anywhere, trapped inside by a powerful blizzard. Just her and Gavin.

"Strip."

"Excuse me?"

His lips quirked with faint amusement. "Get out of those damp clothes before you catch pneumonia. I suggest you jump in the shower and get warm. I'll toss your clothes in the washer."

Her cheeks felt hot. What did she think he was asking her to strip for? To have sex with him? How embarrassing. *Get your mind out of the gutter, Madison.* "Give me a minute." Lifting her chin, she marched to the lone bedroom.

The bedroom was just as nice and comfortable, courtesy of the small fire that burned in the antique woodstove. Gavin had lovingly refinished it himself. The great stone fireplace in the living room was nice and functional, but he'd fallen for the charm and ageless grace of the old wood-burning stove.

Madison glanced around. The king-size bed was still here, as well as the pine dresser and matching nightstand. Nostalgia hit her hard at that moment. This was where she spent some of the happiest days of her life with Gavin.

Hearing a sound behind her, she whirled around. Gavin motioned to her jeans and sweater. "Clothes?" At her hesitation, he gave her an amused smile. "I've seen it all before."

Madison ignored that and went into the bathroom, slamming the door shut. Shivering, she hurriedly peeled off the parka, her sweater and undershirt. Next came her damp jeans. She bit her lip. Should she take off her underwear and give him that too?

"All of it, Maddie," his voice boomed from the other side of the door.

Did he read minds now too? Irritated, she pulled off her underwear, thinking now was not the time for modesty. Opening the door, she cracked it just enough to extend her arm outside and drop her clothes. Shutting herself in once more, she walked into the shower stall and turned on the water. In no time at all, the room was immersed in rising steam. Madison stepped gratefully under the hot spray.

Soon, she felt close to normal and wasn't freezing anymore. Grabbing a plush towel from the rack, she wrapped it around her securely before pulling the door open. Her small case sat on top of the bed. Madison grabbed her clothes and quickly donned them. She hadn't really counted on being snowbound, and she only had one day's change of clothes with her. The rest of what she had packed were toiletries plus an extra pair of underwear and socks. With any luck, the storm wouldn't last more than a couple of days at the most.

She ran a brush through her damp hair, took a couple of deep breaths and left the sanctuary of the bedroom.

Gavin was placing steaming bowls of chicken soup on the table, along with a couple of thick sandwiches. "Hungry?"

"Yes. Thank you." While she'd been in the shower, he'd changed into a fresh pair of jeans and a flannel shirt. The casual clothes enhanced his sexy masculinity. *Stop! Don't even start thinking of him that way again.* But she was fooling herself, because she couldn't keep her eyes off the tight backside encased in soft, well-worn jeans when he stood up to get their drinks. When he slipped into the chair across from her, she quickly averted her gaze, pretending a serious interest in the hot soup.

Madison tried to follow Gavin's lead and act nonchalant, but failed miserably. Thick, uncomfortable silence descended between them. The cabin seemed to have shrunk in size, dominated by his presence, further fraying her sagging defenses. She dragged much-needed oxygen into her lungs, only to realize it was permeated with his scent. Again and again, her eyes were drawn to him. As surreptitiously as she could, she examined his face. He looked the same, in fact, even better than the last time she'd seen him months ago. His hair was a little longer, but it suited him somehow. Lips that she'd loved to nibble on seemed to taunt her with their tempting presence. He could make her weak with just one kiss. One stroke of his damp tongue would trigger an avalanche of reaction from every single one of her nerve endings.

Her pussy clenched.

Madison groaned silently. Even now, after months of separation, she was reacting to his presence like she was in heat. What had happened to all her avowals of putting Gavin completely out of her life? It was a joke. Just like it was fate's cruel trick that she'd ended up stuck in this cabin with him while a blizzard raged outside. Once again, her eyes strayed to his lips. Her nipples tightened under her shirt, reminding her she still wore the rings he gave her. Slow, syrupy wetness pooled between her legs. This was a man who could turn her on with just one scorching look. Desperate to stop her runaway thoughts, she blurted out the first thing that came to her mind. "Thanks for dinner."

Gavin shrugged. "It's no big deal."

What now? Madison didn't know what to say after that, so she kept her mouth shut and just ate. After she was done, she brought the dishes to the sink. Gavin followed suit. "I'll wash up," she offered. There weren't many dishes, and she was done in no time at all. Madison wiped her hands with a dish towel, lingering by the sink, desperately wishing she could hide in the bedroom. She couldn't sneak away, no more than she could stop her eyes from being drawn to Gavin as he stared out the window, his hands on his hips. For a moment, she looked her fill. She'd been on intimate terms with that body, spending endless hours exploring every mouthwatering inch of it. Again, her senses responded to just being this close to him. Her gaze strayed lower, irresistibly drawn to his taut buttocks. *Stop looking at his ass.* When she looked up, Madison was shocked to see his reflection looking right back at her, the glass giving him a clear view of her face. *Oh, great.* He'd caught her checking him out!

Madison flushed. "Ah, um, maybe I can start to sort through

some of the personal items I left here and decide which ones I'd like to take with me."

When he faced her, he looked faintly amused. "All the stuff's in there." He pointed to the antique trunk that doubled as the coffee table before positioning his big body in the chair next to the window.

Determined to divert her wayward thoughts, she sat on the throw rug and pushed open the heavy lid. The first thing she saw was their wedding album. Right after they were married, she and Gavin had spent a month here at the cabin. Foolish romantic that she'd been, she'd asked the photographer to ship the photos up to her. She hadn't wanted to wait until they got back to Los Angeles to see them. She traced their embossed names on the cover. Against her better judgment, she flipped it open.

Madison was assailed by memories as she looked through picture after picture of her and Gavin. Smiling. Kissing. Laughing. Gazing into each other's eyes. Oh God, this was killing her. With more force than was necessary, she closed the album and put it aside. She reached inside the trunk once more and pulled out more photos. This time they were the ones she'd taken of Gavin chopping firewood. She'd caught him in the act of swinging the ax, a soft sheen of sweat glistening damply on his tanned skin. She'd taken several pictures of him, even one where he'd jokingly flexed his muscles for her.

The next one was of her, asleep, with only a thin sheet slung across her body. She remembered that one too. Gavin had ended up slipping into bed with her and gently waking her up with hot, deep kisses that inevitably led to other, more pleasurable, things.

Releasing a shaky breath, Madison dropped the entire stack of photos on top of the wedding album. This was harder than she'd thought.

"Had enough?" His dark, compelling eyes were locked on her.

Madison's pulse jumped. "I didn't think it was going to be this difficult."

"We had some happy times here, Maddie."

"Yeah, we did." It was hard to speak past the lump in her throat. A burning question hovered on the tip of her tongue. She'd been silently debating the wisdom of asking it, but how could she not? She needed to know. "Why are you selling the cabin?"

"It's outlived its usefulness. I don't intend to come here like I used to."

She was the reason. Madison was certain of it. The thought didn't sit well with her at all, triggering confusing feelings of remorse. "But you *love* this place. This was where you could get away to think and write. You restored this place, picked every piece of furniture that's in it and once told me this is where you found peace. How can you let it go?"

Gavin gave her a long, enigmatic look. "Don't ask questions, Maddie. You might not like the answers."

Her heart thumped anxiously. "I want to know why."

"This cabin is filled with memories of our life together and I don't want to remember that anymore. Is that honest enough for you?"

She flinched. "I'd hate for you to lose one of the things you love the most just because of what happened to us."

"I don't need it anymore. I find that I don't need a lot of things since our divorce became final."

"I'd really rather not talk about the past. This cabin—"

Gavin's dark eyes narrowed. "Why not talk about it? I've got nothing to hide. I didn't cheat on you."

Madison turned away, unwilling to venture into their turbulent past. That only seemed to incense him further.

"You refused to listen to my explanation, refused to believe me." His tone was dangerously cold. "*You* left *me*."

Madison trembled as she grappled with painful memories. She felt on edge, unsettled, her emotions seesawing dangerously. "We can't undo what's been done."

"You're *so* goddamn positive that I cheated on you."

"I *saw* you," she snapped, goaded beyond endurance.

"You gave up on us. You didn't want to try to work things out." The cold anger in his voice lashed at her. "You threw away what we had without even giving us another chance. Instead, you let the poison your mother planted in your head dictate your actions. Don't even pretend I'm to blame for everything," he finished tautly.

Madison uncoiled her legs and stood. She blinked back the tears, trying to regain her composure, staring at the greedy flames that licked at the split logs in the hearth. Fighting was not going to get them anywhere, and rehashing the reason for their divorce was a moot point.

The silence was tense and uncomfortable. How were they supposed to coexist while trapped in the storm? There was nothing to be achieved by being at each other's throats. She'd come here to let go of the past, for God's sake, not dredge it up again.

Armed with this conviction, she faced Gavin. "I don't want to fight. Whatever happened in the past is over. None of that matters anymore. I know you've . . . moved on." Under his unrelenting stare, she flushed and tried to smile. "I mean, I've seen your picture in magazines. The woman you're with, she's very beautiful."

Gavin crossed his arms over his chest. "If I didn't know better, I'd think you were asking me if I'm dating her." His eyebrow rose in faint challenge. "You lost that right when you divorced me, Maddie."

Her smile died a quick death. "Forget it. I don't know why I even mentioned it."

"Are you jealous?"

Her face felt hot, all the way to the tips of her ears. "Of course not," she replied quickly. Too quickly. "I, ah, I'm dating someone too." As soon as the words were out of her mouth, Madison wanted to smack her forehead. What on Earth had possessed her to say that? Was it her way of salvaging some pride after finding out her ex-husband was dating again? "I just think it's time we put the past behind us and try to become friends," she finished lamely.

Gavin's face was carved from stone. Had she not been reeling from the big fib she'd just told, Madison would have recognized that as a sign of impending doom. "You're *dating* someone," he repeated, his voice low and throbbing with intensity.

A cold knot formed in her belly when he pushed from the chair and came toward her. She took a step back. "Th-that's a good thing, right? I-I mean, we . . . we shouldn't let what happened to us get in the way of living normal lives again. You know, bitterness warps the mind and all that," she said breathlessly.

He didn't stop until he was only inches away from her. Awareness hit her squarely in the chest, gathering in the already sensitive tips of her breasts. She had the strongest urge to rub them against him, to find relief from the need pulsing in her pussy. "What are you—" Madison jumped when he grabbed her hand and placed it on the front of his jeans.

Oh God. His cock was thick and hard beneath her palm. "This is what you do to me, Maddie." His breath washed over her, as hot and urgent as his words. "I look at you and I get a fucking hard-on. I imagine you naked, laid out on my bed for me to feast on." His hand tightened over hers, forcing her to clamp around the long shaft under the soft, worn denim. "I want to see your nipples adorned with the rings I gave you. I want to lick and suck them until you beg me to bite you."

Madison shuddered, her knees almost buckling from under her.

"I want to spread your legs and lick you all over. Most of all, I want to suck you through your little clit ring." He pulled her tighter against him, thrusting against her hand. Of their own volition, her fingers curved around him, molding his shape eagerly. "Are you still wearing it?"

Madison swallowed. She felt feverish, her blood turning molten as it raced through her veins. "Gavin, I—"

"I want to fuck you, Maddie, so bad I can almost taste it. I jack off at night thinking of you tied up in my bed, remembering your pussy wrapped around my cock like a wet glove while you begged me for more."

A whimper escaped her lips. Hunger exploded inside her, drowning out the persistent voice that warned her not to let him do this. She'd been too long without him, too long denied his touch. She was starving for him.

"Most of all, I remember how your ass clamps so sweetly around me as I fuck you there. That's what I think about when I come, Maddie. That gets me through the night. But in the end, it's not enough. It's never enough." With his other hand, he cupped her nape and tipped her face back. "You still think we can be friends?" he snarled, jerking her hand away and thrusting her from him. He went inside the bedroom and slammed the door shut behind him.

The silence in the cabin was deafening.

Madison trembled, panting hard, falling back on the couch. Need vibrated through her body, concentrating in the soaked folds of her sex. She squeezed her thighs together, moaning softly. How was she supposed to stay here with Gavin and not go insane from wanting him? She looked at the bedroom door, hunger eating away at her common sense. For months, she'd fooled herself into thinking she didn't want him anymore, that she was over him, that she could move on with her life. Yet tonight, as soon as he'd touched her, every cell in her body came to stinging, pulsing life. The pain of betrayal, the months of separation and the bitterness of divorce melted away. She was right back where she'd started, with Gavin holding her body and her heart in the palm of his hand.

The inevitable was about to happen. She'd lost the war when he'd rescued her from the storm. From the first moment she'd seen him again, the chemistry that had always simmered between them had begun to work its magic on her susceptible senses. It was undeniable. Unstoppable. Irresistible.

She moved toward the closed bedroom door and opened it. Gavin stood by the window, stiffness lining every muscle, his fists clenched as he looked out at the dark night. When he eventually faced her, Maddie was singed by the intensity of his gaze.

"You have five seconds to get out of here. I'm *this* close to throwing you on the bed and saying to hell with the consequences."

Madison trembled, awash with need. She couldn't get beyond wanting to be with Gavin again, beyond having him inside her once more. Let tomorrow take care of itself.

"I'm warning you. I'm hungry, Maddie. I won't be easily satisfied." His eyes pierced her with heat. "Get out now while you can."

With shaking fingers, she gripped the hem of her sweater and pulled it over her head, tossing it off to the side. Holding his gaze, she unbuttoned her jeans and shimmied out of them. The air was so thick she could have cut it with a knife, but she didn't waver. In moments, she was completely naked, her body bared to his gaze.

Gavin sucked in a harsh breath.

Madison knew she was playing a dangerous game, but she could no more stop this than she could stop breathing. Tonight was about Gavin.

"You had your chance," he growled. In no time at all, he covered the distance between them, grabbed both her hands in his and pulled them over her head. "No regrets."

"No regrets," she confirmed huskily.

He pushed her against the wall, at the same time clamping his mouth on hers, wasting no time in preliminaries as he thrust his tongue inside in a blatantly erotic kiss that devoured her. It was unrepentant, carnal and hot.

Her mind turned hazy with wanting. "Let me touch you."

"Hell no. If you do that, this will be over before we even start." With his knees, he nudged her legs wider apart, forcing her to ride him. The denim rasped against her aching clit.

It felt *so* good. "Oh, yes. Right there."

With one hand, Gavin fumbled with the button of his jeans. Madison moaned, consumed with urgency. "Hurry."

"Damn it," he muttered in frustration before he finally got the button through the hole. He pushed his zipper down, his massive erection spilling against her belly.

The feel of the soft skin encasing his hard flesh drove her insane. "Gavin," she cried out. "I need to touch you."

With a curse, he finally let her go so he could push his jeans down his thighs. Madison instantly wrapped her hands around his cock, fisting it, sliding up and down, fascinated by the broad, bulbous head where a drop of liquid already quivered on the slit. She bent to lick it.

"Oh no, you don't." Gavin cupped her ass and lifted her against the wall. "You'll get that later."

"I want it now," she moaned, automatically wrapping her legs around his hips.

"I've got to fuck you now, Maddie," he gritted out. "I've got to feel your pussy clenching around me or I'll go insane."

He'll go insane? She was teetering on the edge of madness as the ridged head rubbed against the slick opening. With one mighty thrust, Gavin impaled her to the hilt. She uttered a shaky sigh, lost in the bliss, her eyes closing as she absorbed the delicious feeling of having him inside her once again.

"I've come home," he rasped against her skin.

Madison opened her eyes and met his. An incredible feeling of tenderness overcame her at his words. She wrapped her arms around his neck and pressed her lips to his, unable to come up with a response. The kiss soon turned urgent, rapacious. Gavin slapped a hand on the wall and braced his legs on the floor. His hips thrust inside her with ever-increasing speed, catapulting them swiftly into that place where only the two of them existed.

"Yes. Yes. Yes," she chanted, her breath hissing at every slide and push. The rhythmic friction created the most delicious feeling.

"I'm sorry, babe," Gavin panted, his warm breath mingling with hers. "It's been too long."

"Don't be." Madison tightened her inner muscles around his cock. Biting her lip, she felt the first tingling gathering in her lower belly. The first splash of his seed against her inner walls triggered her climax. Delirious, she cried out as she came.

"Fuck. *Maddie.*"

She savored the sharp pleasure of their orgasms. Gavin had always loved coming with her, loved the feeling of her inner muscles contracting tightly around his shaft as she milked him. Tears gathered in the corners of her eyes at the all-consuming pleasure. After months of separation, this first joining had been quick and intense. She'd only now realized just how much she missed this physical closeness with Gavin. She'd been starved for it.

Long after she stopped trembling, Maddie couldn't bear to

let him go. Her mind was still buzzing with satisfaction when he moved them over to the bed, gently laying her down. She sighed, burrowing into the soft mattress, basking in the soft aftershocks that still pulsed through her. Her eyes drifted shut. She'd rest, just for a moment. It felt so good to be in his arms again.

FOUR

GAVIN EXAMINED THE FAINT signs of satiation that edged Madison's serene profile as she slept. Unlike her, he couldn't sleep at all. He'd been jolted by the shock of what had just happened. The whole feverish encounter left him reeling, both from the pleasure and the unexpectedness of it, and he had yet to recover. He couldn't believe that Madison—his ex-wife—was in his bed once more.

When she'd divorced him, he'd resolved never to see her again, never to speak to her again, and most of all, never to touch her again. She'd broken his heart and put him through hell. Despite all that, when he'd realized she'd gotten lost in the blizzard, he'd driven like a madman through winding, desolate and icy roads trying desperately to find her, praying that he wasn't too late. When he'd opened the car door and seen Madison again for the first time in months, he'd known right away the battle was lost. His anger and resentment melted away like snow under a hot desert sun. He snorted. It'd been appallingly easy to forget all his resolutions about this woman, who still had a stranglehold on his heart *and* his cock.

In the dim light of the bedroom, her skin glowed with a soft, luminous sheen. She moaned and rubbed her foot against his before shifting to lie on her back, presenting him with a full view of her body. His gaze strayed lower, devouring the picture she made. God, she was so fucking hot he couldn't get over it. Full breasts, small waist and rounded hips. The very first time he'd seen her, he'd fallen like the proverbial ton of bricks. He'd foolishly thought that once he'd had her in his bed, the intensity would lessen. He'd been wrong. He only wanted her more.

There wasn't anything he'd asked that she hadn't done. He'd loved her lack of inhibition, her eagerness to play. Maddie had enjoyed being tied up, blindfolded, handcuffed and restrained. Their bedroom had become a playground, a place for adventure that added spice to their new marriage. But in the end, all that had paled in comparison to how right he felt with her. In the short time they'd been married she made him happy, brought laughter into his life and soothed his frustration on days he couldn't write anything that made one iota of sense. She'd never complained when he immersed himself in his writing for hours on end, always there for him when he finally emerged. Their life had been perfect until the day she'd caught him with Kimberly outside his hotel room.

His jaw tightened. Kimberly was a pain in the ass who couldn't quite accept that their one-night stand was just that. The thing with Kimberly had been over before he'd even met Maddie, but he'd been a fool to get involved with her in the first place. The woman had ambushed him outside his hotel room that fateful day. He'd fired her on the spot, but the damage had already been done. He'd already lost his wife.

Madison uttered a soft sound. Gavin stared at her face, peaceful in sleep. The feelings he'd tried to suppress for so long clawed their way to the surface, wrapping around his heart until he couldn't breathe. What had made him think he was over her? The desire, the *need* to claim her physically, had never gone away. It was a constant, gnawing ache that had been his sole companion during the long, lonely nights after their divorce.

Madison was here, within reach once more. They were alone in a remote cabin, stuck in a blizzard. This was his chance to win her back, to rekindle the love that had always existed between them and to prove to her that they belonged together. She still wanted him. He'd have to build on that to win her heart back, because tonight he'd realized one thing. He could *never* let Madison go.

She's mine. She'll always be mine.

Touching one nipple, Gavin rubbed it until it stiffened. Her breasts had always been ultrasensitive, made even more so by the gold rings she'd willingly worn for him. He leaned down and lapped at it, alternating between sucking and gently biting, insistently drawing her from sleep. He knew the exact moment she woke up by the way she arched into his mouth.

"Hi." He skimmed his lips across the fragrant valley between her breasts, sniffing the delicate, feminine scent of her skin as he traveled across to the other one. With his tongue, he traced the full swell in ever smaller circles, teasing but never quite touching the waiting tip. "You still wear my rings."

The deep breath Madison took brought her flesh closer to his mouth. "I-I just never had the time to . . . to get another set," she moaned.

As excuses went, that one was lame. Gavin didn't argue, instead pulling her into a sitting position. He quickly reached into the bedside drawer and pulled out leather ties. "Arms over your head, Maddie."

Excitement glowed in her eyes. Madison raised her arms, crossing one wrist over the other with unabashed eagerness. He bound her to the headboard, piling pillows behind her to cushion her back and leaving enough room that she could shift to her side if necessary. She licked her lips, her breath coming faster. Gavin pushed her legs apart, positioning himself in between before sitting back and just gazing at her. His cock rose long and stiff between his legs. It seemed all the blood in his body pooled between his legs. Madison's gaze fell on his shaft, hunger written plainly on her features.

Instead of giving in to her silent plea, he cupped her breasts in his hands, kneading them exactly how she liked it, alternating between gentle squeezes and firm pinches, worrying the tips with his fingers. "I used to suck your nipples for hours, Maddie, remember? It drove you crazy when I clamped these."

Madison trembled, her hips subtly rising on the bed.

"Tell me what you want," he invited, his own senses rioting at her responsiveness.

"You know what I want," she replied in a helpless, breathless voice. "Please."

"This?" He used his teeth to pull at the stiff crest before biting down on the pliant flesh.

She shuddered, her breath catching sharply. Her eyes were glazed with lust. *"More."*

He sucked her briefly, enjoying the little sound of distress she made when he pulled back. Again and again, he manipulated the tips through the sexy gold rings, driving her arousal higher. He used his mouth, his teeth, his lips and his hands to stimulate her further, loving the soft, breathy moans she uttered.

Gavin slid his fingers down the flat plane of her belly, coasting over smooth, silky skin. Madison had gone still the instant he did that. Hot anticipation shone in her beautiful face. He cupped the backs of her knees and pulled them up. In this position, she was completely open to him.

He parted the puffy, soaked lips of her pussy. Savage satisfaction filled him to see the hood ring piercing her clit and the fragile little "G" pendant that hung from it. He thumbed the swollen nubbin, gathering her juices and swirling them around the pulsing spot. Driven by a compulsion he couldn't resist, he asked, "Have you slept with anyone?"

"Have you?" she countered huskily.

He didn't even hesitate. "No."

"B-but that picture in the magazine—"

The little catch in her voice told him it was a difficult statement for her. Gavin looked into her eyes, wanting her to see the truth of what he was about to say. "Had they printed the entire picture, you would have seen Wesley standing on the other side of the woman in the red dress, who happens to be his sister, Susan. She works for the museum that had the gala that night." Madison remained silent. It rankled that she didn't believe him instantly, but he was determined to work through that. "At this point," he continued quietly, "I don't need to lie to you, Maddie. We're divorced. It doesn't matter if I've slept with anyone or not."

She flinched at the truth of his words. "You're right, of course. It's none of my business."

"But I *am* telling you that there's been no one since you left me." He placed his palm over her mound. "You said you were moving on. What exactly does that mean?"

A shadow of unhappiness flickered in her eyes. "Maybe we shouldn't talk about this at all. It's only going to lead to trouble."

He grimaced. "True. Talking never did us any favors." He pulled back, cutting off any physical contact. Did her refusal to answer mean she'd already slept with somebody? Possessiveness rose to his throat, threatening to choke him. To even think of another man's hands on her body, touching her, kissing her, was like a jagged blade cutting through him.

Madison went still. Gavin's handsome face flashed with something that looked suspiciously like pain. The unexpectedness of it surprised her. Was it the natural reaction of a man to the thought of his ex-wife sleeping with somebody else? Or was that hurt unique to him because he still cared? Was it even possible?

This was dangerous territory they were entering, one that could potentially bring more heartache to her later on. Yet when Gavin had declared in that utterly serious tone that he hadn't slept with anyone and had no reason to lie to her, she believed him. Their divorce was over and done with. Any confession he made about being with somebody else was of no consequence. Even so, she was relieved and strangely happy to know that he hadn't. "I haven't slept with anyone either."

His breath hissed in at her admission. "I'm glad."

"Me too."

"I think it's time to reacquaint your body to my touch."

Heat swept over Madison. There was no need for any reacquainting. Her body had never forgotten its master. Her nerve endings were already singing, eagerly waiting for the gentle bite of his teeth, the merciless pounding of his cock—even the sting of his hand on her ass.

"Maddie?" he prompted as he gently pulled once more at the delicate gold nipple rings.

Madison drew in a sharp breath, dazed by the familiar pleasure-pain that radiated from the aching tip. God, it had been so very long. Hunger tormented her, licking at every inch of her skin. She couldn't stem the needy whimper that escaped her lips as he continued to play with her, stoking the fire inside her with stunning ease. They were creating their own tempest that could rival the snowstorm that raged outside.

Swallowing, Madison dropped her gaze to Gavin's straining cock. It was swollen, thick and heavily veined. It was hungry for *her*. Stinging heat rushed to her vagina, soaking it with even more moisture. Her clit throbbed with sharp anticipation.

"Look at me."

Something stirred within her at the quiet command in his voice. She knew what it was. It had always been inside her. It was the very basic need to submit to his every wish.

"I want to play, Maddie." Gavin delivered a light, stinging slap on her bare mound. Pleasure reverberated through every cell in her body. Intense, hot lust curled from her inner muscles and spread inexorably from the tips of her toes to the ends of her fingers, coming together to merge in her sensitized nipples. "I'm greedy." He slipped his fingers inside her once more, delving deep, bringing a gasp to her lips. "I want to do everything at once."

Her senses were battered by the prospect of once again experiencing all that they'd shared together. "*Oh yes.*" She was barely able to say the words.

Gavin captured her lips. Madison responded with everything she had, running her tongue along his lower lip before delving deep inside to absorb his unique flavor.

His fingers worried her nipple through the ring, pulling, pinching, squeezing. Every touch intensified the heavy ache in her lower belly, just enough to keep her teetering on the edge, hungry for more.

Gripping her hips, he shifted her lower body slightly to one side, exposing her ass. The ties holding her wrists had enough play that she was able to move comfortably. Even canted to her side with her wrists bound over her head, she was still able to lock her eyes on him, wanting not just to feel everything but to see it. Sliding his hand caressingly over one buttock, he rubbed her skin lazily. She held her breath, knowing what he was about to do. Gavin had an obsession with her ass.

He was not one to disappoint. Slipping his right hand in the warm crevice, he trailed his fingers down to her anus and teased the puckered orifice. Swirling lower, he delved into the crease, gathering up moisture. When he finally came back up and rubbed against the tight ring of muscles, gently slipping past it, Madison released the breath she'd been holding, her lips slightly parted.

"It's been a long time, Maddie," he murmured gruffly. "I'm dying to be here." He worked in another digit, easing past the tightness, getting her used to being penetrated *there* once more.

It felt so good. She moaned when he slipped his thumb inside her, working it in until his palm was flat against her mound. She began to undulate against him.

The feeling of being deliciously helpless swelled as he continued to work her with his magical fingers. Through the fog of pleasure clouding her mind, she knew she was getting close, so close . . . When he pulled back, she moaned in protest.

"Shh," he murmured. "I'm not going to rush this." His face was a mask of hunger, calling forth a deep, answering need inside her.

Gavin settled once more between her splayed legs. His gaze was dark and hot. "This will always be with us, Maddie. You can't deny it, and neither can I."

It was the truth. She'd realized it as soon as she'd stepped inside the cabin. No matter what had happened between them in the past, no matter what would happen to them when they left the cabin, *this* would always be there, between them.

Gavin shifted to his knees. Madison swallowed at the sight of him, naked and aroused. Beautifully sculpted from his wide, muscled shoulders to his flat, trim waist and the long, thick cock that jutted proudly from a nest of dark curls, Gavin took her breath away. "I want you in my mouth," she whispered.

He stood on the bed, bracing his long legs on either side of her, positioning the wide, bulbous tip right at her lips.

"Suck it," he instructed hoarsely.

Opening obediently, Maddie trembled as he slowly drove the head between her parted lips. He was huge, wide. She rubbed her tongue just under the ridge of the head, exactly as he'd taught her, and earned a soft grunt in response.

Gavin went in carefully, feeding her one delicious inch at a time. She breathed through her nose as she took more and more. Her cheeks hollowed as she sucked his flesh, moistening him on the long, slow slide back up before pulling him in deep once more.

"Come on, babe," he whispered roughly, his free hand threading through her hair. "You can take some more."

Even as she took a couple more inches, there was still plenty left. Madison relaxed her throat and sought to take him deeper, loving the way he tightened his hand on her hair, reminding her he was in control.

"God, yes. Just a little bit more. I want you to take the whole thing."

She took him until she could take no more, until he was touching the back of her throat. He had both his hands in her hair now, guiding her movements during the long, slow suck she gave him.

"You always knew just how to suck my cock," he groaned. "Like that, babe."

He was almost more than she could handle, her lips stretched impossibly wide. Her nipples tightened and wetness dripped down to her upper thighs. She'd always enjoyed taking him between her lips, loved giving him this pleasure.

Gavin was fucking her mouth, alternating short strokes with longer, deeper ones. "God, yes. Get it nice and wet, Maddie. It'll be inside you soon, babe," he whispered, urging her on.

Moaning, Madison caressed with her tongue the thick vein that ran under his shaft before rimming the head and then sucking him deep. He let her go on for another minute, his hands clenching and unclenching in her hair before he finally pulled out of her mouth altogether. At the soft sound of protest she made, Gavin grimaced. "No more, or this'll be over before we even start."

As he stepped off the bed, Maddie admired the lean, muscled strength etched in the graceful line of his spine. Gavin might be a bestselling author, but he wasn't a sedentary one. He regularly worked out in the gym and ran up to five miles a day. Even his feet were as beautiful as the rest of him, long, narrow, perfectly shaped. A sharp thrill went through her. For tonight, at least, he would be hers again.

When he turned to face her, Madison caught her breath. He held a large butt plug in one hand and a tube of lubricant in the other. Anticipation kicked her sharply in the stomach. His progress back to her side was slow and deliberate. Her eyes were wide as she watched him squirt a thick line of lube on the plug, spreading it with his hand. She shivered. It had been so long . . .

Gavin didn't have to tell her what to do; she already knew. She raised her hips when he slipped a pillow underneath her, and opened her legs obediently. He worked his finger in first, gently stretching her, lubricating the little puckered opening. Old habits die hard, so she knew to look at him while he rubbed the tip of the plug against her, never breaking eye contact, letting him see everything she felt. Deliberately relaxing, she was nonetheless unable to control the sudden jump of her pulse when he worked the tip of the plug inside her ass. Holding the toy in one hand, Gavin put the other to good use, manipulating her aching clit until she arched off the bed. Moments later, he finally eased the plug past the tight ring of muscle.

Madison let out a long, low whimper as it slid in all the way, until the cold, flat base rested against her bottom. She pulled deep, shuddering breaths into her lungs, feeling stretched to the limit. Gavin ran his palms up and down her inner thighs, patiently letting her get reacquainted with one of their favorite toys.

"Tell me it feels good," he commanded gruffly.

She couldn't deny it. "Y-yes."

"You're so sexy, Maddie," he muttered, bending to lick a distended nipple. "Lying there with a plug up your ass, begging me with your eyes for more." He kissed her, his tongue delving into her mouth. "I need to taste you."

She writhed on the bed, as much as she could in her position. At the first touch of his mouth on her pussy, she trembled violently. Gavin was a master at everything he did. Every lick and lap, every foray inside her slit was measured to drive her insane. When he pushed the plug in and out her ass while he ate her, she toppled over the edge. With a cry, she bucked against him and came.

He rode it out to the last tremor before he got to his knees. He slid his hands behind her knees, pulling her legs up before positioning the plumlike head of his cock at her entrance. His progress was slow, the tight fit made even more snug due to the plug still lodged in her backside.

"Jesus." He breathed roughly. He held her steady when she would have moved. "Easy, baby. It's a tight fit."

Madison whimpered, her breath hitching sharply as he slowly worked his way inside her. "Gavin," she moaned, tortured and pleasured. He merely grunted in response, gritting his teeth as he slowly slid in to the hilt. She couldn't breathe, couldn't think, filled to the brim. Tossing her damp hair away from her face, she pleaded, "Fuck me now."

Gavin pushed in and out, his pace agonizingly slow. Eyes glittering darkly, he rubbed a thumb over her lips, slipping it into her mouth. Madison bit the fleshy part of his finger.

"Harder. I want it harder," she begged shamelessly. It had been too long since she was with him like this.

"Damn it." Gavin moved incrementally faster, driving her against the headboard. Pleasure exploded inside her, an insistent throbbing that battered her senses. In a low voice, he told her how much he wanted her, what she was doing to him, what he was feeling. His erotic words washed over her, his words of praise—sometimes gentle, sometimes frankly sexual—heightening her pleasure. When he gently pinched her nipples, she moaned and asked for more, craving the pain and the pleasure that went along with it. Her breath came in heavy pants as he stroked in and out of her slick channel with long, mind-blowing thrusts that jammed the plug even deeper in her ass.

It was too much. With a scream she had no hope of holding back, Madison gave in to the exquisite release. She shuddered convulsively, gasping, whimpering as he plowed on without mercy, giving her no quarter. A second later, Gavin groaned and she felt his hot seed jet inside her. The bedroom was filled with a cacophony of soft moans and whispers.

Gavin slumped over her. He released her wrists from their restraints, pulled them down and rubbed her arms gently. Madison lay limp and boneless against him, drained and satiated. He arranged her so she was lying on her side before gently pulling out the plug. He got up and went to the bathroom, returning with a warm washcloth and tenderly cleaning her. Madison didn't utter one word of protest when he came back to bed with her after he was done.

Drowsy with satisfaction, she snuggled against him. "Gavin," she murmured softly before she gave in to sleep.

FIVE

THE WIND WAS STILL howling when Madison woke up. Rubbing her eyes, she glanced at the small clock radio on the bedside table, surprised to see it was almost nine o'clock in the morning. Gingerly shifting under the heavy arm that lay across her waist, she took in Gavin's sleeping face. A thick lock of dark hair fell across his forehead, his lashes formed half-moons on his cheeks. His nose was far from perfect. It had a slight bump in the middle, something he'd acquired in a fight when he was a teenager. His lips were beautifully shaped and had the power to turn women into weak-kneed, lust-crazed creatures. Including her. Resisting the temptation to look under the thick blanket, she tiptoed out of bed. Gavin must have gotten up sometime in the middle of the night and added more logs to the woodstove, for the fire was still going. She stood by the window watching the snow flurries that fell endlessly on the already white ground. The storm hadn't abated.

Madison moved into the bathroom and turned on the shower, shivering slightly in the cool air. Steam rose as she stepped into the tiled cubicle, raising her face to the delicious heat of the water. Now that it was morning, what was she going to do?

She picked up the shampoo, squirted some on her hand and worked her hair into a lather. Last night proved that she was still susceptible to Gavin. Nothing had changed. It had been like that from the moment they first met. Their eyes had locked across the room and she had known with the first sting of hot awareness that she would end up with him . . .

"Hello," he greeted her with a sexy smile. "I'm Gavin Cahill."

His dark brown eyes were like velvet. "Madison," she replied, her voice husky. He was standing close—so close that the expensive wool of his suit brushed against her dress. He was much taller than she, even in her heels she had to look up at him.

When his gaze dropped to her lips, she'd licked at them nervously. He was staring at her hungrily, making no effort to mask it. The music, the buzz of conversation, the clinking of wineglasses faded into the background until she was aware only of him.

"Let's find a quiet place."

There was no asking, no hesitation, just a direct invitation to leave with him. "Uh, th-the party," she stammered. "Wouldn't it be rude to just leave?"

"Do you want to stay?"

She could smell the mint on his breath. Their lips were mere inches apart. "Not really," she admitted huskily.

He trailed his hand down her bare arm before capturing hers. "Let's go, then."

Without a thought of the friend who she had come to the party with, Madison willingly let him pull her through the throng and out the ballroom door. Silence enveloped them as he took her farther down the carpeted hallway of the large estate, seeming to know exactly where he was headed.

"Where are we going?" she asked breathlessly.

"Right here." He pulled her inside a darkened room, a small lamp illuminating the desk in the far corner. In the dimness of her surroundings, she could only make out the stacks of books on built-in shelves and plump leather couches in the middle of the room.

"What are we—"

He backed her against the wall and swooped down to take her lips. Her mind scattered into a million pieces and she responded instinctively, opening her mouth to let him in. He swept inside her mouth like he owned it, thoroughly kissing her senseless. By the time she became aware of her surroundings once more, the halter top of her dress was down to her waist.

"Beautiful," he muttered, palming her breasts. When he squeezed her nipples, she moaned. When he inserted a thigh between hers, she obligingly parted her legs. And when he growled as her dress got in the way, she didn't stop him when he pulled it up her legs and bunched it around her waist. She rode his thigh, slightly off balance, forced to hang on to him. He sucked on her neck and kneaded her ass, sliding his hands inside the silk of her panties. She was whimpering, fevered, wanting more. She'd never done anything like this, had never let a perfect stranger take such liberties. Her knees almost buckled when he took her hand and placed it on the erection that strained against the front of his trousers.

She didn't even think of stopping. It was all so urgent, so demanding, that her head reeled. There was a desperate hunger to the way they touched each other, sweeping aside all common sense and caution.

"I need to be inside you," he murmured harshly.

"I know," she replied urgently. She felt his fingers as he made quick work of his pants. "Hurry." In the next second, he freed himself. She looked down and swallowed, marveling at the beauty of his flesh. He ripped her underwear and she gasped, not in shock, but at the heat of his hand as he cupped her mound.

"So hot." He shifted slightly away and fumbled impatiently with his wallet. He handed her a foil packet. "Put it on me."

She bit her lip, tearing open the square. His groan reached her ears as she rolled the condom down the length of his shaft. He lifted her off the ground, wrapped her legs around his waist and smoothly slid into her pussy. Their simultaneous groans of pleasure broke the silence.

To Madison, it was unlike anything she'd ever felt before. She caught her breath, only to release it slowly as he began to thrust in and out. It wasn't slow, it wasn't tender. It was a mad coupling combined with the sheer desperation of needing to have each other. Her orgasm hit her hard. She shuddered, holding tightly on to him. She was dimly aware of Gavin following her, feeling the delicious swell of his cock as he came.

When he gently put her back on her feet, she straightened her clothing, at a loss for words. Picking up her torn panties, Gavin slipped them into his pocket. "Let's go." He took her hand once more and led her out into the hallway where a few people were chatting. She blushed and averted her eyes as they emerged into the warm evening air. He took her to his house and she spent the night. She didn't want to let him out of her sight. She got ready to go home the next day, already thinking of when she could see him again, when he suggested she just pack up some clothes and spend another night with him.

One night turned into two. Two turned into three and so on. More and more of her things ended up at his place until she finally stopped going home altogether. By the end of the first month, they were living together.

A month after that, they were sitting out on the terrace, enjoying the balmy night air and looking at the twinkling city lights. Madison leaned against Gavin and listened as he talked about his latest book and the publicity tour that was sure to follow. She loved listening to the sound of his voice, deep and low, intimate, as if she was the only person in the world he wanted to talk to.

Gavin chuckled. "Maddie, are you listening to me?"

Rubbing her cheek against his chest, she closed her eyes in pleasure. "Uh-huh." She could sit there forever and just listen to him talk, enclosed in his arms, feeling loved.

He fished something out of his pocket and held it in front of her. It was a diamond ring, square cut, set in a simple platinum setting. She twisted around and faced him, her heart beating as fast as a jackhammer.

"I think it's about time you made an honest man of me, don't you agree?"

"Oh Gavin."

"Marry me, Maddie," he said gruffly. "Let's make this permanent."

She must have said yes, because the next thing she knew, he was slipping the ring on her finger. Gavin insisted they marry soon. Two weeks later, they were married in a simple ceremony with only close friends and family in attendance.

After the wedding, her mother had pulled her aside. "I certainly hope you know what you're doing, Madison."

She blinked. "What do you mean, Mom?"

Janice inclined her head over to where Gavin stood, surrounded by his friends. "A man like that, you think he's going to stay faithful to you?"

"Mom," she chided, shocked that her mother could say such a thing.

"I only want you to go into this with your eyes wide open. Men like Gavin Cahill will never be satisfied with just one woman. Look at your father. Believe me when I say that you need to protect yourself and get ready for any eventuality."

Madison fought to keep her voice light but she failed. "Gavin loves me and I love him. He's not like Dad."

Janice scoffed at that. "We all start out with the best intentions, honey. But mark my words, even the strongest of men succumb to temptation."

Unable to listen any longer, Madison murmured an excuse and left, weighed down by sadness. Her mother's bitterness over her husband's repeated betrayals had warped her view of men and marriage. Over and over again, she'd hammered into Madison that men were not to be trusted, planting in her young mind a real fear of infidelity. Why today, on her wedding day, would her mother choose to spread her bitter poison?

Madison's head began to throb and she headed swiftly to the ladies' room, needing a moment alone. Gavin suddenly appeared, a look of concern on his face.

"Maddie?"

The tightness in her chest eased as she looked into his eyes. His very presence comforted her. Gavin would never cheat on her. Her mother was wrong about him.

He smoothed the wisps of hair away from her face, his touch tender. "What's wrong?"

The worry in his voice lessened her anxiety. She mustered a smile. "You made me the happiest woman alive by making me your wife." She would have preferred that nothing marred this day, but she had to get it off her chest, had to hear him reassure her. "I just want you to know that I love you."

His dark eyes softened. "I love you too."

She rubbed her cheek against his palm. "You know that . . . that if there's anything that would drive me away, it's infidelity." She rushed on. "I've seen what it can do to a marriage. I don't want that to happen to us."

Gavin pulled her close, tipping her face up to press a gentle kiss on her lips. "I would *never* be unfaithful to you."

His voice rang with sincerity. Just like that, all Madison's doubts melted away. She hugged him tightly, closing her eyes. "I know. I just needed to hear you say it."

With a sigh, Madison pulled herself back to the present and rinsed her hair. She'd been naïve and trusted him completely. Closing her eyes, she reached for the soap and jumped when it was placed in her palm.

She opened her eyes to see a very naked Gavin standing in the shower stall with her.

He grinned. "Good morning. Did you leave me any hot water?"

She tried not to let her gaze stray lower. Just having him this close was enough to raise her temperature. "I'm sure there's a lot left."

Stepping close to her, he adjusted the nozzle so the water would hit them both. "Still, it might be better to shower together. All in the name of conservation, of course."

Not knowing what to say, feeling off-kilter, she didn't demur when he started soaping her. His touch was as hot as the water when he rubbed the soap against her skin, lingering on her breasts. Madison reveled at the sheer sensuality of his touch. He was determined to get her clean, soaping and rubbing every crevice, every curve. When he wandered between her legs, she stopped him with her hand.

Gavin grinned. "I'm making sure you're clean everywhere. Come on, Maddie, open up."

She obediently opened her legs, willing to play the game. Maybe because in the back of her mind, she knew this was temporary. A fantasy she was living while the storm raged outside and they were isolated in this cabin in the woods. For a short time, nothing else existed except her and Gavin. Not their divorce, not his infidelity, and certainly not all the anger and pain she'd bottled up.

Just for a little while, she reassured herself, she'd play along and live out this surreal dream of being with him again. She'd enjoy it while she could.

Gavin was thorough. By the time he was done, she'd been soaped from head to toe, and her breathing had turned heavy. He handed her the soap, clearly expecting her to return the favor. Madison eagerly ran her hands over corded muscles that flexed under her touch. Wanting him to be as affected as she was, she soaped him thoroughly, taking special care with the hard flesh that rose high and proud between them.

When he finally rinsed, his lips were pulled into a tight line and the teasing grin was gone. He kissed her, their wet bodies sliding against each other. Her eyes fluttered shut. There was something about long, deep, intimate kisses that spoke more than words could say. She lost awareness of time, their lips melded to one another. By the time he let go, she was clinging to him, grateful for his arms supporting her.

Madison lowered her face, trying to hide how a simple, poignant act like kissing could affect her so deeply. Only in the past twenty-four hours had she realized exactly how much she'd lost when their marriage fell apart. It hit her hard, pressing like a heavy weight on her chest.

Trying to stop her churning thoughts, she dried off and combed her wet hair while Gavin brushed his teeth. The scene was reminiscent of old times, when they would share a shower at the start of every day. The simple intimacy of the situation struck her hard, adding to the already deepening feeling of loss. She missed sharing her life with him.

The lights flickered for a moment before coming back on.

Gavin grabbed a towel from the rack and wiped his face. "The power's probably gonna go out soon. I'm surprised it didn't go out last night." He wrapped the towel around his hips and opened the door. "Don't take too long. I'll make us some breakfast."

Another burst of nostalgia hit her. Even though she'd loved cooking for him, Gavin oftentimes insisted on making their meals. It was his way of unwinding after a long day of writing. She would arrive home from the coffee shop to find him in the kitchen whistling softly as he cooked.

Though it was difficult to ignore the flood of painful memories, it did her no good to dwell on the past. Madison twisted her damp hair into a coil on top of her head and dressed. She emerged from the bedroom just in time to see Gavin put eggs and bacon on a plate. The scent of fresh coffee wafted on the air, and slices of bread popped up from the toaster.

Going on autopilot, Madison poured Gavin a cup of black coffee. She hadn't forgotten that part. After fixing her own, she handed him the mug and sat down at the table.

At that moment, a particularly strong gust of wind rattled the windows. Startled, she whipped around to stare outside. The weather hadn't let up. How long was this storm going to last?

"It'll keep up for probably another day or so," Gavin stated, answering her unspoken question. "Don't worry. I've got all the supplies we'll need in the shed out back."

She chewed on her toast. "You're going to miss this place when it's sold."

"This was the one place where I could write with no interruptions. The isolation worked well for me."

Her heartbeat tripped. "What about your writing?"

"I'm looking at a house somewhere else."

Madison stilled. "Far away?"

"I'm thinking somewhere in Europe. Maybe a nice place outside of London."

Dismay filled her at the thought of him a whole continent away. "Th-that sounds great." She tried to smile but failed.

"What's important is you'll be able to do your work. I know you'll miss this place though."

"It's time to move on. I've been here since July."

Her eyes flew to his. He'd been here since . . .

"I've been here since the divorce became final. The only time I went back was for that museum gala I'd promised Wesley's sister I'd attend." His expression was intense as he leaned forward. "Why are you surprised? You didn't expect me to seek solitude and lick my wounds? Did you think I'd go out and party the very same day?" He frowned. "You expected me to just shrug off the fact that you filed for divorce and go on my merry way?"

She couldn't deny that she'd thought exactly that. "I thought you'd be happy that you were free."

"I was devastated, Maddie." His dark eyes flickered with anger. "Then I was pissed. Pissed that you could trust me so little and leave me so easily."

That left her speechless.

Gavin pushed his plate away, his jaw tight. "I'm going to the shed to get some more firewood and get the generator ready." Walking to the door, he shrugged on his parka and pulled on thick gloves before stepping outside.

Madison couldn't move, shocked and dumbfounded. All this time, Gavin had hidden away in this little cabin licking his wounds. Unable to sit there a minute longer, she quickly washed the dishes and put them away. But still he hadn't come back. Peering out the window, she couldn't make anything out. Getting worried, she pulled on her parka and followed him outside. Heading to the side of the cabin, she found Gavin loading up a cart with various items. It was snowing so hard she could barely see in front of her, but she went to him anyway.

"What can I do to help?" she asked, raising her voice to be heard over the wind.

If he was surprised to find her there, he didn't show it. Instead, he handed her a bag of canned goods to add to the ones in the pantry. She quickly walked back in the warmth of the cabin and put them away. Gavin followed not far behind and closed the door. The cart was full of firewood and bottled water and other things she couldn't see.

"The generator is ready to go anytime the power goes off. So don't worry, we're not going to die in this storm."

"I'm not worried," she replied cautiously, trying to gauge his mood.

The sudden crackling of a radio broke the thick silence between them. Gavin strode to the corner where his computer was and pressed a button on the ham radio she hadn't noticed was there. He talked to a man who identified himself as the sheriff. From the sound of it, Gavin had a pretty good rapport going with the man, who was checking to make sure he was okay.

Madison wandered over to the window and sat looking out. He'd stayed here alone for months after their divorce became final. He'd sought solitude. He'd wanted to get away.

But that little voice in her head was quick to remind her that all this had happened because she'd caught him with another woman.

Frustration hit her. God, she wished she could just clear her thoughts. She was confused. Her emotions were jumbled. She couldn't shake off memories of her life with Gavin, even though she knew it was no use rehashing the past. Feeling Gavin's gaze on her, she reluctantly turned.

Just then, the power suddenly went out. Although it was not yet noon, it was dark outside. The fire in the hearth cast dancing shadows on the wall. When Gavin started to turn on a gas lamp, she stopped him. "It's nice like this. Maybe we could just save the lamp for tonight when we'll really need it?"

He shrugged and sat across from her.

"How's your mother?"

"Fine," he replied curtly. "Thanks for asking."

She bit back a sigh, refusing to be deflated by his demeanor. "I liked your mother, Gavin. She was always nice to me."

"At the moment, she's enjoying herself on a Caribbean cruise." He paused. "She liked you too. Always has." The close relationship he had with his mother was something she'd never had for herself. Marilyn Cahill had been warm and caring, eager to get to know her daughter-in-law.

Once again, Madison's gaze strayed to Gavin. She resisted the urge to fidget, something she always did when she was nervous. His mood was difficult to read, and she didn't know what else to say. This uncomfortable silence was hard on her nerves.

"How's the coffee shop?"

"Thriving," she replied with a small smile, grateful that he'd initiated conversation. "The store next door to me is closing. I'm thinking of taking that space and expanding."

"Things are going that well, then?"

At least they were talking. "Oh yes. Right now, I have four part-time employees, college students who need extra money. I like interacting with people, meeting customers, getting to know regulars." She drew her knees up under her chin. "When I was growing up, I helped out at my aunt's coffee shop every summer. It was then I realized I had a knack with people."

"You've made a success of it. You should be proud of yourself."

Madison flushed. "It's something I can truly call my own. When we were together, it helped keep me busy too. I mean, as soon as we came back from our honeymoon, you went back to writing."

"I was under a deadline at the time, Maddie."

"I know that," she rushed on. "I wasn't implying anything. It's just that, the times we were together, most of them were spent in—"

"Bed," he finished for her. "You don't have to remind me."

"It's the truth. Talking was the last thing we did. And then you were busy with your book tour and, well, you know the rest."

A thoughtful look came over his face. "You think we rushed into getting married without really knowing one another?"

"We really *didn't* know one another, did we?" Her smile was rueful. "There are still so many things you don't know about me."

"You told me a little about your father."

Squirming uncomfortably in her chair, she shot him a chiding look. "Yes and let's not go there right now."

Gavin stared at her broodingly. "I've been a selfish bastard, haven't I? I married you then buried my head in my work, only coming out long enough for mind-blowing sex." He ran a hand through his hair. "Was I a lousy husband?"

A wave of sadness hit her. "No. Not lousy. Just . . . busy."

"Is that why you decided to surprise me that day at the hotel?" he suddenly asked. "Because we hadn't been spending enough time together?"

"Well . . ." she hesitated, realizing they were venturing into extremely sensitive territory. "I just thought it would be nice to surprise you."

"I'm sorry for putting my work before you."

"It's in the past, Gavin." Her voice was heavy with the regret that weighed her down. "There's nothing we can do to bring it back now, is there?"

Gavin abruptly pushed himself out of the chair and opened the door, pulling his parka from the coatrack.

"Where are you going?"

"For a walk."

"In this weather?" He didn't answer and stepped outside. "Gavin—"

The door slammed. He was gone.

Madison debated whether to follow him outside, but decided to just stay put. He knew the area well, even though a thick blanket of snow was currently coating it. That thought did little to ease her apprehension. Anything could happen out there. "Damn it, Gavin. What a stupid thing to do."

She sat by the window, anxiously waiting for him to return. The snow fell rapidly, and the intensity of the storm hadn't lessened. Peering outside, she could see nothing but white. Where was he? It was freezing outside, and visibility was near zero. Her glance strayed to her watch again and again as she counted the minutes. When he failed to return after fifteen minutes, her anxiety deepened. She chewed on her lip. Gripping the windowsill, she searched for any sign of him, even a glimpse of his dark parka. Nothing. Time crawled by. Madison paced in front of the window, hoping to sight him right away. She sat down. She got up again. After half an hour, she was wringing her hands. Her nerves were stretched thin. *I'm going to kill him. What if something happens to him out there?*

Cursing her stupidity for not following him, she agonized and worried about him. *Please let him be okay. Bring him back to me.* She teetered between anger and tears, biting her nails nervously. Talking about the past never did them any good. When would they learn not to dredge up what had happened during their brief marriage? It was over. Finished. They should've left well enough alone. Now Gavin was out there somewhere and she was terrified he was hurt or trapped in this awful weather. She eyed the radio he'd used earlier. How hard could it be to figure out how to use it? It looked simple enough. She'd just made up her mind to try calling the sheriff when she heard the heavy thud of boots on the porch. Before he could even open the door, she'd beaten him to it.

"Where the hell have you been?" she demanded, her anger born out of fear. "I was so worried!" She shut the door behind him and glared at his back.

Gavin shook the snow from his head and carefully put his parka back on the coatrack. When he faced her, his features were grim. "Were you worried I was going to die and leave you here all alone?"

Fury swelled to her throat so fast it almost choked her. "Of all the stupid things to say." Tears welled up in her eyes. "I thought you got lost, hurt or worse, buried under all this stupid snow! You're such an ass, Gavin." Madison pushed him aside, stalked into the bedroom and slammed the door. She sat at the far end of the bed, quickly swiping away her tears. What an insensitive boor. How could he think that her safety was the reason she was worried? *This is what I get for caring what happened to him at all.* It seemed like one way or another, they always ended up hurting each other.

She stiffened as the door opened. The bed dipped as Gavin sat behind her. Refusing to look at him, she tipped her face away, still simmering with anger.

"I'm sorry." His voice was low, quiet. "I didn't mean to worry you. I was actually in the shed freezing my nuts off. I needed to think." Madison closed her eyes when Gavin laid his hands on her shoulders and began to knead softly. He ran his thumbs over her nape, burrowing under the tendrils of hair that had escaped from her twist. He worked his way down her back, his fingers pressing with just enough pressure to get rid of the tension that tightened her muscles. "Okay?" he murmured against her ear.

Under his soothing touch, her anger melted away. Madison knew he was trying to make amends. "Yeah." It felt so good to be in his arms, knowing he was here safe with her. She didn't stop him when his fingers drifted to her front and pulled off her sweater off and unclasped her bra.

In the glow of the embers in the woodstove, her rings glinted softly. Gavin rolled his palms over her nipples. She moaned softly. He pushed her to stand up and turned her around to face him, working on her jeans. Shadows danced on the angles of his face, highlighting the slash of his cheekbones and the dark intensity of his eyes. Placing her hands on his shoulders, she obediently raised her legs one after the other and kicked free of her jeans and underwear. The atmosphere was hushed, hazy. Neither of them said a word, as if by unspoken agreement. Words would have ruined the moment.

He tugged her back down onto the bed before quickly shedding his clothes. Naked and aroused, he knelt between her parted legs, his hooded gaze sweeping over her.

Gavin ran his palms up and down her body, heating her with his touch, spreading fire everywhere. When he came to her breasts, he pinched the tips. She moaned at the sharp, piercing pleasure-pain. He drew his hand over the slight bump of her belly before coasting down to the roundness of her hips. With a fingertip, he traced her hip bone and swirled over her bare mound glistening with moisture. Without any warning, he delivered a light slap to the bare mons.

Madison shuddered.

He did it again, this time aiming his hand so that he hit her swollen clit dead-on. She moaned but didn't move. She knew this game well, had played it many times with him.

In quick succession, Gavin delivered four more taps to her pussy, all in varying degrees of intensity but always hitting the little nub that swelled impudently from between the wet labia. Madison bit her lip, her breath coming in quick pants, loving the delicious sting of the blows on the sensitive mass of nerves. *More.*

His eyes were locked on her mound. "So pretty. Plump and pink." A finger swiped moisture from the cleft, spreading it around lazily. Her pulse jumped crazily as he delivered another tap. She rose off the bed, arching closer to him. But the warning tap he delivered on one buttock made her sink back down on the soft mattress. "Don't move."

Pushing her legs apart, he flicked at the ring with his finger. The brief movement jarred the stiff button, and she moaned. He played with her, working the sensitive point until she felt like bursting. Helpless against the need ripping through her, she undulated her hips, trying to get his finger to slip inside the sopping slit that so needed him. "Gavin—"

"Not yet." Positioning his big body between her legs, he pulled open the puffy lips and blew on her, sending the delicate pendant bumping against the swollen nub. Madison trembled, in tune with every little thing that happened to her down there. With his tongue, he licked the swollen nub, tracing and shaping, lifting and gently tapping.

She clenched the sheets until her fingers hurt. She couldn't stand it. Gavin alternated between deep and firm licks to light, barely there touches. She panted, moaning softly, pleading incoherently. Anything, *anything* to let him know how much she needed him to fuck her now.

"Patience, Maddie," he instructed her in a voice that throbbed with heat. "You can't come yet." He buried his face between her legs, working his tongue in the soaked crevices, sinking deep inside her.

She reared off the bed, a cry breaking from her lips. "Oh God." The need for release frayed her control. Sweat broke out on her body as she desperately tried to hold back. Even the deep, measured breaths she took only provided temporary relief. "Gavin, I don't think I can wait," she cried out in desperation.

He ignored her plea, eating her with an intensity that shredded her restraint. Madison shuddered violently. When he gently bit down, she cried out. "I'm coming," she gasped. "I can't hold it . . ."

Sharp pleasure slammed into her, her pussy clenching tightly as she came. His name was a litany on her lips as she rode out the sensations. Gavin was merciless, pushing her up and over after the first intense wave. Madison was delirious from the sensual assault, racked with powerful aftershocks of pleasure.

He held her in the circle of his arms until the tremors gradually ebbed, soothing her with gentle touches, murmuring sweet words in her ears. The bed dipped as he got up. When she was finally able to open her languorous eyes, the sight before her made her go weak at the knees.

Gavin knelt on the edge of the mattress, spreading a thick line of lubricant on his palm. His eyes were locked on her as he coated his erection liberally, from the broad head to the root. His intent was plain, and she wasn't about to stop him. She didn't *want* to stop him.

"Get up."

Madison stood gingerly, her thighs heavy with renewed lust. She greedily eyed his beautiful body as he sat on the bed and leaned against the propped-up pillows and headboard. Excitement raced up her spine as she waited for what was going to happen. Gavin spread his legs, his shaft rising from its nest of dark curls like a thick sword. He let her look her fill for a moment, taking his well-oiled cock in his fisted hand and caressing it with slow, deliberate motions. Maddie trembled, knowing what was to come, helpless against the tide of lust that swept over her.

He indicated the thick tube lying on top of the sheet. "Prepare yourself."

Her knees almost buckled under as she picked up the tube of lubricant. His eyes were hooded, half closed, but she knew he was watching her closely. Jagged anticipation streaked through her. She was already looking forward to the forbidden. It was the most basic and primal act of possession, one that she wouldn't deny him. Her hands trembled as she applied the thick lube between her buttocks, dipping inside the tightly puckered muscle again and again, knowing it would ease his entry. When she was done, she licked her lips and waited.

"Come here."

Madison was under his spell, bound by his will, unable to do anything else but obey. Getting on her knees, she moved to his side of the bed.

"Straddle me."

Her heart was trying to beat its way out of her chest as she swung one leg over him. Shaking, she shifted until her knees were on either side of his waist.

"Open yourself for me, Maddie." Gavin's voice was low and hypnotic.

She did as he asked, holding her buttocks open, biting her lower lip. It was difficult to maintain her position when she was quivering so much, but somehow she did it.

Gavin rubbed the lip she'd bitten, soothing it with a soft touch. "Take me inside you."

Madison descended in slow increments, pausing when she felt the head of his cock against her puckered entrance. Taking a deep breath, she pushed down gently, slowly, forcing herself to relax, feeling the broad tip ease inside the tight muscles. The lubricant aided his entry, but it was still a very tight fit.

He grunted but remained perfectly still, letting her set the pace, letting her take him in.

Madison took in a couple more inches, savoring the exquisite combination of pain and pleasure in taking him this way. Tossing her head back, she desperately held onto what little control she had left. Gavin played with her clit, gently tugging at the ring, swirling around it, adding to her arousal. She paused, reacquainting herself with the hard flesh impaling her ass. With a slight shudder, she took more inside her, never letting up until he was seated to the hilt. She was on sensory overload, her breathing uneven and raspy. This was the ultimate mastery of her body.

He slid his hands up to her breasts. Gavin worked the tight buds into aching tips, every tug and pull calculated to drive her insane. "I've waited so long for this to happen again. Move, babe."

Gripping the headboard with white-knuckled intensity, Madison obeyed. She slid all the way up until he almost slipped out, before gliding back all the way down. The dark curls tickled her wet pussy as she undulated above him. Her ears buzzed with the pleasure as she took him deep again and again.

Gavin took her breast and suckled hard. Madison moaned, her lust-glazed eyes locked on him as he pulled at the nipple caught in the ring. The slight pain intensified all the other sensations swimming through her as she bounced on his lap.

Gavin slipped his fingers inside her slit, crooking the digits and starting a mind-blowing pumping motion. She whimpered a plea—for what, she didn't know—when he thumbed the aching bud, rubbing sensuously without interrupting the in and out movement of his fingers.

"Tell me how you feel, Maddie."

"I feel . . . I feel . . . " she trailed off, unable to form an answer.

"Good?"

"Y-yes," she breathed, moving faster. "It feels so . . . I can't . . . Oh Gavin—"

"Fuck me faster," he growled.

Under the shadow of the flickering firelight, she did as he bade her, taking him deep with ever-increasing speed. Her skin glistened with perspiration, their damp breath mingled. Gavin wrapped his other arm around her waist, holding her tight, all the while plunging his fingers in her pussy and sucking the nipple closest to his mouth. Stars exploded behind her closed eyelids. Madison gritted her teeth, skating on the edge of insanity, knowing she wouldn't last for long.

"I want to feel your ass clenching sweetly, tightly, on me. Come, Maddie," he rasped.

The floodgates opened. She cried out as her orgasm exploded through her body. Intense, almost painful, pleasure rolled through in a giant wave, robbing her of all thought. She clamped down on his fingers; she clamped down on his shaft. "Gavin. Gavin," she chanted mindlessly as she absorbed the pain and pleasure of their joining. He cupped her nape and drew her lips down to his. Madison poured everything she felt into the kiss. She never wanted it to end.

"Maddie," Gavin groaned, thrusting, his cock swelling impossibly bigger a moment before he blasted his seed inside her. Madison sought his lips, her tongue delving within to tangle with his in a heated duel. She couldn't get enough of him, clenching around him as he rode out his own pleasure. Her heart pounded in her chest, gradually slowing back to normal until the very last shudder was wrung from her body.

"Whatever else that may have happened between us, Maddie, we have *this*. We'll always have this."

Madison buried her face in his neck, silent tears coursing

down her cheeks. She wept for what was and what could have been. Her heart ached, and for a moment, just for a moment, she wished she could wipe away everything that had happened between them and start over. He was right. They did have this. But would it be enough to carry them through the pain and uncertainty they would have to endure?

It wasn't. Trust was something that was earned, not freely given. They could never go back. Their time together in this cabin was just a dream, a fantasy they were living out while the storm raged outside.

Madison didn't say a word as Gavin cleaned her up, her heart twisting at the gentle way he cleansed her with a warm, damp cloth. Afterward he cleaned himself before sliding under the sheets with her and gathering her in his arms. Neither of them said a word. There was nothing left to say.

The storm lasted for a couple of hours more, then miraculously in the late afternoon, it stopped. The dark clouds parted and the sun peeked through, a feeble beacon of brightness that instead of making her happy, only intensified her sadness. The storm was gone and soon—as soon as the roads were cleared—she was going home, leaving Gavin for good.

Once he moved out of the country, she'd probably never see him again.

An engine started outside and revved. Madison pushed aside the sadness closing in on her. *Stop being silly,* she scolded herself. This time with Gavin had been nothing but a dream. Now it was time to go back to the real world, back to the lonely reality of her life.

Gavin met her at the bottom of the steps, standing next to a gleaming black SUV. He helped her inside before stowing her bag in the trunk. Silence reigned in the car as they drove through town. She shot him a puzzled look. "Aren't I supposed to get off here?"

"I'm taking you to the airport." His reply was curt, and he didn't even glance at her. As a final blow, he turned on the radio, filling the truck with soft jazzy music, discouraging any conversation. Madison stared out the window, taking in the blinding white of the snow-covered countryside. She didn't know why he was taking her to the airport. Things had been strained since they'd woken up that morning. Gavin was in a strange mood, brooding and quiet. At this point, plagued by her own depressing thoughts, she didn't even want to risk conversation.

Madison breathed a sigh of relief as he pulled into the airport terminal parking lot much later. The tense atmosphere had been nearly unbearable, the air thick and uncomfortable. She got out of the car, mentally readying herself to say good-bye. When Gavin pulled out an expensive-looking suitcase along with her bag, she frowned. "What are you—"

He merely turned away and headed into the building. Clamping her mouth shut, Madison hurried to keep up with his longer

SIX

THE ROAD CREWS WORKED all night to make the road passable. While Maddie showered and got ready, Gavin remained in constant contact with the sheriff, making arrangements for the local garage to pull her car from the ditch she'd driven into and return it to the local rental agency she'd gotten it from. "Put the charges on my tab," he instructed the person on the other end before turning off the radio.

"I'll pay you," Maddie assured him quietly, emerging from the bathroom. "Just send me the bill and I'll take care of it."

"It's no big deal. Are you packed and ready to go?" At her nod, he strode to the door. "I'll meet you outside."

Madison took one last look around before slinging her purse over her shoulder and picking up her overnight bag. The personal items she'd chosen to take were all carefully packed in a box, ready to be shipped. It wasn't much, just some early pictures of her and Gavin, plus the wedding photos and a few personal items. She looked around once more. This was probably the last time she'd be in this cabin, which held so many memories of her life with Gavin. Soon, this chapter would be forever closed.

stride. When he didn't go to the airline counters, she finally pulled his arm to stop him.

"I need to check in."

"Not over there, you don't" was his calm reply. "I'm going back to L.A., you can ride with me." He continued walking, emerging in a hangar for private planes and charter jets.

"I can take a regular plane," Madison protested, having to almost run to keep up with him. "Gavin, will you *stop*?"

He finally did and gave her an impatient frown. "Our flight is scheduled to take off in twenty minutes. We have to board now."

"I didn't know you had your own plane," she blurted out like an idiot.

He shrugged. "It's chartered. I don't like flying. I like to be as comfortable as possible and commuter airlines are certainly not that." He glanced at his watch impatiently. "We're on a schedule here, Maddie. And don't give me any nonsense about not wanting to fly back with me. I'm going to L.A. too, so why not go together? Any more questions?"

She shook her head.

He headed for a jet that was idling on the runway. Madison followed his instructions like an automaton, choosing a seat in the plush cabin and buckling up. Gavin spoke to the pilot before closing the door to the cockpit and taking the seat across from her. Soon afterward, the plane taxied down the runway and took off. Gavin looked out the small window, appearing deep in thought.

In a way, she was glad he was ignoring her. This whole day had exhausted her, emotionally and spiritually. She felt like she'd been through the wringer, and it wasn't over yet. To say that her feelings were conflicted was putting it mildly, but she chalked it up to just being with him again. Whenever he was around, she just couldn't think straight. Once she was back on solid ground, on her home turf, she'd see things clearer and realize that she and Gavin were never meant to be together. This was only temporary. The time they'd spent together at the cabin would have to last her a lifetime.

Madison gasped in surprise when Gavin unceremoniously unbuckled her seat belt and yanked her out of her seat and pulled her into his lap. "What are you doing?" she asked, her heart beginning to thud heavily in her chest.

He didn't answer. Instead, he kissed her. Madison moaned under the onslaught. It was fraught with frantic hunger, mixed with an element of desperation. The misery that plagued her at the thought of never seeing him again was buried under the avalanche of need that welled up in her. She wanted this, needed it, just as much as he did.

Slipping his hand under her sweater, Gavin pushed it up and over her head in one quick movement. He disposed of her bra easily, exposing her breasts to his gaze. Her nipple rings glinted in the dull cabin lights as he bent and laved the stiff tip with his tongue.

Her mind went fuzzy. She whimpered when he sucked her deep into his mouth. Balanced precariously on his lap, she arched and offered him the other, bringing it close to his mouth, quivering in need as he lavished it with the same attention. Liquid heat traveled like electricity along her veins, raising her temperature, bringing instant flooding to her pussy. Needing to touch him, she fumbled with the buttons of his shirt, whimpering a faint protest when he didn't make a move to help her at all. Gavin was too busy laving her breasts, licking every inch of skin within his reach. Knowing he found so much pleasure in her body was more potent than any aphrodisiac. This time, pleasing him, taking him higher than he'd ever gone before, was very important.

Madison climbed off his lap and pulled him up. With a greed born of desperation, she pushed his shirt off his shoulders and fastened her lips to his skin. He tasted so good. She knelt, working on the fastening of his jeans, moaning in triumph as she pushed them down his muscular legs to the floor. On the way back up, she skimmed her lips up his thigh, bypassing his cock, and slowly slid up his chest to end at his neck, suckling the skin softly before she stepped away from him.

She shook her head when Gavin made to reach for her, motioning him to sit back down. In the isolation of the cabin, their eyes made contact and for a brief moment, Madison allowed the love she still felt for him to shine through. In that instant, they shared what was probably the most honest moment between them. Love and regret shone in her eyes, the same two emotions mirrored in his gaze.

She shimmied out of her jeans, slowly pushing them down her legs, taking her underwear along with them. Naked, she stood before him, feeling not one iota of shame or embarrassment, or reluctance or second thoughts. This time was for him.

Propping a leg next to his thigh, she moistened a finger with her tongue before trailing it down to one stiff nipple, slipping inside the gold ring and tugging gently. His eyes flashed with heat, glued to her finger as she swirled it around and around the distended crest.

Sliding her finger down over her belly, Madison reached between her legs and was instantly engulfed in warm, sticky moisture. Widening her stance, she slipped her fingers inside, tracing her labia, dipping in and out, circling from side to side. With her other hand, she drew back the lips, exposing her swollen button and the ring, along with the gold pendant. Madison never took her eyes away from him, noting his heightened color, the flared nostrils and the muscle in his jaw that ticked. Gavin was aroused, highly so. He wrapped his hand around his engorged flesh.

Giddy with desire and nearly out of her mind from the need tearing at her, Madison caressed herself in front of him, uncaring that just beyond the cabin door were the pilots, and that one could walk in at any moment. Gavin was as indifferent to the threat of discovery as she was, never taking his eyes away from her glistening labia.

She massaged her clit, going around and around, under and over. At his impatient growl, Madison rubbed her fingers against his lips, coating them with her moisture. Gently slipping inside the warm cavern of his mouth, she shivered as his tongue lapped hungrily at her, cleaning her fingers meticulously, sliding between each digit and savoring her taste.

"No more games." Gavin curved his hands around her buttocks and pulled her close, burying his face between her legs. Her knees buckled under her and Madison clutched the seat for support. He ate her voraciously, slurping his enjoyment, greedily inhaling her scent before plunging his tongue inside her slit.

Madison cried out, closing her eyes at the sharp pleasure that pulsed through her. She let him do what he wanted, offering her body to him without any words. Holding her tighter, Gavin explored every single inch of her dripping pussy, lashing at the bundle of nerves nestled between the folds before taking it between his lips and sucking hard.

She shuddered and bucked in his arms. He groaned, the rough sound humming over her skin. She bit her lip and tried to hold still, but found that she couldn't, grinding against his face. "Oh God, Gavin."

He thumbed the hot bud, devastating her with the slow and deliberate way he rotated the fleshy part of his finger against it. Nearly insane, she ground her hips against his hand, needing firmer, harder contact. But he denied her even that, and continued to thumb her lightly, almost casually.

"Please," she cried softly. "I need more."

He finger-fucked her in measured beats, adopting a slow, lazy rhythm that didn't even begin to satisfy her. A strong tremor rocked her. "Gavin, hurry."

He stroked her faster. Madison opened her legs as wide as she could, inviting more of his touch, consumed by the need thundering through her veins like molten lava. He pulled away and stood, turning her as he positioned her in front of him. He pushed her legs wide apart and bent her slightly at the waist. Without hesitation, he plunged inside her, taking her from behind.

Madison moaned in bliss. She didn't want gentleness at this time—she wanted it rough and primal. "Yes . . . yes." She shivered as he pulled out entirely before plunging back in again. His hands latched onto her breasts, squeezing and pinching her nipples, driving her insane.

"Fuck me harder," she begged with mindless abandon.

His hips slammed against hers, making quick slapping sounds as he fucked her deep, again and again. Her senses whirled. Her heart pounded. Madison cried out again and again, uncaring if anybody else heard her pleas.

Gavin released his hold on her breasts, wrapped a hand in her thick hair and tugged her head back. He placed his lips in her ear and swirled his tongue around the soft shell before whispering, "Come for me."

As if his words triggered her release, a huge wave of pleasure slammed into her, robbing her of breath, wringing a harsh cry from her throat. Gavin didn't stop pounding into her through the shudders that racked her body, stroking in and out until he let out a mighty groan and went over the edge. She couldn't move, satiation rendering her boneless. Limp, she barely stirred when he reached for her clothes and dressed her. He pulled on his shirt and jeans before he sat back down and pulled her back onto his lap.

"We belong together, Maddie. Can't you see that?"

Her heart tore in two at his words. She placed a finger on his lips. "Gavin, no."

"Yes," he countered in a low, intense voice. "I love you, Maddie. Until the day I die, you will be the only woman for me. These last two days proved that we can be together. I want to try, Maddie. I want you to give us another chance."

Madison swallowed the lump in her throat. "We'll just end up hurting each other again."

Gavin took her hand and placed it over his heart. "I don't know what else I can do or say to make you believe me that I didn't cheat on you. I can only swear that what you think you saw that day was not what happened."

She closed her eyes, feeling the strong rhythm of his heart under her palm. His voice rang with sincerity.

"I didn't lie to you then and I'm not lying to you now." He closed his eyes and held her tight. "If you truly think there's no hope for us, that you can never trust me, then tell me now, Maddie. Tell me you don't love me anymore and I'll leave you alone forever."

Madison hid her face in her hands and let the tears flow. Did she really want to go back to long nights of dreaming about Gavin when she could have the real thing? Life without him was an empty existence, one day blurring into the next. Before long, life would pass her by and she would lose this chance to be with him again. No other man could ever make her feel the way Gavin could. But the fear was still there, squeezing her heart. But the love she felt for Gavin fought for equal space, reminding her of its existence, stronger and longer lasting than the fear she harbored. The love never really went away.

She buried her face in his neck, soothed by the warmth of his skin. "My father was the local football hero," she began in a soft voice. "The small town he grew up in worshipped him. He could do no wrong. My mother was the high school girlfriend he got pregnant. They had to get married before they had me."

"Maddie, you don't have to tell me this."

"I want to tell you the whole story. I want to explain, somehow, why I'm the way I am."

Gavin kissed her forehead. "All right."

"It wasn't long before he got tired of being tied down to one woman." Madison breathed deeply. "He made it known that he wasn't satisfied with my mom, that he wanted to play around. She couldn't stop him, enduring the humiliation over and over again as he went from one woman to another. People looked the other way. What's worse, they blamed my mom. It was somehow her fault that her husband strayed."

"Jesus."

"She became very bitter. Finally, when I was about nine, we left him. All my life, she'd warned me about not trusting men. Men are incapable of being faithful, she said. Men can never be satisfied with one woman. On the day of our wedding, she told me I was a fool to marry you. That we would never last, that you weren't the type to stay faithful to me." She sniffled. "I tried, Gavin. I really tried to put her words out of my mind."

"Then you saw me with Kimberly."

"I was crushed. Most of all, I was devastated that my mother had been right. All I could think about was getting away from you as soon as I could, before I got hurt even more." She stared into his eyes, wanting him to understand. "I told myself I should have seen the signs. Kimberly used to call at home when you weren't there and drop little hints about your 'relationship.'"

"She *what?*"

Madison nodded. "She was your publicist. I couldn't complain about her presence around you. She told me you'd been lovers, that you and she had an arrangement. She didn't care that we were married. She still wanted you. Don't you see, Gavin?" she asked. "What was I supposed to think after all that? I tried to ignore her, tell myself that you couldn't possibly be sleeping with her. That she was lying. Then you left for your book tour." Her voice broke. "You know what happened next."

"I slept with her once, long before I met you. *Once,*" he emphasized. "And the woman never got over it. She kept thinking there was more to it than just a one-night stand." Gavin sighed, stroking her hair. "Maddie, I'm really sorry she subjected you to all that bullshit. Had I known, I would've put a stop to it immediately and fired her right away."

"I thought I could handle it," she murmured, still hurting from the memories.

"It's my fault too," he admitted in a low voice. "I should have tried harder to get you back. But I was angry and proud. I wasn't going to make a fool of myself and beg you to come back when you didn't want me anymore. I damn near killed myself drinking, just to forget about you."

"I'm sorry I didn't believe you." She'd been foolish and blind, wallowing in the pain, not realizing what she'd lost. "Can you forgive me for not trusting you?"

"Our past makes us the people we are. You can't help yours." He gently drew her hair back from her face. "I'm not letting you go again."

Madison swallowed, tears flooding her eyes. She didn't deserve this strong, caring man who still loved her despite what she'd put them both through. She cupped his face. "I love you."

He pulled in a sharp breath. "Do you really think you can trust me, Maddie?" he asked, utterly serious. "I need you to do that before we can move forward."

"Yes." Her words rang firm and sure.

Gavin held her close. "I will never willingly hurt you."

She rubbed her cheek against him. "I know. It's not easy to erase the painful memories of my childhood, but I'll work through it. You mean more to me than anything else."

"We'll do whatever we can to make it work. Anything, Maddie. As long as we're together. Any doubts, any questions, we'll handle it together."

Madison buried her face in his neck. "All right."

His arms wrapped around her. "I thought of all sorts of things that I could do to persuade you to stay with me when we got back to L.A.—I even thought about keeping you locked up at home until you'd listen to me."

"Locked up, huh?" She licked his ear. "I think I like that idea."

"Yeah?" He slipped his hand under her sweater. "I even have handcuffs and whips. Plus all the toys we need."

Madison laughed happily. "Sold. You can have me."

"But you have to be good, otherwise, I'll have to spank you."

She licked her lips. "Sounds exciting."

"You're mine forever, Maddie."

She skimmed his cheek with her lips, smiling. "Forever. That sounds nice. Is that a promise?"

"It's a goddamned guarantee." He kissed her deeply. "Marry me again."

Happiness chased away the last remaining doubt in her heart. "Yes. Yes." She rained kisses on his lips. "I'll marry you whenever, wherever you want. And this time, we'll make sure its forever."

Epilogue

AVIN STEERED HIS WIFE into a quiet corner of the art gallery and palmed her ass. "This party sucks. Let's go home, babe."

Madison giggled. "Will you stop it? This is Kylie's boyfriend's first show. She'll be crushed if we leave so soon."

"You call this art?" he drawled in her ear. "A three-year-old can draw better."

"Shh. Don't say that out loud. Kylie really likes him."

His finger brushed against her nipple, lingering for a longer touch. "What happened to that Dave something-or-other?"

She leaned closer, pushing her breast against his hand. "He's *so* last week." When he gently pinched her nipple, she bit back a moan. "No fair. You can touch me but I can't touch you."

He chuckled. "You're welcome to touch me anytime."

"Hello, Gavin."

At the sugary-sweet voice, Gavin stiffened and turned around. "Kimberly."

Madison's blood began to simmer as she faced the stunning woman dressed in a revealing black gown.

"Darling, it's been a long time. You're looking well." She devoured Gavin with her eyes.

Madison stepped forward. "There's nothing you have to say that we're interested in hearing," she snapped, deliberately being rude. She barely restrained herself when Kimberly released a dramatic sigh, casting a disparaging look at her strapless red gown. *At least I don't look like an overly made-up doll. I bet she looks horrible without all that war paint.*

Kimberly's perfectly shaped eyebrows rose. "Your wife's scary, Gavin. No wonder you preferred me, darling."

His jaw tightened. "I never preferred you, Kimberly. You just couldn't take no for an answer."

Kimberly's laugh grated on Madison's nerves. "Did I get you in trouble that day at the hotel? That was just a small payback for how you treated me like shit, like I was some groupie." Her eyes glinted with malicious triumph. "Even though we didn't have sex, what's important is *your wife* thought so. That was enough for me." She tossed her head and turned toward Maddie. "Although what he sees in *you* is beyond me."

Madison clenched her fists. It would be so easy to give in to her anger and hit Kimberly. She wanted to wipe that smirk off her face, but in the end, the other woman wasn't worth it. "It's simple, really. He loves me." She cocked her head, stepping close to her. "Do you know that there are *several* places on the body where I could hit you and not leave a mark? Now why don't you leave us alone before I do that?"

Kimberly paled beneath her makeup but lifted her chin. "I've got somebody else now. Way better than Gavin. You can have him." She disappeared into the crowd.

Gavin burst out laughing. "Bravo, babe. That was good."

Madison grinned, wrapping her arms around him. "Can you ever forgive me for believing you would be attracted to that . . . that *bitch*? I was so stupid."

Gavin smoothed a hand down her back. "Nothing to forgive. That's all in the past, Maddie. We've started a new life together. Consider what happened tonight closure."

"I'm sorry for not trusting you. To think of all the time we wasted and the pain I could have spared both of us."

"Forget it. What matters to me is that we're together again and that you trust me."

"I *do* trust you."

"That's enough for me. I'll happily spend the rest of my life proving that I love you and no one else."

"I don't deserve you," she murmured.

He gave her a wicked grin. "You can make it up to me as soon as we get out of here."

"I'd love to." Her eyes swept over the crowd. "Although I really would've loved to have kicked that woman's ass."

Gavin laughed. "Sheathe your claws, woman. She's not worth it. Now kiss me."

"With pleasure." She leaned up and gave him a hot, tongue-tangling kiss.

He held her tight against him. "Come on, let's go home."

RIDE A COWBOY

DELILAH DEVLIN

One

The house Katelyn Carter had bought sight unseen was kind of like her—weathered by storms and in need of a lot of TLC.

After a quick glance around the empty road, she set her truck into park and stared. She let her eyes blur and tried to imagine how the old house must have looked once upon a time before the harsh South Texas sun baked its exterior. She wasn't encouraged. Even from behind her dirty windshield, she could tell the one-story ranch needed a lot of work, and at the very least, a fresh coat of paint.

A lone tear streaked down her face, surprising her, and she sniffed. One last cry—she deserved that much. Then no more feeling sorry for herself. She had too much to do and a whole new life stretching in front of her.

A loud honk sounded and Katelyn swung her gaze to her rearview mirror to find that a dusty, older-model pickup truck had pulled up behind her. She swiped away the tears with the back of her hand, and then stuck her arm out the window to wave the driver past.

Instead, the driver-side door opened and a tall Texan in faded jeans and a cream-colored cowboy hat stepped onto the pavement.

Katelyn cursed under her breath and quickly tilted down the mirror to see whether her mascara had smeared. She didn't really care what a stranger thought—that was the old Katelyn. Still, some habits die hard.

When boot steps stopped beside her, she glanced up . . . and found herself trapped within a moss green gaze that raised the temperature within her cab a notch. The rest of him was just as captivating. Dark brown hair peeked from beneath his hat. His jaw was angular, his chin chiseled. Shallow crow's feet surrounded those amazing eyes and crinkled when he frowned—as he was doing now. But they were wrinkles cause by the sun, not the weathering of a few years, like hers.

Damn! Here stood the first man she'd met since her separation who made her think of all the steamy possibilities, and he was too young.

She didn't realize she'd cursed out loud until his soft chuckle washed over her like a silky caress. Her cheeks flamed instantly.

"Women don't generally cuss me 'til *after* they know me better," he said, his baritone voice thick as molasses.

The timbre and tone of his voice appealed too much. She lifted a single brow, trying for off-putting and hoping he didn't notice her lashes were still wet from tears. "Obviously, they're not too discerning."

His smile dimmed and his eyes narrowed, sweeping over her face and body hunched behind the steering wheel. "Not from around here, are you?" he asked, leaning closer.

She reminded herself she was alone, in the middle of a country road, with a large, predatory-looking man looming over her—and she'd just insulted him. She hit her automatic lock button.

"Whoa," he said, lifting his hands. "I didn't mean to scare you, ma'am."

Ma'am! Now she really did feel like the spinster librarian she was.

"Look . . ." He straightened away. "I just stopped to see if you were having car trouble."

"Funny, but I wasn't having any trouble at all 'til you stopped," she said, making sure he understood her unsubtle dig, and hoping he'd take the hint and leave.

The cowboy looked around and then down the gravel road toward her home, before returning to give her a questioning glance. "You lost then? The main highway's about three miles behind you."

"Nope, I know exactly where I am." She kept her response terse and lifted her chin. No way was she going to encourage the conversation to continue, no matter how handsome the man was—or more to the point, *because* he was so attractive. "Not that it's any of your business. I was just double-checking the address."

He pushed back his cowboy hat and leaned down again. "Well, I wouldn't want you to waste any more of your valuable time," he said, his gaze raking her face, "but you're at 118 Amman Road. The letters are worn off the mailbox."

The longer he stood there, the more certain she became she needed him gone. Something about him, his steady gaze and his large sturdy frame, made her . . . want . . . something more, something she was better off not having right now. "Then I'm in the right place," she said, keeping her expression challenging.

His hand rubbed the back of his neck and he shook his head. "Well, I'll be damned," he said softly. When his green gaze returned, his expression was hard to read, but intense, almost searching.

Katelyn shivered. All that attention from a handsome man unnerved her. She needed time alone to dam up her defenses against her unwanted reactions. Handsome she'd had and wasn't what she needed now.

"Seein' as how you don't need any help," he said, "I'll be on my way." One last glance with a naked promise she couldn't misinterpret, and he left . . . taking Katelyn's breath right along with him.

In the mirror, her gaze clung to his broad back and nicely rounded backside until he reached the door of his cab and glanced back. She whipped away her gaze and hoped like hell he hadn't caught her looking at his ass. Sinking in her seat, she burned with embarrassment while he passed by, giving her one last smoldering glance.

Katelyn's heart slowed and her hands released their tight grip on the steering wheel.

He was just a man—he had nothing she needed or wanted—*ever again*. Except maybe sex. She did miss that. But she'd never have sex with entanglement again. Complicating that fact, she'd come to a small town to start her life anew and couldn't afford the kind of scandal a fling with a younger man would cause.

Pushing thoughts of the tall cowboy aside, she pulled onto the long gravel drive and forced her mind back to what needed doing before she could rest that night. Hard work was what she needed—not anything the young cowboy had to offer.

And looking at her new home, she guessed she'd get plenty of cowboy antidote. A long day's work lay ahead of her—and that was before she could unpack the U-Haul trailer laden with all her worldly belongings. She squared her shoulders. She'd make it through the next couple of days like she had the last few years—one step at a time.

Her gaze lifted beyond the house to the field of ripening buffalo grass and broken rock behind the chain-link fence surrounding the two-acre property. The landscape was so different here.

Atlanta had just revealed the first hints of spring. Crocuses had pushed up through the lawn. Daffodils bloomed beside the porch where she'd planted them during the first year of her marriage to Chris, when she'd still had so much hope for their future together.

Here, the few live oaks that dotted the landscape looked like bushes in comparison to the tall pines of her former home.

And good Lord—the heat! Only April and already eighty degrees and climbing fast.

Katelyn opened her door, grateful for the stirring breeze. It was Monday; Thursday she started her new job and she wanted all her things in their proper place before she began her new life. She'd begin as she meant to continue—building order out of the chaos her world had been.

Besides its less than pristine appearance, she quickly discovered another problem with her new home—the ancient air conditioner didn't work. She raised every window she could and propped open the back door to let a breeze waft through the house. Warm though it was, the temperature outside was still better than the stale heat inside.

After wrestling with her bed frame, mattress, and small nightstand, she decided to get a good night's sleep and start again early the next morning. She lay down on top of cool crisp sheets and sighed her relief. But despite her fatigue, she tossed on her mattress, unable to fall asleep.

She would have liked to blame her restlessness on the warm weather. But the temperature of the room had little to do with the heat pooling between her legs and everything to do with the cowboy in the faded jeans.

After pounding her pillow for the second time, she surrendered to her body's demands and did something she'd only recently developed the skill to accomplish, masturbating to orgasm being something her husband had considered a theft of his own pleasure.

Moonlight glared through the top of the window and obscured her view of the front yard, but she relaxed, knowing darkness, being a good hundred yards distance from the road and the spindly oaks in her front yard obscured the view inside her bedroom. She didn't live in the city anymore.

With one last guilty glance out the bare window, she slid her fingers beneath the edge of her panties. And if her mind drifted to the tall Texan in the cream-colored cowboy hat, well, she'd just put it down to a momentary weakness. He'd never know.

Feeling as low as a snake, the cowboy hid in the shadows just outside the woman's window and watched while her fingers disappeared beneath the edge of her pale panties.

Such a private thing to witness. A weakness betrayed. A deep passion exposed.

He'd walked the quarter mile from his house to hers, following an urge so strong he hadn't questioned it. While she'd worked steadily, well into the evening, brushing away a year's worth of dust from her wooden floors and wrestling with furniture, his gaze had followed her efficient movements, roaming the curves of her firm breasts and ass and the tempting length of her legs beneath the frayed edges of her cutoff jeans.

When at last she'd turned off the light, he'd been rewarded for his patient vigil as she'd drawn off her T-shirt and bra and slipped the shorts down her thighs. Although too dark to see the color of her nipples, he'd discerned their size and witnessed them drawing into beaded points when she'd rubbed them as though easing an ache. He'd licked his lips, anticipating their velvet texture on his tongue. Then she'd drawn a small top over her head that hugged her breasts like a second skin and did little to cool his ardor.

He'd grown hungrier by the moment, coveting each sweet curve of her body, determined to stake a claim, and soon. She might be a little older than he'd have liked, but the difference in their ages didn't mean a thing to his cock. The large, hard knot of his erection pressed uncomfortably against the front of his jeans.

But the physical attraction was only part of what drew him, what kept him skulking in the darkness outside her bedroom. The hint of sadness glinting wetly on her dark eyelashes when they'd met earlier on the road had done crazy things to the inside of his chest. The pain-filled defiance in her gaze hadn't deterred him one bit. If any man was going to chase the shadows from her past, it'd be him. The loneliness he'd sensed in her was echoed tenfold in his own heart.

Her low whimpered moan carried on the air between them, tightening his thighs and balls, building a painful urgency he had to relieve. He flicked open the button at the top of his jeans and eased out his rigid cock. He'd share this private act with her, giving the ache a face—*hers*. Blue eyes the color of a clear Texas sky. Hair as pale and soft as corn silk. Her face was etched on his mind, and now on his body.

With his hand closing around his shaft, he joined her, imagining sinking into the moisture her fingers drew from her pussy.

Her thighs parted, her knees rising high and splaying wide as her hips undulated on the mattress.

His hand glided up the rigid shaft, squeezing when he reached the end, then glided back down. His hips pulsed in time with hers, driving his cock within his circled fingers until the friction became nearly unbearable. He dropped spit onto his palm and resumed the rhythm, the moisture easing the movements. He imagined sinking to his knees between her thighs and pressing into her. How hot and tight she'd be, clenching around his cock like a wet fist, like his was doing now.

Her fingers pulled out partway and swirled faster. She must be getting close. Her little clit ached for direct stimulation. Someday soon, he'd purse his lips around it, flutter his tongue on the hard little knot, then suck on it until she came, screaming his name.

Her cry was wispy, restrained, but was enough to push him over the edge, and he spilled cum into the dirt at his feet, jerking his cock those last desperate strokes.

Tomorrow, he'd give her a proper introduction. And learn the name of the woman he planned to make his own.

THE NEXT MORNING sunlight streamed into her bedroom through the bare window. The air was stifling hot, and she lay drenched in sweat, her hair clinging to her face in sticky clumps. She flipped back the covers.

An ominous rattle sounded from the floor, and she froze.

She didn't need to be a native Texan to recognize that raspy rattle. Easing up to stand in the middle of her mattress, she peered cautiously over the edge. A rattlesnake lay on the floor next to her bed in a fat coil, its tail erect and quivering. Even if the snake hadn't paralyzed her with fear, he lay in a patch of sunlight between her and the bedroom door—she wasn't getting out of this predicament by herself.

She needed the cavalry, or at least the local sheriff's department. Moving slowly, she reached for her cell phone on the bedside table. Her heart nearly stopped when the dry rattle grew louder and the snake's head drew back with its mouth open and fangs exposed.

Her hands shook as she punched 911.

"Wendall County Police, how may I help you?" a female voice chimed.

Relief nearly made her weak. "Um . . . this is Katelyn Carter," she said, rushing to get the words out. "I'm at 118 Amman Road. I'm new here and I have a problem." Her voice trembled with fear as she explained her dilemma to the dispatcher. "Can rattlesnakes climb?"

"We'll send a unit right over, ma'am. You sit tight, now. I don't think that snake's gonna do any climbin'."

"Wait!" For the first time Katelyn realized she stood in the middle of her bed wearing only a tiny pair of bikini briefs and a thin white camisole that was transparent due to her own perspiration. Embarrassment warred with her fear.

"Yes, ma'am?" The dispatcher interrupted her thoughts.

"Uh . . . I'm not dressed. Can you send a female officer?"

The woman on the other end of the line chuckled. "Ma'am, we don't have any female officers, but I'll make sure only one fella comes in. You just stay right where you are."

As she powered off her cell phone, Katelyn could already hear sirens in the distance and wondered irritably whether the whole Wendall County police force was responding to the call. It wasn't long before booted footsteps made their way through her house.

One of the officers called out to her, "Miz Carter, you in there?"

Despite her fear, Katelyn cringed inside. The house was a mess—littered with cleaning supplies, wadded packing paper and half-emptied boxes. Worse, total strangers were about to see a whole lot more of her than anyone but her husband ever had. She inched her hand down to pull up the sheet to cover herself, but halted when the snake grew agitated by her slight movement and began to writhe in a tight circle around itself.

Wilting with embarrassment, she replied, "I'm in here."

A broad, amused face peered around the corner of her bedroom door. The officer's gaze widened slightly as it paused on her before seeking out her intruder on the floor. He whistled when he spotted the snake. "It's a big 'un all right. We won't come in just yet, ma'am. I can tell that rattler's gettin' annoyed. We've sent for a rattlesnake wrangler to come pick up this bad boy." He gave her a kind smile. "It'll only be a few minutes. You just hang tight—and don't move, ya hear?"

Long moments passed while Katelyn counted the drops of sweat that slid down her face and the brown and black diamonds that crisscrossed the snake's back. She had just begun to wonder what a "rattlesnake wrangler" was when she heard more voices from the living room and heavy footsteps just outside her bedroom door.

"Ma'am, it's Daniel Bodine."

That voice! Warm as whiskey, it poured over her. Katelyn nearly groaned.

"I'm coming in now. Don't you move a muscle."

A moment later, the cowboy who'd figured in her dreams—hot and sexy dreams—filled the doorway of her bedroom.

As nervous as she was, Katelyn couldn't help noting his broad shoulders nearly spanned the doorframe, and he had to duck to clear his hat beneath it. In one hand he held a long pole with a hook at the end of it; in the other, a white sack.

His gaze met hers briefly, and he nodded once in her direction. A flush of red tinted his cheeks as he moved slowly into her bedroom, then all of his concentration focused on the snake.

As he approached it, the whispery rattle grew louder and the snake's attention moved to him. When its head rose with fangs exposed, the man reacted in a blinding whir of movement, pinning the snake's head to the floor with the hook. Then the cowboy placed the toe of his boot just below its head and tossed aside the pole.

Her heart pounded with fear as the snake frantically whipped its body about.

Daniel grabbed the snake just below the head, then straightened and held it up for a moment, letting it relax its full length toward the floor. He whistled appreciatively. "Whoa, he's a big 'un all right." He dropped it into the white sack and pulled the drawstring closed over it. Finally, he turned to her, his gaze flickering over her before sliding politely away. "It's okay, ma'am. You can come down off the bed now," he said softly.

"Thanks," she said, her voice croaking like a bullfrog, "but I think I'll wait until my legs stop trembling before I attempt it." She hated admitting her weakness and flushed, feeling the heat color her cheeks and spread down her neck to her chest. She wanted to raise her hands to hide her breasts, but knew it was a little late to save her modesty.

"Let me help you down." He stepped toward the bed, his hand stretched out.

"N-No," she said, suddenly breathless. *Don't let him touch me.* After last night, she already felt as though he'd touched her—intimately. She'd come, pretending his fingers stroked her slick flesh.

"It's okay. I swear I don't bite," he said, his voice softer, huskier. His hand closed around hers, and he tugged gently.

Katelyn drew in a sharp breath at the heat of his touch and the calluses that roughened his palms, and let him help her to the floor. When she stood beside him in her underwear and bare feet, she ducked her head and pulled at the cotton camisole that stuck to her skin, aware he could see the dark outline of her nipples through the cloth.

Sure enough, his glance swept down her body and back up.

A warning flashed in the back of her mind, but she couldn't help the slight catch of her breath as his gaze paused on her breasts. But rather than the suggestive comment she expected from the sassy cowboy of yesterday, he tightened his jaw and he looked away.

The telltale sign of awareness and tension had a similar effect on her body and she felt her nipples bead beneath her damp camisole.

He cleared his throat and stepped away. "I'll just put him in the truck and be on my way," he said, his voice now brusque. "I wouldn't want him to scare you again." With a hot glance that said he hadn't really been talking about the snake, he turned on his heels and left the room.

She slumped against the bedpost and wondered what that had been all about and why her heart still pumped madly . . . and not from fear or embarrassment. She blew out a pent-up breath and moaned. Who the hell was she kidding? The look on his face had held a promise. One she was dying to know.

Katelyn, girl, you're in trouble now!

TWO

DANIEL SWORE AND SLUNG the sack into the bed of the pickup truck. For the second time in as many days he'd managed to act like a teenage boy in first lust in front of the prettiest girl he'd ever seen.

Dwight Emerson strode up beside him just as he reached for the door to the cab. "Mmm . . . mmm! Now, if that ain't the way to start off a morning. That there's one pretty filly."

Knowing Dwight had just gotten an eyeful of the woman he'd already decided would be his own, Daniel chose to ignore his friend. It was that or plant his fist in Dwight's grinning face. And he certainly didn't feel like discussing the sexy woman and her sweet assets with anyone. Especially a yahoo like the sheriff.

Daniel just wanted to get away and let the tension dissipate that had gripped his body the moment he'd laid his eyes on her wearing less than his heart could take—and a whole lot more than she'd worn last night when she'd stripped in the darkness. A deep shame still burned through him for his actions of the previous night.

He'd spied on her like a horny twelve-year-old boy.

"Yup, my eyes just about fell outta my head when I spotted Miz Carter standin' in the middle of her bed, all pink 'n' pretty. Didn't know sweat could look so hot." Dwight shook his head mournfully. "Too bad I'm a married man."

"Bet Maria wouldn't be too happy hearing you talk like that," Daniel said, sending him a warning glance. He glanced away and asked the question that was burning a hole in his gut. "What's her first name?"

"You talkin' about Katelyn Carter?" Dwight's eyebrows rose. "Now, she's a little long in the tooth, but it don't look like you even noticed that fact," he said, a wicked twinkle in his eyes.

Oh, Daniel had noticed all right—but he couldn't change the day she was born. Daniel resisted adjusting the crotch of his jeans and narrowed his eyes at his erstwhile buddy. Try as he might, he couldn't push from his mind the memory of her moist, sleep-tousled blonde hair and wide blue eyes. His body was as taut as a barbed wire fence and his groin ached. If she'd looked down the front of his body even once, he'd have frightened the tart-tongued woman even more than the snake.

Wanting to change the subject, Daniel asked, "How do you suppose that rattler got into her house?"

"Cain't be sure, but Miz Carter left her back door open all night. She don't have no screen door on it. That snake was probably just lookin' for a warm spot to spend the night. Cain't think of anyplace warmer, kin you?"

Daniel ignored his teasing and paused for a moment, his hand on the door as he digested that bit of information.

"So, you decided to stay in town for yer vacation?" Dwight's question intruded on his thoughts.

Daniel's gaze drifted back to Katelyn Carter's front door. "Yeah, I've got a lot to do around the place. I'm gonna catch up on chores," he lied. He wrenched open the door of the cab and climbed inside.

"Well, enjoy yerself, and stay away from the station. I want you rested—I'll need you this weekend." Dwight winked slyly at him and cocked his head toward the house. "Maybe you should check on her later. Make sure your new neighbor's doin' all right after her excitement this morning."

Daniel didn't respond as he inserted his key into the ignition. He was way ahead of Dwight.

"You know," Dwight continued, "she could probably use some help unloadin' the rest of the stuff she's got in that trailer. And Daniel . . . I didn't notice no ring on her finger." He winked again and grinned, then touched the brim of his white sheriff's hat before sauntering back toward the house.

Daniel cursed the fact that his interest in the woman was so apparent. He'd have liked to keep it to himself awhile—savor the heady emotions running riot inside him in private. Thank God he had a few days off. He needed time off to get himself under control. By the time he went back, he wanted the heat banked that burned through his body at just the thought of *Katelyn*.

Such a pretty damn name.

The long list of chores he'd hoped to accomplish during his vacation would just have to wait. They weren't nearly as urgent as his need to be around the woman. But first, he had to make a run to the hardware store.

Not that it was gonna be easy convincing her she needed his help.

Last night during the long walk home, he'd thought long and hard about how to get beyond the bone-deep wariness that made her expression defensive and almost brittle. He'd decided not to rush her, to take her slowly—one step at a time.

First he'd gain her trust, then he'd gentle her with his voice and hands. Kind of like breaking a nervous filly to bridle.

Last night he'd grinned at the thought. Today, he wasn't so certain she could be brought around to trust him. Someone had hurt her, made her skittish around men. The man who'd had her before was a damn fool.

Her body was tanned and toned like a model's, and she carried herself like a queen—even when she stood in the middle of her bed in her underwear. She had class stamped all over her face and body.

What the hell did he have to offer a woman like that?

AROUND NOON, Katelyn was busy putting away the last of her dishes into the cupboard when the dull thud of a vehicle door slamming shut echoed through the house. Sighing, she made her way around unpacked boxes to the front door to see who her visitor was just as Daniel Bodine stepped onto the porch.

Desire flushed her skin, unwanted and perverse in its choice of obsessions—which Daniel was quickly becoming. Inside, her body softened and moistened. Outwardly, she lifted her chin and waited.

He pulled off his cowboy hat, revealing chestnut brown hair cut short, but not short enough to hide a tendency to curl.

Her fingers itched to sift through his rich, curling pelt.

Daniel cleared his throat. "Howdy, ma'am."

Katelyn waited behind the screen of her front door, glad for the barrier between them. He was a sight to behold—muscles stretching the shoulders and arms of his pale T-shirt. Her heart pounded just looking into the green gaze that watched her steadily. Pleasure washed over despite her intentions, causing a tingling sensation in places she'd thought numb from years of neglect.

His face wasn't pretty-boy handsome. Instead, it was almost harshly defined and very masculine. Something about the way he stood so still and kept his unwavering gaze on her face told her he was an honest man—but he was still too good-looking for her peace of mind.

"What can I do for you, Mr. Bodine?" she finally managed to blurt out.

The corners of his mouth lifted just a fraction—just enough to warn her he knew she'd been checking him out. "I couldn't help noting earlier," he said, his voice dropping lower, "you don't have a screen on your back door. It isn't safe to keep it propped open like you did last night."

She frowned, not sure where the conversation was leading and not liking what his rumbling voice was doing to her body. She squeezed her thighs together to stop the instinctive yielding. "I kept it open because it was hot as a furnace in the house, but a repairman is coming out tomorrow. I won't have that problem again."

His gaze dropped and he cleared his throat again, twisting his hat in his hands.

She wondered cynically if this feigned shyness was an act he used to convince women to trust him.

When he raised his gaze to hers again, his expression was clear of any humor—and seared her with its intensity. "Ma'am, I know this house has a lot of problems. The previous owners were friends of mine. I take on jobs as a handyman from time to time, and I'd be glad for the work. I'd like to help you get this place to shine again."

Katelyn's breath caught. *How does he do that?* When he looked at her like that—like she was the prettiest woman he'd ever seen—she felt herself melting like a Popsicle in the sun. It was likely a practiced technique, but she was falling for it. Falling into those moss green eyes.

"Ma'am, what do you think?"

Me, think? This tower of a man—any woman's wet dream—could sap her resistance with just a look and that smoky, deep voice.

Katelyn sighed. The little sound that escaped broke the trance that had her leaning toward the screen door. She lifted a hand to her mussed hair, buying some time to get her reactions under control. But touching her hair was enough to remind her, she was a mess and he was probably only staring at a smudge on her face.

Her prejudice against handsome men might be coloring her impression of him. His eyes looked at her steadily without a hint of sexual innuendo. Her gaze turned to the ancient pickup parked in her driveway and she guessed he might need the money every bit as much as she needed help.

If she were truthful to herself, she'd admit the thought of having him underfoot made her feel more alive than she had in years.

Taking a deep breath and hoping she wasn't making a big mistake, she replied, "Mr. Bodine, it's not that I can't do this all by myself—and that would be my preference—but I want things in their proper place by Monday. That door's just one more thing I won't have to do."

"I understand, Miz Carter. You don't really need me."

She gave him a sharp nod. "That's right. If I'm satisfied with your work, we'll talk later about what else you might do for me." She blushed when she realized how that last statement might be interpreted, but a quick glance at his face eased her mind that he hadn't read anything into it.

He still wore the same steady expression. "I'll get started on it right away." He replaced his hat on his head and turned away.

Phew. She released the breath she'd been holding, and then her brain unclenched as she had another thought. "Wait!" she called out to him.

He hesitated on the porch step, and then turned. "Yes, ma'am?"

"I can't afford too much just yet. I start my new job on Thursday."

He appeared to relax.

He must have thought I changed my mind, Katelyn thought.

"That's okay," he said, nodding solemnly. "You can pay as you go. I also know which hardware stores have the best prices—and I get a discount." He smiled and continued to his truck.

That little smile nearly blew her away. A hint of a dimple in his left cheek had her thinking she was in trouble for sure. For a moment she melted, her toes curling against the hardwood floor.

Then she remembered the path those kinds of thoughts

could lead, and she stiffened her spine. Glad she'd let him know up front where she stood, she turned from the sight of his strong shoulders and tightly muscled backside as he hefted a large toolbox from the bed of his truck and slammed the front door shut.

DANIEL STUBBED HIS TOE AGAINST the top step of the back porch and cursed under his breath as he set down his toolbox. Deciding he'd better remove the solid door to get it out of the way while he worked, he reached for a hammer to tap the pins from the hinges. As he worked, he let his mind stray back to his beautiful employer.

Katelyn Carter had thrown him for a loop—again. No woman had a right to look that good with dirt smudging her cheeks and sweat dampening her hair. Looking into those baby blue eyes brimming with suspicion, he'd almost talked himself into believing that showing up on her doorstep so soon was a very bad idea. And letting her think he was a handyman didn't sit right.

Uncomfortable with subterfuge, he still couldn't think of a better way to spend time with the lady. He needed to get his foot in the door before the rest of the unattached males in Tierney, Texas discovered this exotic flower of womanhood. He knew he didn't possess a glib tongue or a pretty face, but usually he was satisfied with what he did have. This morning, however, Katelyn made him wish he was so much more.

Daniel sensed if she knew what kind of hammering and painting he really had on his mind, she'd probably run screaming. As he tapped at the pins, he imagined himself alone with her in the moonlight. He'd start with stripping that tiny excuse for a T-shirt from her body and lick the sweat from between her plump breasts—

"Mr. Bodine?"

Her voice startled him, causing him to jerk, and he nearly mashed his thumb with the hammer. "Yes, ma'am?"

She stood beside him, so close his ears began to burn. That T-shirt clung to her skin like he'd imagined doing. She licked her lips nervously, drawing his gaze upward to follow the pink tongue as it flicked once around her lips.

Daniel lost track of the conversation.

"Mr. Bodine?"

He blushed when he realized he hadn't heard a word she'd just said. "Pardon me, ma'am?"

"Um . . . " She blinked and her glance fell to his lips.

Was she thinking about kissing him too? He pushed back his cowboy hat and leaned toward her. "Ma'am?"

She shoved a glass into his hand and slipped back inside the house before he had a chance to say thanks. Grinning, he was heartened to realize she was just as disturbed by his presence as he was by hers. He chugged down the sweet tea and reached into the kitchen to set the glass back on the counter.

Slipping the hammer out of his belt loop once more, he tapped at the bottom of each hinge to unseat the pins and freed the door from its frame.

When he looked around, she was standing next to him again, a frown creasing the soft skin between her eyes. "I'm sorry. I forgot what I came to ask you in the first place." She blushed and twirled a curl of her blonde hair around her finger. *Definitely disturbed.*

"Shoot," he said, leaning the door against the side of the house.

"I was wondering if you'd help me bring in some of the heavier items from the U-Haul trailer."

"No problem." He wiped his hands on his jeans and walked toward her.

She backed away hastily. "Oh, I didn't mean right this minute."

"No time like now."

They met at the door that separated kitchen from living room, and she stood sideways to let him pass. He inhaled her scent, a heady mixture of lemon furniture polish and her, and tried not to notice when their chests met. The startled awareness that bloomed red in her cheeks had him hardening in an instant. Walking through the house, he was conscious of her shadowing his every step.

He stepped out onto the front porch, noting that she'd moved the trailer in front of the porch steps. "You'll have to tell me where you want me to put everything."

"Oh no, I didn't mean for you to unpack it all by yourself." She moved to unlock the trailer, but when she reached inside to grab the first box, he gently placed his hands on her waist, eliciting a gasp from her. Picking her up, he deposited her back on the porch.

His hands burning from that quick contact, Daniel hefted the box high. Her waist had felt taut, the muscles strong. "I'll let you know when I need your help," he said, his voice gruff. "You just point me in the right direction."

A frown knitted her eyebrows, and her chin rose. "They're all marked. That one says bedroom, so take it on back to my room. You know where it is."

He gave her a sideways glance, careful not to let his face show his amusement at her irritation from his taking charge. "Yep, I'm not likely to ever forget that."

Her face flamed red, and she stammered, "Well . . . well, I'll just leave you to it, then," before she escaped.

Chuckling, he continued on to her bedroom. Katelyn Carter was mighty cute when she blushed. Fact was, there wasn't much about her that he didn't find attractive. She was just the right size—she could rest her cheek right over his heart. She wasn't too fat or too thin—just soft and sexy. Daniel had every intention of finding out just how soft and cushiony those womanly curves, above and below, would feel pressed to his body.

He knew instinctively the real pleasure would be getting to know the parts of Katelyn not visible to the eye.

Whistling to himself, he returned to the trailer again and again. Never a man to question the vagaries of fate, Daniel knew his life had forever changed the first moment he saw her. Tierney was a small town, and he knew most of the unattached women in a hundred-mile radius. None had ever made his heart skip a beat, or tempted him to wrap her in cotton wool and take every care off her slim but capable shoulders. There was something fragile and wounded in her expression that was at odds with the defiant tilt of her chin.

He wondered if she'd realized just how transparent her attire had been that morning . . .

Katelyn tried to ignore Daniel's presence in her kitchen as she continued to labor, unpacking boxes throughout the afternoon. It was getting late when she heard the creak of the floorboards behind her.

He once again had his hat in his hands. "Ma'am, I'm finished. I'd like you to take a look at that door."

She followed him back to the kitchen. The new door was in place, and he had painted the casing surrounding it to match the rest of the frame. He opened it and allowed the door to close again.

"It looks fine," she said quickly, wanting to put more space between them. Standing so close with darkness encroaching around them created an intimacy that undermined her discipline. "How much do I owe you?"

"How about you just run a tab?"

Katelyn nodded, at a loss for anything else to say. He was doing it again—staring at her with that look that made her tremble inside. She touched her hair. "I know I must look a mess," she said, and bit her lip. *God, did I sound like I was begging for a compliment?*

He raised his hand toward her face, slowly, as though letting her get used to the idea before his touch settled on her skin. His thumb smoothed over her chin, rubbing. "You've got a smudge here," he said, his voice a low, sexy rumble that produced a prickling deep inside her pussy.

Her mouth parted around a tiny moan and his thumb slid over her lower lip. Before she had a chance to think better of the idea, her tongue slipped out and lapped the callused pad, tasting salt, feeling the roughness that made her nipples tingle.

Daniel's chest rose and his jaw tightened. His thumb pressed inside her mouth and she sucked it. With a sharply drawn breath, he bored his gaze into hers. "Tell me you don't want me to kiss you, Katelyn."

He'd said the words—torn away the flimsy barrier between unspoken yearning and surrender. She shook her head. "I . . . can't."

His hands cupped her face, gentle and reverent, as he leaned closer. His breath was sweet and brushed her lips first, prompting her to open her mouth. When his lips slid over hers, he murmured and closed his eyes.

Now, Katelyn had shared many kisses in her life. But Daniel's tasted sweeter, made her feel cherished, even beautiful. His fingers threaded through her hair and he pulled her head closer for a deeper joining.

She stood still, letting the sensation of his mouth, pressing and molding hers, draw heat like a small, smoldering ember into a flame that licked over the places he hadn't yet touched—her breasts, her pussy . . . her heart.

He raised his head, dragging in a deep breath. "I should go."

"Yes, you should," she whispered, staring into his heated gaze. Katelyn stood at a crossroads, her destination hers alone to choose. Her body yearned for more of his soft caresses, but she wasn't sure she was strong enough not to want more.

Contrary to what her mind was thinking, she lifted her hand and placed it on his chest, molding her palm to fit the curve of hard muscle that flexed as she caressed.

His body went rigid beneath her touch. "Be sure," he rasped, his chest rising and falling faster.

Be sure? Kate wasn't sure of anything except she needed to be touched, filled—by Daniel. Katelyn stepped closer, aligning herself, chest to hip, with his body. In an instant, stinging delight drew her nipples into tighter, distended points. She swallowed and lifted her gaze to his. "This doesn't mean a thing," she said, her voice tight. "I don't want you to tell me sweet lies and this isn't about forever."

His nostrils flared and his head dipped, his lips hovering above hers. "Katelyn, darlin', who said anything about forever? What about just having fun?"

THREE

TORN BETWEEN EXCITEMENT and a dampening, perverse disappointment, Katelyn rose on her toes to close the distance between their mouths. *This is what I want*—all *I want*.

She believed the lie when his hands closed around her hips to hold her still while he pressed the ridge growing beneath his zipper into her belly. She rose higher, straining closer to his hardness.

He broke the kiss and pushed her away, his gaze burning. "Turn around and face the wall."

Katelyn's eyes widened and her body thrilled to the curtness of his tone. She thought she'd craved a softer, more romantic joining all these years, but the electric excitement, prickling every erogenous zone she possessed, said her body was delighted at his coarse command. With deliberate, breathless slowness, she turned away.

"Put your hands against the wall." His voice was closer, stirring her hair.

Katelyn shivered and braced her hands against the wall, and then waited, her heart pounding so hard she heard her own heartbeat in her ears. The tips of her breasts pressed achingly against her bra. Moisture dampened the crotch of her panties.

She jerked when his hands gripped the notches of her hips and a leg slipped between hers. He nudged her feet, one at a time, until they were shoulder-width apart.

Her breaths were shallow, her excitement rising. Although fully clothed, every part of her was accessible, open for him to explore. *Where will he start? Should I tell him where I need his touch next?* Instead, she bit her lip.

Daniel's hands slid around her belly and slipped beneath her T-shirt. The heat from his palms and the scrape of his calluses set her stomach quivering.

"Easy, now," he whispered, his body pressing closer to her back. His fingers found the clasp of her bra and opened it. The cups parted over her breasts, and in the next breath he held both mounds, squeezing her gently.

Katelyn moaned and pressed harder into his hands, gasping when he thumbed an aching nipple. Her head fell back against his shoulder and his lips slid along her cheek to her jaw and neck as he massaged her breasts, kneading until she whimpered, weak with delight.

"Easy," he whispered. One hand slid down her belly to the top of her shorts and his fingers crept under the waistband, flattening against her stomach until he reached her curls.

His hand rubbed in drugging circles, until she thought she'd scream if he didn't reach deeper. "Please, please, touch me," she whispered.

"Yes, ma'am." The snap opened and the zipper rasped, and then his fingers slid inside her shorts to cover her sex. His fingers swirled in the wetness seeping from within her, and one long, thick finger slipped between her lips to push just an inch inside her pussy.

Katelyn's whole body trembled and her knees gave way. If not for the arm clamped around her belly, she'd have melted to the floor.

"Tell me what you want," he said, his voice harsh now.

A question she'd never been asked and hadn't the capability to answer, she was so carried away with the feelings swamping her body and mind. A strangled "Inside me" was all she could manage.

"Put your foot up on the box."

"Box?" she parroted and looked down, surprised to see the wooden case with her silverware on the floor. She lifted a foot and the distance and angle of her stance opened her further.

His fingers reached deeper into her clothing.

Katelyn sucked in a breath and her belly, dying by inches for him to touch the part of her that wept and clenched.

Fingers combed through the short curls, tugging gently, easing, then tugging harder, until her abdomen trembled again.

"Like that, do you?" he rumbled.

"Uhnnn," she moaned, and she widened her legs again, inviting him deeper between her legs.

When at last his fingertips scraped her wet outer labia, she arched, her hands leaving the wall in front to reach behind her. She needed an anchor, his body to touch. She found his shoulders and neck and draped her body across his front, her bottom rubbing his erection.

One large, rough hand squeezed her breast harder, while the

other delved deeper until he parted her and rubbed around her opening, rimming her vagina.

Katelyn's pussy tingled and quivered, and her hips moved forward and back as she silently begged him to enter her.

Then his whole hand cupped her, warming her cunt, two fingers sliding deep. Liquid gushed from inside her to coat the thick digits and seep beyond to soak his hand. "Katelyn," he said, the word sounding like he'd dragged it from deep inside his chest. "You're so damn wet. Do you know how much I want to taste you?"

Her heart pounded. Her throat closed against a sudden rush of emotion. In all the years of her marriage, her husband's voice had never held that note of anguished desire—*for her*. A sob escaped, and he murmured against her hair, the hand cuddling her breast released it, pulling out of her shirt. Gently, he turned her face upward.

Her cheeks flushed hot and her eyelids dipped. She felt drugged, surrounded, overwhelmed. Her heart beat in her ears to join the sound of her shallow breaths and the wet, succulent sounds below as he drew lush excitement from her body. Her channel convulsed as the moment built, pulsing, clenching around his fingers.

He twisted and stroked, deeper and deeper—three fingers filling her now.

Then a rising blackness overcame her. Her whole world exploded in sliding caresses and the pumping of her hips. She cried out, unable to hold the sound inside.

"That's it, baby. *God!* You're so beautiful."

When she opened her eyes, his were closed tight, his nostrils flaring. She felt the ridge of his cock grinding into her bottom, and she knew pleasuring her had caused him pain. "Daniel?"

He opened his eyes and shook his head, drawing his hand from her panties. He turned her in his arms and held her, pressing her face to his shoulder. "Give me a minute," he said, his voice gruff.

"Why?" She was ready. If he asked her to lie with him now, she would. She wanted more of his kisses. Wanted his cock to fill the empty space inside.

"Because this was for you—and I moved too damn fast."

She grew still in his arms, barely breathing. "I don't understand." Part of her was elated that a strong, younger man wanted her so badly. Another part, not so ready and just plain scared, cried inside, "No, no, no!" She didn't want him thinking this meant any more than it was—just sweaty, consensual sex.

He hugged her close one more time and then set her away, his gaze sliding from the shorts riding low on her hips. He drew in a deep breath. "I'd like to start next on the floorboards of the porch. Tomorrow," he said quickly, like he expected her to object and he wasn't going to give her the chance.

While deep inside she felt a wail of denial rising in her throat, Katelyn relaxed. He'd given them both a reprieve—and her time to think about where she was willing to let this lead, without pressure or desire clouding her mind.

He stepped toward the front door, keeping his back to her. "You have several boards loose. A few might have to be replaced." He glanced over his shoulder, a question in his gaze.

Katelyn nodded. She knew he was right—about the boards and about needing time. For such a young man, Daniel Bodine was pretty smart when it came to knowing how far he could push a woman.

She didn't think she could take having him underfoot for long without doing something that might embarrass them both. "I'm not sure when I can afford more work . . ."

"It won't cost much, and it shouldn't take me long. How about I come by tomorrow morning and get started?"

He was so insistent she thought he must really need the job—or maybe he really did want to come back just to see her. Her heart melted a little. She lifted her chin. "All right, I'll see you then."

He walked out onto the porch and quickly loaded his tools, and then headed to his truck.

She didn't relax until his long, powerful legs disappeared into the cab. He gave her a short wave, and she was startled to realize he knew she'd been watching him all along.

Katelyn uttered a curse word she'd only heard in R-rated movies, surprising herself into a giggle. "That man's a terrible influence," she murmured, pulling her shorts up. Her gaze clung to the trail of dust rising in his wake. "It's not like I want to give him the idea I'm interested in forever."

DANIEL GUNNED HIS ENGINE and let gravel spray behind him as he peeled out of her driveway. The look on her face when he'd been talking about the porch repairs had nearly done him in.

Her lips and eyes were glossy and soft from his lovemaking. Disappointment had turned down the corners of her mouth when he'd turned to leave. Just the thought that he could be sinking into her wet, tight pussy right now had him hard as a post and groaning.

She'd come apart in his arms, shivering and moaning so sweetly, he'd wanted to lay her down on the gleaming wood floors and stretch his body over hers to absorb her ecstasy. He'd never felt more a man than with her sweet cunt squeezing around his fingers and her hips jerking at every rasp of his thumb across her swollen little clit.

He brought his fingers to his mouth and inhaled the scent of her as he licked the salty-sweet flavor of her desire. Katelyn Carter could say this wasn't about forever a hundred times, but her body sang a different tune entirely.

KATELYN FELT AS IF SHE'D BARELY had time to blink and the morning arrived, and she couldn't help the excitement thrumming through her body. She was up before the sun and had a large pot of coffee brewing when she heard Daniel's pickup truck pull up to the house.

"Mornin', ma'am," he called out as his booted heels climbed the porch steps.

Katelyn found herself smiling and realized she was truly happy to see him. She opened the front screen door and called back, "I have coffee made, would you like a cup?"

His slow smile melted the hard knot of anticipation that had rested in her belly as she'd waited for his arrival.

"I could use a jolt of caffeine to get me started today," he said, his rich molasses voice wrapping her like a warm blanket. "Sure I'm not too early?"

"Not at all. I was anxious to get started myself." She drew in a sharp breath and blushed. *God, is every word out of my mouth going to sound like an innuendo?* She rushed on, "The AC's working now, so I'd like to be done with the outside work before the worst heat of the day hits." She opened the screen door to allow him to pass. She didn't realize she hadn't left much room for him to enter until his chest rubbed against hers. "Coffee's in the kitchen," she said to him, suddenly breathless. To herself she thought, *He's going to think I did that on purpose!*

He didn't appear to notice the intimate contact as he preceded her into the kitchen, and Katelyn wondered what law of physics applied when the cozy room suddenly seemed to grow smaller as his tall, broad frame strolled inside. She hadn't forgotten how handsome he was, but she had thought time and the stern talks she'd had with herself the past couple of days would dull the sharp edge of her interest.

She pulled her gaze away and sighed. Even from the back, or maybe especially from that perspective, she was achingly aware of every masculine muscle stretching his T-shirt and of the round, taut buttocks his jeans revealed. It just wasn't fair. Coming or going he was too delicious to ignore.

He cleared his throat, and she blushed again because she realized he'd tried to draw her attention to something he said.

"I beg your pardon?"

He glanced over his shoulder, the corners of his lips curving in a slight smile. "Cups?" he repeated.

"Oh yeah." She walked to the cupboard, took down two and

handed them to him. He poured coffee and she busied herself looking for sugar, creamer and spoons. She needn't have bothered. It turned out they both liked theirs black.

They stood awkwardly, leaning against the counters, sipping from their cups. She looked anywhere but at him, certain she'd betray her thoughts if their gazes connected. Memories of how he'd held her while she orgasmed simmered at the surface of her thoughts. Never had she been so at a loss for words. She was aware of every move he made, of the smell of his aftershave and the way he too avoided looking directly at her.

Perhaps he regretted their intimacy.

Her stomach sinking, she realized she'd been hoping for more all along—more of his kisses, more of the sexy rumble of his voice as he'd coaxed her into opening to him. She wanted to know the sensation of his mouth on her breasts and his cock thrusting inside her.

She'd dressed especially for him this morning. The soft pink T-shirt a deliberately feminine choice. Tucked into the waist of an ancient pair of faded blue jeans, the T-shirt clung to the curves of her breasts.

When she'd dressed that morning, she'd called herself every kind of fool, worrying about what she wore and wondering if he'd approve of what he saw. She'd been too bold, dispensing with her bra for the day.

Earlier, she'd reasoned the heat would make wearing one unbearable. A glance in the mirror that morning had assured her the T-shirt didn't fit *too* snugly.

Unfortunately, she hadn't taken into consideration her reaction to this man. While she held her breath, trying to think of a way to break the uncomfortable silence, her nipples drew tight, the points visible beneath the fabric. Embarrassed, she hunched her shoulders and plucked at the fabric to ease the fit. Glancing up, she caught him before he could avert his gaze from her chest.

Fascinated by his reaction, she watched him cross and uncross his legs, and then take a long swallow of his coffee. His eyes teared up, and she guessed he'd burned his tongue.

She pressed her lips together to suppress a feline smile of triumph. He'd noticed the tips straining against her T-shirt and his gaze had clung—and he was bothered.

The blush on his cheeks as he grimaced through another sip of the scalding coffee somehow reassured her. His reticence pleased her.

He set down his cup on the counter. "I better get started outside, ma'am."

"*Mr. Bodine?*" she said, keeping her voice soft.

"Yes, ma'am?"

She raised her gaze to his. "Don't you think it's a little silly for us to be so formal? Please call me Katelyn."

He released a long breath and nodded solemnly. "And I'd be pleased if you'd call me Daniel." Without waiting for a response, he went out the back door.

His haste to get away had her grinning.

Katelyn went to work as well. The previous two days she'd managed to unpack the boxes, but there was still a lot of cleaning to do. The windows alone would likely take the whole weekend. They were so covered with dirt and grime and many wouldn't open.

Gathering her cleaning supplies, she headed outside to begin her self-assigned task. She didn't question why she needed to start on the exterior of the windows. She was resigned to the fact that she needed to be near her handsome handyman.

All morning long, she savored her awareness of his presence as they both labored. Midday, she saw him pause to wipe a hand across his forehead. His damp shirt stuck to his broad back. She put down her scrub brush and realized she was just as soaked with sweat. She went into the house, enjoying the blast of cool air, and hastily poured two tall glasses of iced tea.

Carrying one in each hand, she went out to the porch. "Daniel, would you like a glass of tea?" She held out a glass to him and he stood to accept it. Once again, she was intensely aware of the height and breadth of the man. Her breath caught.

"Thanks, I could use a break. The heat's a killer today."

She murmured her agreement and tilted back her head for a long sip. When she opened her eyes, he was watching her. His gaze slid away, but not before she noted the tightening of his jaw.

"It's very warm," she drawled.

He finished his drink and set the glass down, his eyes narrowing on her.

"Would you like another?" she asked.

His gaze swept down her body and he swallowed. "Not right now," he said, his voice gruff, "but thanks." He picked up his hammer and a couple of nails and went back to work.

A spring in her step, she went back to her chores as well.

CHIPPING AWAY AT PAINT THAT GLUED one window to its casing, her gaze returned to the porch for the hundredth time that day.

Only now, Daniel was drawing his shirt over his head, baring his broad back and tapered waist. His skin was tanned, and the ridged muscles rippled as he shouldered several long planks.

Her mouth grew dry, and her belly tightened. God, how she wanted him! If the sideways glances he'd given her throughout the morning were any indication, he felt the same way. Their sly appraisals of each other felt like foreplay, building a slow heat that threatened to flicker into flame with the slightest encouragement.

Realizing the direction of her thoughts, she berated herself. She should be ashamed. She was in full-blown lust over a man she didn't even know. The last thing she needed was another man in her life, especially when she hadn't completely shed herself of the last one. She was a fool to stand here drooling over a cowboy.

Placing the tip of the screwdriver into the corner where the window met the casing, she pounded the end with a hammer, working her way along the corner to free the window. She continued to pound away her frustration, until she felt a hand at her shoulder. Startled, she whipped around. Daniel stood behind her.

"Let me see if I can get that open for you."

She moved away and he grabbed the window to push it up. His jaw tightened and his forearms bulged. With a crack, the paint gave and he shoved it upward.

Grinning, he looked back at her. She knew she must have looked like a deer in the headlights, but she couldn't seem to take her eyes off the broad, bare chest that stretched endlessly in front of her eyes.

"Need help with anything else?" he drawled.

The gravelly texture of his voice drew her attention upward. Her heart pounded as she read the intent in is expression and his face drew near hers.

The kiss was light. His lips rubbed softly against hers, never opening. It wasn't a carnal kiss. It was sweetly innocent and exploring. Her hands rose to rest against his damp chest and she felt a ripple of response as the muscles tightened and flexed beneath her caress.

She rose onto her tiptoes to deepen the kiss, but his head lifted. The look he gave her held a solemn promise. She didn't know how to interpret it, and was more confused than ever when he released her and went back to the porch to pry another board loose.

Why had he stopped? Her husband had never kissed her with just his lips, and his kisses always led to sex. Was she confused because she didn't understand Daniel's intent or because she wanted more? *The last thing I should need is another man in my life, especially one who could have any woman he wants.*

At midday she stopped to make sandwiches for them both and delivered the meal on a tray with drinks. She sat opposite him on the porch steps and barely glanced his way while they ate. The strain of the hard physical work, as well as her efforts to ignore her clamoring hormones, had finally left her tired enough to relax next to him and just enjoy the sight of his naked, glistening chest.

He cleared his throat, drawing her gaze upward. "There's a dance Saturday night." He looked away and shrugged. "It's an annual thing to raise money for the volunteer fire department. I'd like to take you."

Startled, she didn't reply immediately.

She guessed he thought she was trying to find some way to turn him down gently, because he said next, "I know I'm doin' things a little backwards, and I 'm sorry I've made you uncomfortable. If I promise to keep my hands to myself, will you let me take you?"

She studied his face. He was handsome, yes. But his gaze met hers directly. He didn't push. He didn't try to seduce her with honeyed words. She realized he was nothing like her husband. And she liked that little bit of uncertainty he betrayed. She wanted to say yes, and see whether this gentle man was everything he seemed.

But would it be fair to Daniel? She should say no for more reasons than the obvious one. *I should tell him now*. But she demurred, not wanting to mention a name that would only make another's presence tangible—her husband wasn't a part of her life now. She wouldn't let him be, ever again.

"Can't we just go on the way we are?" she asked, feeling like a coward.

"And what way is that, Katelyn?" he asked softly.

"Just us." Her hand settled on his arm and glided to his shoulder. "Just this."

His jaw tightened and he ducked his head. "You mean," he said, his voice just as soft, but with a bite that raised the hairs on her arm, "I'm good enough to fuck, but not be seen with you in public?"

Shocked by the blunt words spoken so quietly, she shook her

head and blurted, "We haven't fucked yet." *Jesus, I just said that!* She bolted to her feet.

His hand wrapped around her ankle, holding her in place. His expression was set, his eyes narrowing. "That's right. We haven't." His hand slid up the inside of her leg. "Why wait? It's what we both want."

FOUR

INSIDE, KATELYN SCREAMED, *That's not what I meant!* But she didn't draw away when his fingers slipped beneath the edge of her cutoffs and stroked her pussy through her panties. Her mouth opened around a gasp as molten desire seeped to dampen the silky fabric.

"Want it here? In the sunlight?" he asked, rising to his knees on the top step. His fingers pushed aside the crotch of her underwear and traced the furrow between her labia.

Moisture pooled in her eyes and between her legs. She didn't want his anger, didn't want anything to mar the beauty of the feelings growing secretly inside her. Didn't he understand she was doing this for him? "I'm too old for you, Daniel," she said, surprised by the quaver and the breathless quality of her own voice.

He leaned forward and hooked one hand around the back of her thigh to pull her hips closer, and glided his lips up the tender inside of her legs. "Looks like you're old enough," he murmured and sank a finger inside her cunt.

Her legs trembled, and she gripped his shoulders. "What will people think? I'm old enough to be your m—"

"Aunt?" He gently bit her skin. "Don't stretch the truth."

Her hands gripped his hair to bring him closer to the ache. "For God's sake, I'm forty-one years old, Daniel."

He paused and his gaze seared hers. "I don't give a fuck, Katelyn. I'm not exactly a boy." Then he snaked his tongue beneath her shorts to lick at her sex.

Katelyn moaned and widened her legs. "This is wrong. You know it," she said, swaying on her feet at the lazy strokes he plied her with. "I'm not what you need."

He lapped her, the broad surface of his tongue skimming her lips, the tip insinuating between to tease her with glancing caresses that drove her crazy and had her squirming against him.

When he dragged himself away, his breaths were ragged. "You are everything I want," he said, his voice fierce. His expression was set, his gaze unwavering.

She believed him. He meant it—*now*.

His hands gripped her upper thighs, his thumbs stroking beneath her clothing. He leaned into her crotch and mouthed her through the fabric, his steamy breath penetrating to heat her already molten core. "*Jesus, Katelyn.*" He groaned and pressed his face to her belly. "Take your pants off 'cause I'm gonna eat you right here."

The hoarseness of his command and the hard grip of his hand thrilled her like nothing she'd ever experienced in her life. She stared at him, knowing that once again the pause was for her sake. He'd given her control.

She could deny him now—end this before she sank any deeper toward a love that might leave scars on both their hearts. Or she could take a chance.

Katelyn drew in a deep breath and looked out over her dusty, rugged front yard. She saw beyond the scrubby live oaks standing still as she was in a breezeless, sun-scorched day, to the sky as blue and wide open as her possibilities, and reached for the button at the top of her cutoffs.

Daniel held his breath while Katelyn fought an internal battle that had her lips alternately tightening and trembling. Her gaze was on the horizon and he wished like hell she'd just look at him—*see him* and everything he could be for her—if only she'd trust him just a little.

When she reached for the top of her shorts, his body grew still. A blush stained her cheeks and neck, and her lips firmed with a determination that filled him with pride. She was so damn beautiful and brave, it hurt his heart to watch.

Daniel didn't know how he knew, but his gut told him this was new for Katelyn. Standing in the sunshine with a man at her feet, baring herself slowly to the light and his gaze—he'd seen her hesitation, the flare of panic widening her eyes when he'd issued the command.

He'd heard her shocked gasp when he'd licked the feminine folds between her legs—and *knew* she'd never been pleasured like that before. Forty-one years old and never loved by man—not like he was gonna love her now.

Her shorts slithered to the floor and she hesitated, her fingers at the top of her panties. Her gaze met his, worry and modesty creasing her brow.

"Don't stop now, Katelyn," he urged her gently.

"Must it be here?" she asked, her voice thin and a little high.

His body urged him to say no—he'd take her on her bed, the

floor, the cab of his pickup truck—just so he could taste her, fill her. But instinct told him he needed her broken down a bit, gentled to his command—if he was going to make her his forever. "Take 'em off now."

She swallowed hard and her gaze dropped, but she slid the panties down her long, slender thighs. When she stepped away from them, her hands fluttered by her sides, like she wanted to cover herself. He wasn't about to let her hide from his gaze.

He lifted his hand to the sparse dark blonde hair that covered her sex. She held herself still, her chest rising and falling with her shallow breaths. He combed his fingers through her curls, all the while watching her face. "That pretty pink T-shirt too, sweetheart."

Her eyebrows drew together in a look of pure irritation, but she yanked the T-shirt up.

Then, without waiting for her to finish, he gripped her buttocks and pulled her close.

She yelped and the T-shirt slapped his back, but he was already tongue-deep inside her, his thumbs spreading her lips wide while he swirled as deep as he could reach.

Her fingers clutched his hair hard and her whole body quivered like a nervous filly. She didn't move, didn't breathe, just clutched him close and seeped sweet honey onto his tongue.

He licked higher and rubbed the flat of his tongue on the hood covering the hard kernel of her clit.

Katelyn moaned, a thin sound that gusted with her gasps as he sucked and swirled.

She was close, her cunt tightening and relaxing, pulsing faster and faster. With his thumb and forefinger he lifted the hood, exposing the bright pink knot, and closed his lips around it, sucking hard.

Katelyn cried out and her knees buckled. He held her tight and pressed his face against her belly. "Easy, now."

A soft sob racked her body. "Please, Daniel—I can't stand it."

"Lie down here," he said, and helped her lie on the edge of the porch while he scooted down the steps. He placed her legs on his bare shoulders and stroked her glistening flesh, parting her to take a good look. "You've got the prettiest pussy I've ever seen."

"Don't talk—I might change my mind," she said, moaning the last words as he opened her wide with his fingers and lapped her with his tongue.

"First time a woman's ever asked me not to talk," he murmured. He decided to give her pretty pussy something to swallow and slipped two fingers inside.

Katelyn's hips rose off the porch. "I didn't think men had cunnilingus in their vocabulary," she said gasping.

"It sure ain't in mine either, but it's not gonna stop me from eating you out." He licked the pink petals of her tender inner lips, taking the cream her body offered while his fingers fucked in and out of her tight, hot cunt.

"I can't believe I'm doing this," she said, her hands reaching to grip his hair.

He gave her a quick, wicked glance. "Beg to differ. You're not the one doing."

Her face was red, her mouth open and gasping. "But out here? In the open? Anyone could pull into the drive—the postman, a neighbor—"

He slid a third finger inside her pussy and circled his thumb around the tight little hole below.

Her back arched off the porch, giving him an interesting view of the underside of her creamy breasts. "Don't!"

"Don't what?" he teased, pressing harder on her asshole.

"*That!* Damn you!" She settled down again and glared down at him.

More liquid seeped around his hand and he groaned, knowing how she'd feel clasping his cock. "You like it," he said, and bit her inner thigh.

Her thighs moved restlessly on his shoulders. "Daniel?"

"I know. You're comin'. Close your eyes."

Katelyn's teeth clasped her lower lip and she shook her head.

"Trust me, baby," he said, crooning now. "Close your eyes."

She drew a deep breath and turned her head away, her hands letting go of his hair and reaching out beside her, flattening on the plank flooring.

Her trust was a fragile thing and he vowed not to disappoint her.

With her thighs clasping his neck, Daniel leaned closer and planted hot, sliding kisses on her pussy while his fingers ground inside her, twisting deeper.

Whimpers broke from her throat as he worked his hand in and out. His thumb resuming its pressure lower, working the cream dripping from her cunt into the tight orifice until it relaxed enough to slip the thick tip inside.

She groaned and her hips undulated, countering his rhythm to draw him deeper still.

Daniel fluttered his tongue on her clit, stroking harder as her cries grew louder, and when her voice broke, he drew hard on it with his lips until she came, shuddering and spasming around his fingers. He didn't relent until her legs eased their hold and her body grew slack beneath him.

Although it damn near killed him, he gently pulled away and gathered her into his arms until she straddled his thighs, her head tucked against his shoulder. "You'll go with me Saturday night," he said, kissing her shoulder. With his hand fisting in her hair, he tilted back her head. "And there won't be any more talk about what's right or wrong with us."

Her eyelids lifted and her clear blue gaze met his. "I s'pose if I tried to disagree, you'd just add another word to your vocabulary, wouldn't you?" she said, the corners of her lips lifting in a weak smile.

He smoothed a finger over her lower lip and smiled down at her. "Do you think I have that much to learn?"

The smile disappeared and she leaned in to slide her lips over his, giving him a searing kiss. When she drew back, she said, "I think there are some definite holes in *my* education." She looked down to where her hands smoothed over his chest. "But there's something in particular I want to learn."

"Tell me what it is. I'll add it to the curriculum."

Her mouth curved and her gaze rose to his. "I want to know what it feels like to be filled with you, Daniel."

He blew out a deep breath and tried to ignore the insistent ache beneath her bottom, sure his balls were blue at this point. "I'd like nothing better, sweetheart."

Her head came up. "But?"

"After the party."

A frown creased her brow. "You think you have to bribe me to go?" Her gaze narrowed and she ground her pussy against his erection.

"I think," he said, gritting his teeth, "that you're trying to distract me—but I'm going to get my way."

"Because I'm dying for you to fuck me?"

He gave her a slanted glance. "Aren't you?" His hands clasped her bottom and he butted up against her naked cunt.

Her eyes closed and her mouth opened around a moan. As he rubbed into her open, juicy cunt, she gripped his shoulders tight. "But . . . ah . . . what about you? Don't I get a chance to please you too?"

He inserted a hand between their bodies and palmed a plump breast. "You do. Christ, I need this in my mouth."

She rose and pressed her nipple against his lips, a little smile curving hers. "Seems kinda one-sided."

"I'll get to the other," he murmured, and then opened his mouth wide to take in as much of her tit as he could.

She laughed and clasped his head to her breast. "That's not what I meant." Her inner knees hugged either side his thighs and squeezed. "One thing I do know how to do is give a blow job," she whispered.

Daniel groaned and gently bit the velvet-soft tip scraping his tongue. "Saturday night."

SATURDAY MORNING, DANIEL ENTERED the white sandstone building that had housed the county library for as long as he could remember. His nose wrinkled at the smell of books, a smell he hadn't encountered since his last year of high school.

It wasn't that he was averse to books, or to reading, he'd simply been too busy—at first with the police academy, and then on the job at the Wendall County sheriff's office.

Then he'd purchased the property which adjoined Katelyn's about three years ago when it came on the market for a good price—it being in nearly the same sad shape as Katelyn's house was now. From then on all his spare time had been spent renovating the thirty-year-old house that sat on twenty acres of land. He'd cleaned, repaired and painted in hopes of preparing it for a family, but the right woman had never come along. He thought now, just maybe, Katelyn Carter was what he'd been waiting for.

Daniel stuck a finger in the buttoned collar of his uniform shirt to loosen it enough to breathe comfortably. He was nervous and feeling more than a little foolish, paying a call on Katelyn at her job. He'd congratulated himself on refraining from checking in on her for three whole days. There was no sense in scaring the woman by rushing her off her feet. He knew he'd almost blown it when he'd turned down her generous offer. But sex wasn't the only thing he wanted from her, and he knew she might get cold feet if she got everything she yearned for too fast and easy.

Katelyn needed to want.

She needed to yearn for his touch the same way he was dying to hear three little words from her—with an ache that wouldn't relent.

Today, he just wanted to see her. Even if it was only to let her level a distrustful gaze on him. She thought he was a handyman—something he'd encouraged her to believe—

because he'd wanted the chance to get to know her. That their physical relationship had progressed so far, so quickly, only added to his unease. He hoped she wouldn't be too disappointed or angry at his little deception. But the time for the truth was now.

"Why, Daniel Bodine, if this isn't a surprise. Now I know you're not here to check out a book, so what can I do for you?" The dry raspy voice of Mabel Comstock harkened back to high school and he broke out in a sweat. Just a glance from the little white-haired woman from over the top of her glasses had always been enough to make him squirm.

Remembering his manners, he doffed his cowboy hat. "Howdy, Miz Comstock. It's good to see you."

"Hrmph." Her mouth pursed, and her eyes narrowed, "I know this isn't a social call . . . " One gray brow quirked upward. "Or maybe not for me. You wouldn't be here to visit the newest member of my staff now, would you?"

He felt the heat creep across his cheeks and cursed his lack of composure. You'd think a twenty-nine-year-old man, and a deputy sheriff to boot, wouldn't be intimidated by a tiny curmudgeon of a woman. He cleared his throat. "As a matter of fact . . . Yes, ma'am. I'd like to see Miz Carter . . . if it's not an inconvenience."

Mabel Comstock's eyebrows rose and the corners of her mouth quirked into a semblance of a smile. "Katelyn's in the computer room." When he continued to stare blankly at her, she motioned toward a room at the back of the building. "That room's been in this building for five years—don't be such a stranger, Daniel."

"Yes, ma'am . . . thanks." With relief, he headed to the rear of the library.

Katelyn's back was to the door as he opened it and closed it quietly behind him. She was on her knees on the floor, her torso beneath the table. The view of her backside, heart-shaped mounds that jiggled a little beneath the fabric of her slacks as she tugged at something out of sight, had him grinning. He leaned against the door and crossed his arms over his chest to wait. No sense in spoiling a good opportunity to take in the scenery by announcing his presence.

She muttered something unintelligible before backing out from beneath the table. As her head popped into view, she caught sight of him. "Oh!" She slammed her head against the table as she tried to rise. Tears filled her eyes.

He rushed to help her up. "Are you okay?" He pushed her toward a chair. "Take it easy here for a second. I'm sorry I startled you."

Rubbing her head, she frowned at him, then took in his uniform in one long glance, from head to toe. Her expression was one of dismay. "You're a policeman?"

"A deputy sheriff," he corrected her.

"No, no one said . . . *you* didn't say." She looked at him accusingly, a scowl wrinkling her forehead.

"I assumed you knew." Well, it wasn't exactly a lie. He hadn't mentioned it, but he couldn't have known how much Dwight might have blabbed to her after he'd removed the snake. He knelt beside her so their gazes were level. He didn't want her staring at his uniform. "I guess there are a lot of things we don't know about each other."

Her glance slid away from his. "You're right. We really haven't talked very much."

Daniel bit back a smile and picked up one of her hands, so dainty within his ham-fisted palms, and squeezed it gently before letting it drop to her lap. "How about we spend some time together. You're coming with me tonight, right?"

Her gaze went to the glass door and back. "Daniel . . . I don't know . . ."

He drew a breath and felt a slow burning anger heat his cheeks while tension filled his arms and chest. "We had a deal, Miss Librarian."

Her eyes widened. "I'll still do that," she hissed, "but don't you think you should give . . . the rest a little time? I mean, you're a deputy . . . you have a reputation—"

"Seems the only one worried about the difference in our ages is you, Katelyn. I'm beginning to think it's just an excuse to keep what's happening between us safe. Like our relationship is in a box for you to take out whenever you have needs."

"That's not fair. We hardly know each other. Do you think I'm afraid to commit?"

"I think someone's made you afraid to trust."

Tears filled her eyes and she blinked. "Daniel, we need to talk—"

He shook his head. "After the party."

A fierce frown drew her brows together. "We'll never get around to conversation then."

Daniel smiled. "After you make good on your promise . . . we'll talk."

Her head canted and she gave him an assessing look. "We just had our first argument."

"Not so bad, huh?"

"I survived."

He rose, and held out his hand to help her stand. "You sure you're feelin' all right?"

"Uh-huh," she answered, sounding a little breathless as she stared up.

His gaze dropped to her lips, and they parted. That was invitation enough.

Intending only a quick kiss to her lips, he pressed his closed lips to hers, but was pleasantly surprised when her head tilted to align their noses, and she deepened the kiss. His hands smoothed over her ribs, slid around her back, then spread to embrace her. He pulled her close to him, and she leaned into him with a soft moan. He let her take the lead, and while she never ventured beyond the seam of his lips, her own melted against his.

Suddenly, she broke off the kiss, shoving at his chest, and he released her immediately. Breathing heavily, he fought to calm his racing heart. Glancing around, he found his hat on the floor and brushed it off before placing it back on his head.

His eyes sought hers. Her lips still glistened from their kiss. Choking down an inward groan, he said, "Tonight."

FIVE

KATELYN CHOSE A PINK cotton dress with a skirt that swirled around her calves when she turned. She smiled at herself in the mirror, wondering if this was starting a trend. A brand-spanking-new *pink* life. Her blonde hair was pulled away from her face, fastened with small silver barrettes, leaving the rest to fall to her shoulders. She hoped she didn't look ridiculous and like she was trying to appear younger than she was, but the truth was, the anticipation of seeing him again left her feeling like she was standing on the edge of something wonderful.

And if they ended up in bed together tonight, she didn't believe her secret was a betrayal. He might have access to her body, but this time around she wasn't going to entrust her inner self to anyone else's care before she was sure. However, yesterday she'd called an attorney and begun the process to end her marriage.

This was a victory she wanted to savor alone—she'd proven her strength of will, proven Chris was wrong about her. She wasn't the insecure young woman he'd married. She no longer needed his approval to validate her choices. She didn't need him—she didn't need any man. It was a liberating feeling taking this final step of emancipation.

Every bit as freeing as the rich sensuality of Daniel's kisses. Today, standing in the middle of the library where anyone could see them, she'd given herself permission to love again. Compared to the wicked things he'd done to her before, the kiss had been rather innocent, but she'd initiated a deeper joining, let her hands roam over his body in a possessive way,

Until she'd realized the hard, unyielding surface beneath her palms wasn't his muscled chest, but the Kevlar jacket he wore beneath his uniform. That had been enough to jar her back to reality. She hadn't known he was an officer. He'd kept his own secret.

She wouldn't hold it against him. They had to learn to trust each other and give themselves time to know each other. If the physical side of their relationship was on the fast track, well, *hallelujah* anyway.

The age difference that had rankled and made her feel ashamed might actually be a blessing. Because he was younger, she felt more in control.

A knock sounded at the door, and her heart raced. She grabbed her purse and let herself out the front door. When she finally glanced at the tall man who waited patiently for her finish locking up, he stole her breath away.

Daniel in faded blue jeans had been a sinfully delicious treat. Tonight, he was the full-fledged cowboy in a starched denim shirt with pearl-covered buttons. His jeans were dark, his boots highly polished.

The oversize belt buckle drew her gaze so long she knew he grew embarrassed, because he cleared his throat before saying, "Do you have everything you need?"

Surprising herself, she giggled. She hadn't felt so lighthearted in ages. "I do now."

She grasped his arm and smiled warmly at him, and he responded by crooking his elbow and placing a hand over hers. They looked at each other for a long time.

Daniel cleared his throat again. "If I kiss you now, we won't make it off this porch."

"And that's a problem?"

He nodded, his expression solemn, but his eyes wrinkled at the corners like when he smiled. "Yes, ma'am. I want to dance with you tonight."

She tilted her head and raised a single eyebrow. "And you're telling me this, why?"

"Because I don't want you thinking I don't want to kiss you."

She lifted a finger to her mouth and licked the tip, then traced his lips slowly. "Consider yourself kissed." She lowered her hand and blushed when he continued to stare.

His chest rose sharply and he glanced away. "Shit."

"Problem?"

"Yeah, I have to get through the evening with a hard-on."

She grinned. "That belt buckle's big enough to hide behind."

His gaze narrowed on her. "No, it's not."

A grin stretched her lips wider. "No, it's not," she drawled.

His hands clasped her hips and glided lower. He rested his forehead against hers and squeezed her bottom.

It was an odd embrace, but one she didn't want to end.

"Where's your hat?" she asked, wanting to extend the moment and not really caring about the answer.

"In the truck."

"Hmmm." This close she inhaled his spicy aftershave and the smell of soap on his skin. She wondered if he noticed the attention she'd given her scent as well.

"Did I tell you I love you in pink?" he said, his voice a low rumble.

She shook her head without breaking contact. "Nope."

"Well, I thought it. That very first day you wore a little pink undershirt."

She gave a breathless gasp. "You noticed the color of my camisole? Wait a second, I was wearing white."

"I was only seeing the pink of your nipples through that camisole. It about drove me crazy."

She sucked her lower lip between her teeth—it was that or mash her mouth against his.

His gaze dipped to her mouth and he groaned. "I'm holdin' on by a thread here."

"Not helping?"

"Nope."

She laughed softly. "Do you need a few moments alone to compose yourself?"

"I need more than a few moments."

"A cold shower?"

"Don't think it would relieve the problem a bit."

She dropped her own voice to a purr. "Would it help knowing I'm not wearing any underwear?"

He closed his eyes tight. "Fuck, no!"

"Well, then, you're in luck. I am. Granny panties."

"White?"

She nodded, sliding her forehead against his. "Mm-hmm."

His grip on her bottom turned rigid. "I want to see."

"After the party." She gave him a quick peck on the cheek and pulled away. "Payback's a mother."

DANIEL'S HANDS TIGHTENED so hard the steering wheel groaned. He'd been sweating bullets since he'd helped tuck her and that flimsy little dress into the cab and pointed the truck down the highway. Her sweet floral perfume and the faint underlying hint of arousal had him wishing he hadn't been so stubborn. He couldn't put his finger on it, but something was different about her tonight.

The quick little glances she gave him lingered on his body, burning him. The little wistful sounds that escaped from her pink mouth had him so hard the clasp on the back of his belt buckle poked his rock-hard dick.

Katelyn sighed again beside him, drawing his gaze from the road to the rise of her chest as she inhaled her next breath. "Is it far?"

"No. We'll be there in twenty minutes."

"Long enough," she murmured.

Her tone had him worried. When her hand settled on his knee, he nearly jerked the truck off the road. He gave her a quick glance and frowned when she undid her seat belt and scooted closer to him on the bench seat.

"Katelyn, get your belt back on."

She tugged the ends of the belt in the middle of the seat and buckled them together, snuggling her hips next to his. "Mmmm. That's better." Her palm slid up his thigh and down to his knee again. She smoothed it back up and then casually let it slip between his legs.

His thighs tensed from the pleasure. "Katelyn? I don't know what you're thinking—"

"You just drive and leave the rest to me."

She angled her body toward him and reached for his belt buckle. Her hand slid behind the buckle and Daniel sucked in his breath to give her room to work. A soft *snick* and it loosened, and as quick as he drew another breath she'd freed the button at the waist of his jeans and slid down the zipper.

"Thought we were waiting 'til after the dance," he said, enjoying the change in plans and the fact that she was taking the initiative.

"This is for you," she said. "*After* will be for both of us." She pushed down the top of his underwear, freeing his cock.

Daniel eased back as far as he could on his seat. When Katelyn leaned toward him, he lifted his right hand off the wheel to give her access, and then settled it on her hair.

As she drew close, her breath bathed his hot flesh.

"You know, there are laws against this kinda thing," he said, gasping when her tongue laved the swollen crown of his dick.

"I know this cop," she said, skimming her tongue along the sensitive ridge just below the crown. "Bet he can fix a ticket."

His hand stroked her soft hair and the truck slowed until he realized he'd eased off the gas. He punched the pedal again. "That cop's gonna be sittin' in the cell next to you."

"Sounds like fun." Her tongue glided down his shaft, curving to his shape.

"*Damn*, baby."

"Just keep your eyes on the road."

"Easier said than done." He bit back a groan when she made the return trip up his cock, swirling her tongue along his length until she reached the head.

She stuck the point of her tongue in the little slotted hole at the end and wiggled it.

Daniel bit back an oath and widened his legs, one foot still on the gas, the other leg pressing against the door. "You're gonna get us both killed."

"Not if you do what I say. Don't be such a pussy."

He snorted. "Didn't know you had such a nasty mouth."

"Don't know everything, do you?" With that, her mouth opened over the end of his cock and she took him inside.

He gasped and lifted his hips fractionally, frustrated he couldn't ram upward the way he needed. His hand gripped her hair harder, encouraging her to take him deeper inside her mouth.

Down she came, murmuring and sighing around his cock, her tongue and lips closing tightly, her mouth sucking—deeper still, until his cock touched the back of her throat and he eased off his grip.

But Katelyn had more to give, more amazing depths to plunder. Her throat relaxed and he sank inside as she moved her head up and down in his lap. With his breaths catching her rhythm, he raked her hair with his fingers, the end rushing up to meet him.

When one dainty hand clasped the base of his cock and the

other dug between his legs to massage his balls, he felt the sweet tension begin to unwind. "Baby, back off, I'm gonna come."

She reared back. "Gotta swallow. Don't want to mess up your clothes." Then she sank down again, taking him into the moist, hot cavern of her mouth and beyond.

Air whistled between his teeth and he cried out, fighting to keep the truck between the dashed line and the shoulder of the road while she sucked him off, murmuring her delight and encouragement.

After he'd emptied his balls, she sat back and shook her hair around her shoulders, a feline smile on her lips. "Think you can make it through a dance or two now?"

He pulled the truck to the side of the road and got out, adjusted his clothing and took deep cleansing breaths of air. When he climbed back inside, he snaked his hand around the back of her head and kissed her hard. "Don't ever do that again."

Ten minutes later when Daniel helped her down from the cab of his truck, he barely resisted the urge to shove her back inside. Her nipples poked against the thin cotton of her dress and her hair was a little messy, her lips swollen and her lipstick nearly gone. He didn't want to share the sight of her with any other man. While he smiled down at her, he gritted his teeth. He'd just have to be satisfied with the fact that her pink lipstick ringed his cock.

THE OPEN BAY OF THE firehouse was strung with lights and the music could be heard well before they crossed the road to the parking lot. Food was laid on banquet tables to one side of the open bay. Sodas, punch and pitchers of tea were on a table to the rear. A band played country music to which people of all ages danced.

Katelyn passed the evening in a happy haze. With Daniel's arm curved around her back, she felt proud and protected. His glance never rested on another woman in the room. He introduced her to several people and she felt welcomed. If she caught a few curious stares, warm smiles quickly followed. It appeared she'd worried about her reception at his side for nothing.

The music slowed.

"Would you like to dance?" Daniel murmured in her ear, his arms enfolding her from behind.

She glanced around at the other couples already circling the dance floor. "I don't know how to dance like that," she said, leaning back against his body.

"It's a two-step. It's easy. Trust me, I'll show you how."

She turned and raised her hands to him, giving him her trust in the deepest sense of that word. He grasped one of her hands in his and placed the other on his shoulder before pulling her closer. He began the steps slowly, heedless of the beat of the music, then picked up the pace as she learned. They circled the dance floor, swaying together with the rhythm of the music.

To Katelyn, dancing within the circle of Daniel's arms was a hint of the heaven she'd know later—when their bodies blended and merged while they made love. Their movements now were pleasurable, their bodies perfectly aligned and in sync. When the dance ended, they both smiled.

"See, I told you you could do it."

They had come to a stop in a darkened corner of the room. His hands still rested on her waist, and she tried to forget the other people were beginning a new dance, so near to them.

Daniel watched her as she gathered her courage and lifted her hands behind his neck to pull his head closer to hers. This time her lips caressed his as she learned their shape and texture, first with her lips then her tongue. She followed the closed seam of his mouth, and he opened his lips on a soft moan.

Daring filled her, and she swept her tongue into his mouth, sliding it along his. She tasted the punch they'd drunk earlier and his own unique flavor. She gasped when his tongue began to slide sinuously against hers.

"Would you like to leave?" she asked breathlessly, when she could pull her mouth from his.

He didn't answer, but his flushed cheeks and the starkly drawn features of his face told her he was as desperate for privacy as she was. Taking her hand, he pulled her along out of the dance hall to his truck.

The drive back to her home seemed to take forever. Neither of them spoke, but she was glad for the silence. She didn't want to think; didn't want to change her mind about what she knew would happen.

DANIEL'S HEART POUNDED FAST. He tried to temper his expectations, to keep his excitement in check, because at any moment she could change her mind. Despite her boldness during the drive to the firehouse, he couldn't let his hopes take flight. He'd felt off balance all evening, having surrendered the pace and the direction of this night to her care the moment she had opened her front door.

Everything after that had been a blur. All he could see were her flushed cheeks, softly curling hair and that bit of pink fabric that kept him a sane man. He'd been all too aware of the curious, covetous gazes that had followed her that evening. He knew he'd have some competition for her time soon, if he didn't make his move quickly to place his brand all over her.

When they pulled up the drive she fumbled for her keys and he took them from her shaking hands and unlocked the door. She didn't turn on the light. Moonlight poured through the living room window. Silver tipped her eyelashes and the curls that lay against her shoulders. Shadows settled in the curves between her breasts visible above the bodice of her dress.

"Are you sure about this?" he asked, praying she was.

She didn't reply. Instead her lips parted, and a small, shivery sigh escaped. She moved closer and touched his face with her open palm, and then leaned into him to press small kisses to his chin, along his jaw and finally on his mouth. He let her take the lead, and when she urged him to open her mouth against his, he obliged. Gently, he drew her body closer until he couldn't tell whether it was the beat of his heart or hers that hammered madly at his chest.

Abruptly, she broke the kiss and rested her face against the crook of his neck. "I'm sorry," she said, but instead of pushing away from him she wrapped her arms around him.

He sighed, this wasn't what he'd hoped for, but at least she wasn't showing him the door. "Katelyn, you don't have anything to be sorry for." She raised her head, and he gave her a crooked little smile despite the ache that pressed against the front of his jeans. "We can just talk," he suggested.

She stood in the circle of his arms, looking at him for the longest. Then she pressed her hands against his chest. He let her go and did his best not to reveal his disappointment.

She turned slightly from him and held out her hand. "Daniel, I'm not a sure this is the right thing for us to do . . ."

His heart began to beat faster. "Baby, I'm not asking for more than you want to give."

She led him to her bedroom. Blood sang in his veins, and he tightened against moving as quickly as he really wanted to. Instead, he let her set the pace, surprised when she turned on the lamp next to the bed and slowly drew her clothing off a piece at a time, until she stood naked in front of him.

The bright color on her cheeks, and the way she stood shyly, her hands held awkwardly at her sides, told him she wasn't accustomed to being so bold.

Lifting his gaze to hers, he said, "You're so beautiful you make me ache from wanting you."

Without taking his eyes from hers, he stripped off his shirt, shucked his jeans and underwear and then remembered to search his pockets for his wallet and the foil packet he had tucked inside it. That he lay on the table next to the bed.

A small smile lifted the corners of her mouth. "I hope you brought more than one of those."

He pulled several more from his back pocket and gave her a lopsided grin. "Didn't want you to think I was taking anything for granted."

Glancing up, he saw her wide-eyed gaze staring at his cock, and he let her look her fill. When she finally raised her eyes to his, his voice was tight. "You can still change your mind, Katelyn."

Her own voice was a little hoarse when she said, "Are you crazy?" She sank onto the bed, and he was right there, climbing over her, parting her legs with his knees.

Kneeling between her legs, he ripped open a packet with his teeth and smoothed the latex down his shaft. Then he curled his back to take an erect little nipple into his mouth and suckle as he rooted with his cock between her legs.

Her hands closed around him and guided him inside her pussy.

Even through the sheath, he could feel her moist heat and the muscles of her inner walls clasp his dick. He let go of her nipple and stretched out on top of her, resting on his elbows to look into her face. "Are you all right?"

She nodded, a smile trembling on her lips.

He kissed her mouth and lifted, just their breaths between them. "Think I'm staying here awhile."

A faint smile stretched her full lips. "Feeling warm and cozy?"

"I'm feeling a lot of things, but cozy isn't one of 'em."

Her hands caressed his chest, her fingers circling his flat nipples. "Feel like a ride, cowboy?"

A short bark of laughter caught him by surprise and he rolled, taking her with him, stopping when she rose above him. "Sweetheart, wanna save a horse? Ride a cowboy!"

SIX

HE'D KNOWN SEX would be different with this woman—somehow more, but he wasn't prepared for the rush of emotions that washed over him at Katelyn's first tentative movements.

She was awkward and self-conscious, perched on top of him. He could tell by the frown that wrinkled her forehead and the way her hands wouldn't settle on any one place for longer than a moment.

He couldn't believe she'd never topped a man before—and bit back an oath at the thought of the selfish bastard who'd taken from her, probably humping her like a blow-up doll for all the joy he'd given her.

The fact she knew how to give a blow job, but had never had the favor returned, burned a hole in his gut too. Katelyn deserved so much more.

He reached for her hands and placed them on his chest, then guided her knees alongside his hips. "That better?"

Her nod was sharp, her breaths harsh. "I feel so full."

She felt wonderful—lush and wet as her cunt caressed his length. "Am I hurting you?"

"No." She shivered, her eyes closing momentarily. When they opened again, she whispered, "Show me?"

He reached and cupped the back of her head, pulling her close for a rough kiss. "Just move," he said, his voice harsh. "Whatever feels good is right."

She levered up and lifted her hips, pulling off his cock, then slid down to take him all the way inside again.

Daniel held her hips, helping her lift and fall, again and again, beginning the rocking ride to completion. Gradually, he moved with her, gently countering her moves, until they stroked each other faster and faster. Her sighs and the soft, moist sounds her pussy made as she rode him, filled the quiet room.

Every lesson he'd ever learned in any other woman's bed had only been a rehearsal for this. He held his own painful arousal in check, concentrating instead on her pleasure, gauging her breaths and the rising color in her cheeks to know when she needed more from him.

Keeping his eyes open, feeling every muscle of his body harden and strain, he watched the emotions revealed on her face as they made love. Anguish, urgency . . . painful need.

Feeling her draw tighter above him, and hearing her soft womanly moans, he knew she was drawing near. He deepened his upward thrusts, sharpening his strokes, earning gasps and jagged sobs from her as she clutched his shoulders and met his strokes, sliding up and down his cock until at last she hurtled toward the abyss.

At the final moment when her whole body tightened and strained, he fingered her clit, scraping his callused thumb over the engorged knot of flesh until she cried out, her head flung back.

Daniel's heart felt squeezed inside his chest. She was so damn beautiful, sitting there lost in her release, her body shuddering so hard her tits quivered. Her inner walls clasped and rippled around his cock and he gritted his teeth, wanting to make this moment last and wanting to watch her make the climb again—with him.

In his heart, he knew no man had ever been so determined to give her this joy, and he wanted her to acknowledge what they shared was unique and meant to be.

When at last she collapsed against his chest, he rolled her to the side and pushed back the hair clinging to the sweat on the side of her face.

"That was some ride, cowboy," she said, her eyes closing as she drew in deep breaths. "You took my breath away."

He kissed her, sucking on her open lips to let her breathe, and then smoothed a hand over her hips, gripping her to cuddle her closer and keep the connection. "Think you got this horse broke to saddle?" he whispered, his head tucked on the pillow beside hers.

Her eyes opened and her mouth slid into a grin. "God, I hope not. I'm looking forward to more bumpy rides." Her inner muscles squeezed around him. "What about you? Did I leave you behind?"

"Mm-hmm. Eating your dust." Then he gave her a little dig with his cock, a reminder there was still unfinished business and no one was getting any sleep just yet.

Katelyn laughed softly and groaned. "I don't think I can move. Something's got me nailed to this bed." But her hand reached over to rest on his chest and her palm rotated on his flat nipple.

He leaned closer and sucked on her chin, then gave it a gentle nip. "How about I do all the work? I'm younger—I've got stamina."

Laughter shook her shoulders. "Statistically, I'm just hitting my prime."

He hiked her thigh over his hip and his fingers slipped between her buttocks to graze her tight hole before sliding down to touch were they were still joined. "Think you're ready for another sort of ride?"

Her breath caught and her eyes widened. "Just what do you have in mind?"

"Nothing you won't love, I promise. Nothing you can't take. I want to taste you. Make you come with my mouth. Then fuck you hard to make you come again."

Her breaths coming faster again, she nodded. "All right, cowboy. You're on."

When she tried to slip her arm around his shoulder, he shook his head. "On your belly. I don't want you to watch. Just feel."

"Daniel . . ."

"Trust me." Pulling his cock slowly out of her tight cunt, he kissed her again and then helped her to her stomach, pushing two pillows beneath her hips to raise her bottom. "Remember, I get to do all the work."

She sighed and rested her head on her folded arms. "You have no idea how awkward I feel."

"Sure I do. That's what makes this so much fun."

Kneeling beside her, he started at her shoulders, kissing and massaging the muscle until she relaxed, purring with contentment. Then, slowly, he worked his way down her slender back, licking the notches of her spine, pressing kisses into the dimples at the top of her buttocks.

When at last he arrived at her plump ass, he stroked his cock, making sure the condom was still rolled to the base and nudged apart her legs with his knees.

She opened, groaning softly. "I don't suppose we could turn the light off now?"

"Not a chance." He placed his hands on the sweet curves of her ass, enjoying the feel of sleek silk beneath his work-roughened palms. The difference in their textures, rough to soft, and their skin tones, suntanned to pale cream, made him feel like an outlaw about to steal a sacred treasure.

With both hands, he parted her and lifted her higher until her hips tilted at just the right angle to give him a view of her pretty pink cunt and small rosy hole. "I've been dying for another peek. Wanna spoil my fun?" He almost growled, his throat felt so tight and thick—just like his cock.

She laughed, but the sound was smothered when she buried her face in the bedding.

Although his cock pulsed and ached for relief, he schooled himself to go slow, savor the journey—and bring her past her embarrassment and modesty. With every gentle initiation he provided, he hoped to tighten the cinch around her heart.

He leaned closer and buried his mouth and chin and in the moist heat between her legs. Knowing his beard stubble chafed, he circled slowly, rubbing himself in her juices while her hips jerked and she emitted excited little cries.

But she didn't try to pull away.

His thumbs parted the thicker outer lips and he tongued her

from clit to cleft, again and again, until her hips followed the movement up and down, like she was trying to draw out each stroke.

He almost smiled, but his dick throbbed and his balls drew painfully high and hard against his body. Still, he speared into her, stroking her silken sheath until more salty cream greeted his tongue. He dug his fingers into her, rolling them to coat them all the way past his knuckles then pulled them out to rub the moisture around her pink asshole.

Katelyn bucked beneath him. "Daniel!" she cried out, desperation driving the pitch of her voice higher.

But he was merciless. He drew her pink inner lips between his teeth and sucked them hard while he pushed one finger into her ass.

Her body shivered and her back arched. Her ass, however, drove higher against his mouth and finger, forcing a deeper penetration. He twisted inside her, loosening the tight ring of muscle, then drove another finger inside and fluttered them, back and forth until she was groaning and gasping for breath.

His cock drew so tight he was afraid he'd spend himself if he didn't get inside her quick. Keeping his fingers in her ass, he rose behind her and guided his cock into her pussy, snuggling his thighs between her widespread legs.

He knelt behind her and with his free hand on her rump, he slammed forward, gliding freely into her heat, tunneling fingers and cock as deep as he could reach.

Katelyn's knees pressed into the mattress to find purchase, and then she raised her bottom to meet his strokes, grunting softly with each hard thrust.

He stroked faster, harder, until his balls banged her clit and she keened, her voice breaking as he pounded. Then he felt the rush of cum emptying from his balls in hot spurts to fill the tight latex sheath. He shouted and pumped faster, clenching his teeth as his whole body spent itself in a final violent thrust.

Afterward, he gathered her quivering body close to his chest and soothed her with his hands sliding up and down her back until her heartbeat slowed and she slumped beside him. When she sleepily nuzzled his neck, he pulled the sheet over them and slept.

MORNING DAWNED AND KATELYN woke and reached a hand across the bed to Daniel, but he wasn't there. She pulled on a robe, belting it snugly at the waist, before going in search of him. But he wasn't anywhere to be found inside the house.

His clothes were gone and his pickup wasn't sitting in the driveway. She felt the first tremor of panic begin to tremble in her stomach. Had she been wrong about him? Had he left her as soon as he had what he wanted? He'd left no note of explanation.

She wandered out onto the porch and watched the first rays of the dawn peek over the horizon—vivid, crisp orange and mauve against the harsh gold that rimmed the Earth.

Sitting on the steps, she drew the top of the wrapper closed, and began to berate herself silently. *How could I be such a fool?* She laid her head against her bent knees and gave herself a stern order not to cry.

Then she heard the sound of a vehicle as it roared down the

driveway. She didn't look up when footsteps ran up the porch and paused beside her. She couldn't look up when she heard Daniel's worried voice speak to her. "Sweetheart, I meant to be back before you woke."

"I thought . . . " she whispered, her voice thick with tears. "I didn't know if you were coming back." A moment later she was in his arms. Ashamed of her distrust, she hid her face against his shoulder as he rocked her. Finally, she raised her face to meet his gaze. "I'm sorry. I'm acting like an idiot."

"It's okay, sweetheart. Trust takes time, and we're just getting to know each other."

She relaxed against him, enjoying the feel of his solid chest beneath her cheek. "So, why did you leave?"

"I went back to my place to pick up the tools I need to start work on the eaves today. You were sleeping so soundly I didn't want to wake you. I'm sorry now, I didn't tell you."

She hugged him hard and pressed her face against his neck. He was apologizing to her, and she was the one who should be ashamed. But she held on to her silence for just a moment longer, savoring the feelings that washed over her. Love enfolded her as he rocked her in his arms.

"Strange as it sounds, Katelyn, you hardly know me, and I don't know nearly enough about you. Why should you trust me? How 'bout we talk? I know there's something bothering you, but there can't be anything so terrible we can't face it together."

It hurt so much to look into his face and see the love shining in his eyes. *How do I tell him?* She shook her head, knowing what she was about to say would make a difference. "I'm married . . . "

It didn't take more than a moment for him to react. It was as if a shutter closed over his face. He drew away from her emotionally, even before his hands lifted her off his lap and left her body.

Panic flared and stilled her heart. "Daniel, please let me explain."

"I think you summed it up just fine, ma'am," he said. He rose to his feet, turned on his heels and marched toward his truck.

She ran after him on bare feet, heedless of the stones in the driveway, "Please, Daniel. Wait!"

He slammed the door to his truck and started it up. She stood beside his window, but he wouldn't look at her.

"Daniel, let me explain."

He began to drive away, but she ran beside him, desperate now for him to hear her. "I'm separated—I've already filed for divorce. Daniel, wait." The truck pulled away, and at the end of the drive, he gunned the engine.

Slowly, she became aware that she had been standing there a long time, staring at the empty road. She wiped her tears on the sleeves of her robe, and turned back to the house.

She had plenty of work to do. She would get through this pain the same way she always had. She just needed to keep busy. Never mind this time the agony cut so much deeper than her husband had ever managed to do.

HOURS LATER, SHE PAUSED TO WIPE the sweat from her forehead. She dropped her scrub brush into the dirty water and decided to get a fresh bucket before she tackled the last window.

She heard a footstep behind her and spun on her heels.

Daniel stood there. His face was pale, his mouth a tight line. His expression was harshly etched.

Afraid she would just break down and cry in front of him, she turned away and dumped the bucket of water.

"We need to talk," he said, his tone hard, the pitch deep and strained.

She added soap to the bucket and began to fill it with water, ignoring him. He wouldn't listen to her before, why should she listen now? She reached for the pail, but his hands stopped her. They settled on her arms and clasped her tight.

He stood so close she could feel him against her back. "Katelyn, stop."

"Let me go, Daniel. I have work to finish up here."

"We're gonna talk. I shouldn't have left the way I did earlier. I'm sorry for that."

As strong as the relief that sang in her heart, anger blasted hot and furious. "Sorry?" She shook off his hands and turned. "You didn't even give me a chance to explain. Where was your trust? You demand it from me, but the first time yours was tested—"

"I had to get away . . . to think. I was too mad to make sense of anything you wanted to tell me. I needed a little time."

"Well, now you have plenty of it," she snapped. "I'd like you to leave."

"I'm not goin' until you settle down and talk to me."

"I don't have to do what you tell me to. There's nothing left to say, and I have work to do." She turned her back on him, picked up the pail and stalked toward the window.

She heard a muttered "Damn it, Katelyn" just before she heard the sound of him walking away. That made her even madder. His affections could only be a pale thing compared to hers if he could give up so easily.

Well, it's better to know now, she told herself. Convincing herself it was better this way, she closed her mind to the pain and scrubbed the dirty window.

Weary and heartsick, she finished up and decided she'd had enough for the day. Too little sleep the night before, and too many emotions that morning, had left her exhausted.

She entered through the back door and headed straight for the shower. The water soothed her aching muscles, and she let her tears mingle with the spray jetting down on her. After she dried off, she went in search of fresh clothing. She had just pulled an age-softened T-shirt over her head when the sound of banging from the front of the house registered.

Every admonition she'd given herself earlier, trying to convince herself she was better off without a man—especially one who quit when the going got rough—disappeared. She'd been lying to herself.

Heart pounding, she walked through the house and looked out the front window. It was Daniel. He was there on her porch, prying a board free. He hadn't walked out on her after all.

But was he here to finish the job or because he wanted another chance? She suspected the answer was up to her.

He must have sensed her watching, because he looked up. She couldn't read his expression before he turned his attention back to the crowbar and the board he'd almost worked free.

Unsure how she'd be received, she hesitated. She prayed she hadn't been misreading him all along. If he returned even a small portion of the love she felt for him, it would be enough.

Pushing open the screen door, she took a deep breath and walked out onto the porch. He ignored her now, and kept working. She didn't mind, deciding it would be easier to get through the explanations without him looking right at her.

"I'm sorry I shouted at you earlier," she said softly. "It was childish of me. I wanted to hurt you like you hurt me when you left this morning."

A board creaked ominously before it split. Daniel tossed down the crowbar and began to pull at the board with his hands.

He wasn't going to make this easy for her. And she knew she deserved it. She had been the one to lie. Or at the very least, omit an important piece of information.

"Please just listen, Daniel." She eyed his back. His head was cocked to the side, and his motions slowed, so she knew he was listening. "I was wrong not to tell you about my marriage," she began. "I don't consider myself married anymore. My husband and I have been apart for more than a year. Our marriage wasn't a good one."

Pausing, she realized it was easier to say what she had to without him looking at her, but she needed to read his expression. She didn't know if she was reaching him.

"My husband was very controlling. And while he didn't ever hurt me physically, he made me feel . . . small and stupid. He also made me feel very *unsexy*." She heard him snort and she rushed to continue. "And there were other women. A lot of other women. Chris said he needed them because I wasn't woman enough for him." She turned away and stared sightlessly at the expanse of rugged buffalo grass before her.

"I believed him for the longest time. I don't know what

changed in me, or when it occurred that I didn't have to take it. I moved out. And at first I thought I was doing it to punish him, and make him see how much he had hurt me. But then I started to realize I liked my life better without him. That was when I decided to leave Atlanta. I couldn't really let go of my past if I stayed there."

He didn't stop working, and she started to feel anxious that maybe none of what she was saying mattered to him or excused her.

"When I came out here to Texas, it was to get as far away from my old life as I possibly could. The last thing I wanted was another man. And trust one? I didn't think I ever could again."

The board came free in his hands, and he tossed it on top of a growing pile next to the porch. He picked up the crowbar and inserted the end between two old splintered boards high in the eaves over the porch. The muscles in his arms and shoulders bunched and sweat dampened the back of his shirt.

Needing to be closer to him before she could say what she needed to say next, she stepped behind him and put her arms around his waist, pressing her cheek to the wet circle between his shoulder blades.

He stilled immediately.

"Daniel . . . " Squeezing him fiercely, she whispered, "I'm sorry I didn't tell you. I felt that if I shared this, somehow I wasn't being strong. And I didn't want you to know how stupid I'd been. You've shown me more about passion and what love is supposed to be in the past days than I ever experienced in years of marriage to him. Every time you pushed, it wasn't just because you wanted something for yourself. You were giving me the world, but I was too scared to accept or see that." Frightened because she didn't sense any change in his rigid stance, she went for broke. "But I want you to know . . . *I trust you.* And I love you with all my heart."

She felt his chest expand as he took a deep breath. He lowered his arms and set the crowbar on top of the rail. Then he placed both hands over hers and squeezed them gently. They stood there for long minutes, relaxing, savoring.

"You're not wearing a thing under that T-shirt are you?"

The question, and his deep smoky voice, made her smile. She bit him playfully on the back, and she felt his response in the ripple of his stomach muscles beneath her hands.

Pulling free of her grasp, he turned quickly, grabbing her around her waist. Before she had time to even gasp in surprise, he sat her down on the porch rail and stepped between her thighs. Their faces were level now, his gaze spearing into hers.

"No more secrets," he said firmly.

"No more secrets," she promised, and her heart began to expand with hope.

"We will be married, Katelyn."

It wasn't a question, but she nodded a moment before his mouth pressed against hers, and his hips pushed against the part of her that ached to be filled.

Pushing the T-shirt up her body, Daniel's lips left hers only long enough to pull it over her head and fling it the ground. "I need to be inside you."

She understood. He needed to stake his claim.

Her hands were just as busy, opening the snap of his jeans to free him. He lifted her from the rail, and her arms clung to his shoulders as her legs wrapped tightly around his waist and he lowered her onto his cock.

He took a deep breath, and rested his forehead against hers. "Damn it, Katelyn. You're more than enough woman for me. I won't ever play around on you."

Her eyes grew damp again. "Daniel, I believe you. But right now no more talk, you have to move."

"You keep telling me that. Thought all you women liked to talk."

Katelyn wound her arms around his shoulders and leaned her forehead against his. "This one likes talking just fine, but right now, I can't think. Fuck me, cowboy."

His mouth twisted in a wicked grin and he tilted his hips to stroke his big cock all the way inside her. "One cowboy coming up, ma'am."